New York Time

Ruth Ry

Ashes of Dreams

Widowed at a young age, Amanda Jeffrey is left on her own to raise three small boys, tend to her ailing father-in-law, and maintain a languishing horse farm in 1880s Kentucky bluegrass country.

But when she suddenly must rely on the assistance of a handsome Irish immigrant, the hopes and dreams that Amanda believed long buried in ashes begin to smolder and spark to life inside her once again.

0-425-20151-1

New York Times bestselling author

Ruth Ryan Langan

Paradise Falls

A young woman's enchanting
journey of love and self-discovery.

**In 1890 Massachusetts, after her father's death,
Fiona Downey must leave her college and
take a teaching job in rural Michigan.
Now, living with the Haydn family in Paradise
Falls, she is drawn into the complex
relationship between two brothers—and is torn
between her desire and her lifelong hopes.**

0-425-19484-1

Available wherever books are sold or at
penguin.com

b071

Also available from
BERKLEY SENSATION

Berkley Sensation titles by Ruth Ryan Langan

PARADISE FALLS
ASHES OF DREAMS
DUCHESS OF FIFTH AVENUE

DUCHESS
OF FIFTH
AVENUE

RUTH RYAN LANGAN

BERKLEY SENSATION, NEW YORK

THE BERKLEY PUBLISHING GROUP
Published by the Penguin Group
Penguin Group (USA) Inc.
375 Hudson Street, New York, New York 10014, USA
Penguin Group (Canada), 90 Eglinton Avenue East, Suite 700, Toronto, Ontario M4P 2Y3, Canada
(a division of Pearson Penguin Canada Inc.)
Penguin Books Ltd., 80 Strand, London WC2R 0RL, England
Penguin Group Ireland, 25 St. Stephen's Green, Dublin 2, Ireland (a division of Penguin Books Ltd.)
Penguin Group (Australia), 250 Camberwell Road, Camberwell, Victoria 3124, Australia
(a division of Pearson Australia Group Pty. Ltd.)
Penguin Books India Pvt. Ltd., 11 Community Centre, Panchsheel Park, New Delhi—110 017, India
Penguin Group (NZ), Cnr. Airborne and Rosedale Roads, Albany, Auckland 1310, New Zealand
(a division of Pearson New Zealand Ltd.)
Penguin Books (South Africa) (Pty.) Ltd., 24 Sturdee Avenue, Rosebank, Johannesburg 2196, South
Africa

Penguin Books Ltd., Registered Offices: 80 Strand, London WC2R 0RL, England

DUCHESS OF FIFTH AVENUE

A Berkley Sensation Book / published by arrangement with the author

PRINTING HISTORY
Berkley Sensation edition / March 2006

Copyright © 2006 by Ruth Ryan Langan.
Excerpt from *Heart's Delight* copyright © 2006 by Ruth Ryan Langan.
Cover art by Leslie Peck.
Cover design by George Long.
Interior text design by Kristin del Rosario.

ISBN: 0-425-20889-3

BERKLEY SENSATION®
Berkley Sensation Books are published by The Berkley Publishing Group,
a division of Penguin Group (USA) Inc.,
375 Hudson Street, New York, New York 10014.
BERKLEY SENSATION is a registered trademark of Penguin Group (USA) Inc.
The "B" design is a trademark belonging to Penguin Group (USA) Inc.

PRINTED IN THE UNITED STATES OF AMERICA

10 9 8 7 6 5 4 3 2 1

For my family—my one true treasure

And for Tom—my one true love

PROLOGUE

———◆◆◆———

Kerry, Ireland—1882
St. John Of the Cross Home for Foundlings

"OH, LANA." SOBBING, twelve-year-old Siobhan Riley threw her arms around her best friend's neck, careful not to touch the red welts that marred her flesh from her latest caning at the hands of Mother Superior. "I can't bear that you took another beating on my account."

"Hush, now. Do you want to wake the others?" Lana Dunleavy shoved a tangle of dark hair from her eyes and glanced around the cramped dormitory, where more than a dozen girls of all ages were sleeping on thin pallets on the floor.

She had been here for five long years, since she was eight. Siobhan had arrived at the foundling home weeks later, at the age of seven. Lana had taken one look at the skinny, lost, and completely terrified little girl and had become her fierce defender. It was Lana who had comforted Siobhan when Mother Superior ordered her lovely mane of honey hair to be shorn almost to her scalp to teach her humility. It was Lana to whom Siobhan turned in the night when the terrors woke her, and Lana who saw that the sickly girl got enough to eat when she was too weak to walk to the refectory with the others. And it was Lana's dream of a better life, in a land far away called America, that fueled Siobhan's imagination and kept her hopes alive when their miserable existence became more than she could bear.

"It isn't fair. You stole that piece of bread for me. And now look what it's got you."

Lana managed a wry smile. "Better I got the beating than you. I've had more experience."

"How can you laugh? One of these days Mother Superior is going to break that rod."

"Or my back." Gingerly, Lana touched a hand to the small of her back and winced.

"I pray every night that we'll be rid of this place forever, Lana. Do you really believe that one day we'll be free to go to America?"

"I do. Yes." The words were whispered fiercely.

"Tell me again what we'll do there."

"We'll live like queens, in a fine, big house." Her voice softened as she repeated the dream that had become her litany of hope.

"You forgot about our garden."

"I did, didn't I? We'll pick roses from our garden and sip tea in our parlor."

"And we'll stay together always. Promise?"

"Promise."

While Siobhan fell into a fitful sleep, Lana lay awake and closed a hand around the tiny pouch she wore on a string at her waist. Inside the pouch were the treasures she'd secreted, to keep them from being confiscated when she'd been brought to the foundling home. Her mother's ear bobs. Her father's ring, which had belonged to his father before him. They were all she had left of her former life.

It was time to flee, she told herself. Though she'd heard horror stories about life beyond these walls, of children roaming the streets without so much as a crust of bread and being forced to work for cruel taskmasters who took delight in beating them for the slightest infraction, she was half inclined to think they were lies spread by the nuns to keep their unhappy charges in line. Besides, could life on the streets be any worse than what she'd endured in this place? She could barely recall her life before. Her mother's face was already fading from her memory. But she knew she'd been happy and loved. And now, there was nothing except this miserable regimentation that began at dawn with prayers and a bowl of thick gruel, and days of scrubbing and polishing, along with the occasional lesson in reading and writing and sums. She was grateful for the education, but at what price? It was expected that most of the girls would stay and enter the convent. From what Lana had seen, it wasn't for her.

She knew how to work hard. Wouldn't someone outside these walls be willing to pay her for her work? If she could earn enough for passage, she and Siobhan could live the dream.

Aye, it was time, she thought. While the bruises were still fresh enough to stiffen her resolve, it was time to make plans to leave this place. By whatever means possible.

"LISTEN NOW, SIOBHAN." Lana caught her friend's hand and glanced around for some sign of fat Sister Annuncia, who was always lurking around a corner, hoping to catch a miscreant and move up a notch in Mother Superior's eyes. "There's no room for error."

Her friend's pallor revealed the depth of her terror. "We'll get caught, Lana, and Mother Superior will beat us."

"She beats us anyway. Why not risk it for freedom?"

"If it's so easy, why hasn't anybody else slipped away?"

"Because they're not as smart as us." *Or as desperate,*

Lana thought. "Listen to me now. We'll have but one chance to make good our escape. When the farmer delivers his crop of potatoes, he empties the sacks into that wheelbarrow and hauls them inside to the refectory."

Siobhan nodded. "He's done it for years. But what has that to do with us?"

"When all the sacks are empty, he stores them in the back of his cart before going to get his pay from Mother Superior. He'll be gone only a minute or two. That's when we'll hide under the sacks."

"And if he spots us?"

Lana tried for a casual shrug. In truth, her nerves had her twitching with excitement. "Anything is better than nothing. If we're caught, we'll take our beating and make plans for the next time."

"They'll separate us. Mother Superior warned us that if we got into trouble one more time, she'd see that we were never allowed to be together again. I'd die if I couldn't be with you, Lana. You're the only one who cares about me."

"I'll not let anything bad happen to you." Lana touched a hand to her friend's arm. "Listen. Already I hear his cart. It's time."

She pushed Siobhan ahead of her, and the two were standing breathlessly by the back door when the farmer pulled on the reins, bringing his horse and cart to a halt.

Without a word, Lana picked up a basket and dragged Siobhan with her as she knelt in the herb garden just beyond the refectory and began pulling weeds, all the while surreptitiously watching the farmer trudge to and fro with his crop.

Finally, she set aside the basket of weeds and caught Siobhan's hand. "Now!"

"I can't do this, Lana." Trembling like a leaf in the wind, Siobhan clapped a hand to her mouth to stifle the cry that sprang to her lips. "I just can't. You'll have to go without me."

"And leave you to the mercy of Mother Superior? You

wouldn't survive in this place a day without me. You're going."

Lana gave a determined tug, dragging her friend along. When they reached the cart, she looked around and, seeing no one watching, shoved Siobhan ahead of her into the back of the cart. When she was certain the girl was completely covered, she crawled in beside her and carefully covered herself.

"Not a word," she whispered fiercely. "Do you hear me? No matter what happens, you're to do and say nothing."

They heard the door open and close and the sound of booted feet on the cobbles. The footsteps paused, and a man's voice said, "What's this?"

Lana froze and felt Siobhan's fingers clamp around her wrist in a death grip. Though she'd long ago despaired of heaven hearing her, she began to pray as she'd never prayed before. It wasn't strength she prayed for, or even freedom. She prayed that Siobhan could contain herself without bolting like a frightened rabbit, exposing their scheme.

"One potato fell from the barrow," the farmer muttered under his breath.

He tossed it into the back of the cart before pulling himself up to the driver's seat. "That's one Mother Superior paid for and didn't get. First time ever that she didn't get the best of the bargain."

Chuckling, he cracked the whip and the horse strained in its harness. The wheels groaned in complaint as the cart lurched through the gate and started rolling along the lane.

Siobhan relaxed her grip, and the blood began flowing once more through Lana's wrist. When she could feel her fingers, Lana lifted a corner of the sack and gingerly felt around until she found the potato. Snagging it, she hugged it to her.

The two girls lay cramped beneath the potato sacks for more than an hour until the cart came to a halt. At the sound of voices, Lana braced herself, wondering if this would be the moment of discovery. She and Siobhan remained as motionless as death, listening to the farmer's footsteps recede.

Hesitantly lifting an edge of the sack, Lana peered around in the gloom.

Seeing no one, she sat up, stretching her protesting muscles. "Come on, Siobhan."

"Where are we?" The girl popped up beside her, rubbing her eyes.

"It appears to be a village. Our good farmer has gone into the tavern, presumably to spend Mother Superior's coin. Hurry now. We must run."

Siobhan breathed in the scent of ale, and meat roasting, and bread baking. "Couldn't we go inside and beg something to eat?"

"Not here. We're still too close to the foundling home. I want to get as far away as I can." She caught her friend's hand and urged her away from the village and across a field of wild grass growing taller than their heads.

As the gloom of evening turned into dark of night, they continued running until the lights of the village were far behind. Wheezing and giddy with the first taste of freedom, they crept into a farmer's hay barn. Huddling together for warmth under a blanket of sweet hay, they shared the raw potato, skin and all, and fell asleep in each other's arms.

Aboard the HMS Griffith in the Atlantic Ocean—1885

"Mrs. O'Connor." Lana skidded to a halt before the cluster of well-dressed women who had staked a claim on the area of ship's deck beside the stairs, assuring them a steady stream of fresh air.

Lana never walked when she could run. And she was always running, always in constant motion, seeing to the dozen or more chores she set for herself each day, crossing them off in her mind as each one was completed.

In the midst of these well-dressed passengers sat the heavy-set woman who reminded Lana of her childhood tormentor, the prune-faced Mother Superior. Bushy brows were drawn together in a perpetual frown. Her jowls moved like a turkey's wattles each time she spoke. Her eyes narrowed on Lana as she approached.

"I've decided to pay your price, Mrs. O'Connor."

The older woman's eyes widened with surprise. "I thought you said you'd never part with your mother's ear bobs."

"I didn't think I could. But I find I'm in need of that shawl." Lana nodded toward the stingy bit of cloth poking out of the woman's satchel.

Nearby, the other women eyed this group in sullen silence, though most of her fellow passengers were too busy struggling just to keep body and soul together to care about creature comforts like shawls or bonnets.

"Let me have a look at them then." Bridget O'Connor held out her hand.

With a twinge, Lana cast a final glance at the gold filigree wires, each ending in a tiny gold birdcage. Inside rested matching blood-red rubies. It seemed odd that, though she could no longer remember her mother's face, she could see those ear bobs in her mind's eye, glittering against perfect porcelain skin, framed by raven-black hair. If she breathed in deeply, she could even smell her mother's scent. Memories, and these few bits of jewelry, were all she had left of the mother she'd lost too young.

She'd kept them all these years, resisting the temptation to sell them for food when she'd been desperately hungry or to barter them for a warm place to sleep. But now they were all she had left, and Siobhan's need was greater than hers.

The old woman's eyes glittered with greed. "I suppose they're worth my shawl."

And a great deal more, you old biddy. Though the thought hammered in her mind, Lana spoke not a word. She'd learned early in life, at great price, to hold her tongue, take what she could, and be happy to get it.

"Here you go." Mrs. O'Connor handed over the shawl with barely a glance at the girl. Her gaze was fixed on the jewels, already tallying how much they would fetch from a dealer when she arrived in America.

Lana carefully folded the shawl before dashing across the deck of the ship to find the old man who was selling fish. After agreeing to trade her boots, which his wife admired, she ran barefoot toward the lower deck in search of her friend.

After surviving on the bleak streets of Dublin, laboring for pennies, and sleeping in everything from cow barns to castle ruins, Lana had saved enough to book passage to America. But survival was just as bleak aboard the HMS *Griffith,* where they fought for a place to sleep along with hundreds of other desperate immigrants, bound for New York.

Out of breath as always from her frantic efforts to keep them in food, clothing, and shelter, Lana was alarmed to find Siobhan lying in a corner, in the throes of heavy labor.

"God in heaven. It's way too soon. Here." Moving quickly, Lana wrapped her friend in the shawl and thrust the food into her hand. "You'll need this for strength."

"I couldn't." Siobhan shrank from the sight of the smoked fish and didn't stop shuddering until Lana tucked it away in her pocket. Then her hand clamped around Lana's wrist. "Find Billy. Tell him it's time. He has to come now."

"I'll fetch him. Just . . ." Feeling suddenly helpless, Lana patted her friend's hair. The thought of hard work never troubled her, but when it came to the mysterious matter of childbirth, she was lost. "Just don't move until we get back."

That brought a smile from the girl's twisted features. "I

wish I could run far away, but because I can't, I'll be here. See that you hurry."

Once again Lana found herself rushing up the stairs, bracing for the blast of wind off the Atlantic that blew her two steps backward for every forward step she took. The deck was cold and slippery beneath her bare feet, but she bravely pushed her way through the cluster of men hunched in their threadbare overcoats, watching the dice roll against the far rail of the ship.

"Billy! Billy O'Malley."

The young man who'd tossed the dice was too intent upon the outcome of his roll to even glance her way. At a shout from the crowd, he grinned and held out his hand to collect their bets. "Three in a row. Who's with me now, lads?"

"I am, Billy."

"Me, too, lad. You've the touch."

"There's none finer than you, Billy, when the luck's with ya."

Fists holding money were raised over Lana's head as the men, eager to side with a winner, held up their bets.

"Billy." Lana barely paused to catch her breath before blurting, "Siobhan's time has come. Hurry. She needs you."

He flicked her a glance, and the boyish smile that could be so charming turned to a sneer. "Babies never come on time." He turned to the others. "Isn't that right, lads?"

"Right you are, Billy," an old man with a thatch of white hair and skin the color of aged leather said with a wink. "Ye could be there, feelin' lost and helpless for hours before ye'll get the chance to greet ye'r firstborn."

"You see?" Billy nudged Lana aside. "You stay with her. I'll be along when I'm through here."

"But she's in terrible pain and calling for you, Billy. She doesn't want me. It's you she needs. What'll I tell her?"

He was already snatching up the dice. "Tell my wife I'm busy looking out for her future in America."

As Lana turned to race back to her friend's side, she could hear the shouted curses and then the wild cheering when the dice stopped rolling.

Her mouth set in a grim, tight line. Aye. He'd looked out for Siobhan, hadn't he? Getting Siobhan to persuade Lana to sell her father's ring to book passage for one more. Bartering her only warm shawl to buy whiskey. Losing their lone blanket on one toss of the dice. He'd taken all and given nothing in return. Nothing, Lana thought with a blaze of fury, except the babe in her friend's belly. But Siobhan was blind and deaf to his faults. She'd been so starved for love, she'd closed her eyes and ears to the truth while Billy O'Malley filled her mind with sweet promises and her heart with false hope. But hope wouldn't put food on their table. If they had a table. Or put a roof over their heads when they docked in America.

Her friend's desperate situation only hardened Lana's resolve. No man would sweet-talk her out of her dreams. Not now. Not ever.

The darkness of Lana's descent seemed even bleaker after having breathed the fresh air above. Her friend lay where she'd left her, moaning softly. All around her were pale, frightened women and children, all looking the other way to avoid seeing her pain. The fetid air, ripe with unwashed bodies, overflowing chamber pots, and those too ill to do more than lie in their own waste, made breathing belowdecks almost unbearable.

Lana knelt and took the girl's hand in hers.

"Billy?" The word was little more than a whisper as another pain ripped through Siobhan's young body.

"He's coming. Hold on, Siobhan."

"Can't. Baby's coming. Oh, Lana, it's coming now." Her body bowed up as the pain grew in intensity until she looked as though the pale flesh would simply burst like overripe fruit.

Her nails dug into her friend's hand as a scream was torn from her lips.

Minutes later, the baby slid free and began bleating like a tiny lamb.

Lana tore away her own petticoat and gathered the baby into it. Having never seen a newborn, she could only stare in awe before placing the tiny bundle in her friend's arms. "Look, Siobhan. A boy. You have a son."

"Colin." For the first time in hours, the pale young woman managed a real smile. "That was my da's name." She examined the tiny fingers and toes, the smooth, bald head, the perfect little features. "Isn't he beautiful, Lana?"

"He is, yes."

"I know it would make Billy happy to have his son named after him, but I just can't help it." Siobhan looked from her infant to her best friend. "I hardly remember my da. Colin Riley. He was dead before my sixth birthday. It seems only right that his grandson be named for him."

"It does indeed. I was lucky." Lana lay a hand over Siobhan's. "My da lived until I was nearly seven." And her mother had been gone before her eighth birthday.

"Promise me something, Lana." The new mother's eyes were fixed on her friend's face with a fierce light. "Promise me that if anything should happen to me, you'll see to wee Colin Riley O'Malley's future."

"Now, now. What a thing to ask. He has you, Siobhan. And Billy."

Siobhan's fingers closed around Lana's wrist. "I know Billy cares about me in his own way, but he'd have never married me unless he had to. If I hadn't gotten . . ."

"Don't say that." Lana drew away. Though the lie didn't come easily, she knew it was necessary, to soothe nerves already stretched to the limit, to offer hope to a friend who'd had so little of it in her young life. "Billy will settle down once he's in America. You'll see. He'll be a grand, loving husband and father."

"Just give me your word that you'll always be there for Colin. I couldn't bear to have him go through what we went through. Alone. Except for each other, we were so alone. And I'd have never made it without you, Lana. Until I found you, I wanted to just curl up and die. It was you who got me through those years. You're everything I'm not. You're so strong and tough and smart. You think ahead and plan, and all I do is drift with the wind and get myself into trouble. Please, Lana. Tell me you'll always be there for my babe."

The very thought of this helpless little babe living as she had sent a knife piercing Lana's heart. She touched a fingertip to the infant's cheek and wondered at the feeling of love that bloomed within her, like a candle in the bitter dark of night.

Tears pricked her eyes, and she blinked them away. "I promise you, Siobhan. I'll love him like my own. And I give you my solemn vow. He'll never, ever have to face life alone as we did."

"Oh, thank you. Thank you. You can't know how much that means to me."

Lana watched as her friend's eyes closed and she drifted on a sweet cloud of contentment, half awake, half asleep, still clutching the infant to her heart.

Life had to be better in America. It had to be, Lana thought, with a sense of desperation as she leaned against the cold, clammy wall of the ship. For she was never going back. She would do whatever it took. Pay whatever price required. If it killed her, she would make a better life.

For Siobhan.

For wee Colin.

For herself.

ONE

———◆———

New York City—1890

"You're late."

At the sound of the heavily accented voice, Lana turned to Mrs. Genovese, the Italian woman who lived across the hall from Siobhan. "I am. Yes."

"The bambino has been waiting for you. How that one loves being with you."

Lana had to swallow the grin that tugged at her lips. Siobhan was fond of her neighbor and grateful that Mrs. Genovese had a son near in age to little Colin. But she fretted about the fact that the woman knew more about her business than she cared to share with a perfect stranger. Not that it could be avoided. The walls of this Lower East Side tenement were thin, and anything above a whisper was heard by the neighbors on either side, as well as those living in the tiny rooms above and below. It was impossible to keep secrets in such cramped living quarters.

"I love being with Colin, too, Mrs. Genovese."

Just then the door to Siobhan's apartment opened, and the little boy danced out ahead of his mother. The two young women embraced as they always did, needing that physical touch to affirm that they were indeed free of the past and safe, at least for the moment.

"Will you come with us, Siobhan?"

The young woman held back. "Not today. I've so much to do still."

Lana glanced at the tiny room overflowing with other people's laundry. "Not even an hour to spare?"

"Maybe tomorrow."

"All right. I understand."

As Lana turned away and started down the stairs, Colin snatched at her hand. "Will you buy me an apple, Auntie Lana?"

"I might." Lana's eyes danced with a teasing light as she looked down at the chubby little hand in hers. "As soon as you show me you can write all your letters on the slate."

"I will."

As soon as they were outside, Colin dropped down to the sidewalk and reached for the slate and piece of chalk Lana carried in her pocket. She knelt beside him as he began meticulously printing his name. Studying the way the sunlight glinted on his pale hair, she felt such a welling of emotion. She loved everything about this lad. The way his tongue, caught between his teeth, moved with every dip and curve of the chalk. The way those blue eyes looked up into hers with such trust. The way he tried so hard to please. He was the dearest thing in the world. In fact, he was her entire world.

"I can't wait until you're old enough to read. Oh, Colin, the places we'll travel in books. We'll sail across oceans. Visit exotic places where the sun shines every day and it's never cold."

"Are there really such places?"

"There are, yes. I've read about them. And so will you. We'll learn the names of all the islands in the Pacific Ocean, and we'll discover what foods the people eat, and what strange animals live there."

"Da said it's a waste of time for me to learn such things. He said I should be learning ways to earn my keep."

"At five?"

"He said you're never too young to work. He said he was already on the streets at my age. Da said I should forget about my letters and learn the old ways so they won't be lost."

"The old ways? Nobody speaks Gaelic in New York, Colin. It's not that I think it should be forgotten, for it's a truly lovely language and there's something about hearing it that just soothes the heart and soul. But this is America, love. To make something of yourself here, you'll need to speak like an American."

Just then a group of children dashed past them. Boys in ill-fitting pants and shirts, girls in dresses fashioned from their mothers' cast-off gowns, shouting loudly in a mixture of Greek, German, Italian, and broken English.

"Is that American, Auntie Lana?"

She laughed. "I suppose it is, love. At least to them. But I want you to learn all you can." She pointed to the slate. "And that means starting with your ABCs. Now let's see you write all the letters."

"And then you'll buy me an apple?"

"I will. Yes." And the moon and stars, as well, if she could.

A short time later she tucked the slate and chalk in her pocket and caught the lad's hand. She had to hurry her steps to keep up with his as he danced toward the fruit wagon in the middle of the square.

As he did every day, Colin took long minutes looking over every apple in the cart before making his choice. The old vendor, who spoke not a word of English, had come to expect this daily ritual. When Colin finally settled on a perfect, unblemished piece of fruit, she paid the vendor her penny and walked slowly beside the lad while he devoured his treat.

Because she worked evenings and late into the night at a tavern on the docks, Lana was able to see the lad and his mother every afternoon. This precious time together was special to both of them, and she knew it gave Siobhan a brief respite from her tedious existence.

"That was grand. Thank you, Auntie Lana." Colin swallowed every bit, even the core and seeds, before pausing on the broken steps of the cramped tenement he called home.

Through the open windows of the tiny rooms drifted curses in a dozen different dialects. The smell of food cooking couldn't mask the stench of garbage rotting beneath the stairs on this hot, steamy day. Above them, the sunny sky could barely be seen through the laundry flapping on ropes strung from one window to the next.

"About time you got back."

At the sound of Billy's voice, the happiness in Colin's eyes fled, replaced by a look of wariness. Despite his tender age, the lad had learned to gauge his father's many moods.

Billy O'Malley had been blessed with a handsome face and a heavy dose of fine Irish charm. As Lana had witnessed, he used it lavishly on the ladies, as he'd once used it to have his way with Siobhan. Poor, love-starved Siobhan. But beneath the charm, beneath the carefully cultivated smile and the pretty words that flowed so easily from his lips, lay a cruel, self-centered shell of a man. Billy's only ambition lay in winning enough on cards or dice to fill his need for whiskey. Once drunk, he would spend his last dollar on the women who plied their trade on the streets.

Siobhan had been forced to take in other people's laundry to have enough for her son to eat. As for the lad, his father barely took notice of him, except to remind him as often as possible that he was a burden.

"Get upstairs. Your mum's waiting for you. And don't stop to talk to that old biddy across the hall."

"Mrs. Genovese is a good neighbor. Be certain to tell her I said good-bye, Colin." Lana bent down, kissed the boy, and then straightened and watched as he dashed away without a backward glance.

"Slumming, are you, Lana?"

She merely turned away, calling over her shoulder, "Tell Colin and Siobhan that I'll see them tomorrow."

"If I say you can."

She didn't pause. To do so would only let him know that his words mattered. She wouldn't give Billy O'Malley the satisfaction of having any power over her, though God knew he tried to.

When they'd first arrived in New York, Lana had lived with Billy and Siobhan, paying for the use of a blanket in the corner of Colin's room and helping with the infant's care, aware that her friend needed a hand with the rent and the demands of a new baby. But when Billy's lecherous advances became intolerable, Lana had moved out rather than risk confiding in Siobhan. The pain and humiliation would have merely created another burden for her already-overwhelmed young friend.

Now Lana slept in a small storage room in the back of the tavern where she worked—and was grateful for it. Though the owner deducted a precious dollar from her pay each week for the use of it, she figured it was worth it. She missed sharing a room with Colin, but she'd soon learned that she loved having a place all to herself. It was the first time in her life she'd known such a luxury. At the foundling home, more than a dozen girls lived in each room, forced to sleep on pallets on the cold wooden floor. Here in America, she now had a cot, a small dresser, which she'd salvaged from a nearby building damaged by fire, and a window overlooking the wharf. She kept the room scrupulously clean. And though the smell of seawater and dead

fish was strong in the summertime, it was oddly soothing
as well. There was something about it that reminded her of
home, for her father and his father before him had been
fishermen.

She hurried down the crowded streets, past the food ven-
dors, past the cluster of boys taunting two bigger lads who
were standing toe to toe in a bloody battle, fists raised, jaws
clenched. *Would that be Colin's fate?* she wondered. Would
he be forced to defend himself while friends and strangers
alike stood around shouting taunts? Was it a ritual all lads
must pass through to reach manhood on these mean
streets?

She felt a tiny finger of fear along her spine. What
chance did the lad have, with a mother beaten down by the
cares of the world and a father who thought only of his
own selfish needs? *But he has me,* she thought fiercely. *And
I can make a difference in his life. I will make a difference.*

She rounded the corner and stepped into the Blue Goose
Tavern. As she waited for her eyes to adjust to the dimness
of the interior, she made a silent vow to work harder, to earn
even more, so she could find a way to help little Colin. She
had an obligation, after all. She'd been the first to welcome
him into the world. That made her the closest thing he had
to a real aunt. If the rest of the world should fail him, she
thought, his Auntie Lana would always be there for him.

"About time you got here." Wilbur Hasting, owner of
the Blue Goose, was busy filling a tray with foaming
glasses of ale. His bushy white eyebrows were drawn together in a perpetual frown. His spectacles had slipped to
his nose, and he peered over them as Lana approached.

"I'm early."

"So are they." He nodded toward a table in the corner of
the room where four men sat playing cards.

Smoke curled over their heads as one man shuffled and
began to deal. When they picked up their cards, the air was
filled with a smattering of curses.

"Take this." Wilbur indicated the tray. "And see that you keep their tumblers filled, girl."

She took hold of the heavy tray and circled the table, setting a drink beside each player.

She recognized old Stump McGraw, so named for the wooden leg the doctors used to replace his missing limb that he claimed had been snatched by a shark when he'd been a young sailor on his first tour of duty across the Atlantic. Beside him sat Toomy Davis, who had to weigh nearly three hundred pounds. Toomy was so wide that Wilbur insisted he use two chairs whenever he joined in a card game. Wilbur Hasting was nobody's fool, and he wasn't about to allow a customer to break up perfectly good furniture. Across from Toomy sat Ned Lancaster, a local merchant who loved playing cards more than he loved his thriving mercantile business, which he left to the care of his long-suffering wife and three strapping sons. Ned was fond of finding new blood for the game. Because the fourth man at the table was unfamiliar to Lana, she assumed he was Ned's latest sucker. Poor thing. After tipping one too many ales and having his pockets emptied, he'd stumble out like all the others, dazed, drunk, and wondering what hit him.

"Good girl." Ned lifted the tumbler of ale to his mouth and took a long drink before wiping the foam with his sleeve. He closed an arm around her waist. "Keep 'em coming, Lana, my sweet."

"I'm not your sweet." She slapped his hand away. "And I've warned you about touching me, Ned."

"So you have, Lana. So you have." He chuckled. "But how's a man supposed to keep a thought in his head when he's looking at someone as dazzling as you?"

"You'll be even more dazzled if you should forget again. One whack with this tray, and you'll be seeing stars." She set the last glass beside the stranger and was rewarded by a quick grin.

Was he laughing at her? The very thought had her sending him a scathing glance, which only caused his smile to widen.

She brought her hands to her hips, ready to do battle. "Do you have something to say?"

"Not a thing." His voice was low and warm with laughter. "I know better than to invite a bashing from that tray."

"I believe it's my call. Can anyone beat two lovely ladies?" Ned lay his cards face up and glanced around with a sly smile, drawing the stranger's attention back to the game.

"I only have deuces." The stranger's smile grew. "Of course, I have three of them."

In that instant, Lana was so startled by that flash of white teeth, the glint of humor in those smoke-gray eyes, she could do no more than gape.

Most of the men who came into the Blue Goose were missing teeth, or limbs, or brains, after a lifetime at sea. This one not only seemed to have all his parts, but they were put together in a way that was most pleasing to the eye. Besides that, he seemed to have a sense of humor as well. She'd seen the laughter lurking in those eyes and had heard the hint of it in his voice.

Forcing herself into action, Lana stepped away and returned to the bar where Wilbur was busy wiping a glass with his dirty rag.

"Who's that?"

The owner shrugged. "Don't know his name. Said he was a rolling stone, so the others have taken to calling him Stone. Likes poker. Ned's latest fish. That's all I know."

"Doesn't look as down and out as most of them."

He paused, glanced over, then back at her. "Oh, I don't know. Anybody who can play cards at this time of day couldn't possibly have any sort of worthwhile job, now, could he?"

She shrugged and had to admit that Wilbur was right.

The man was no doubt just another in a long line of con artists who frequented the tavern, which had become a haven for lowlife actors, artists, and cons. Respectable men wouldn't be hanging out in a tavern in the middle of the afternoon, playing poker.

She picked up a rag and began wiping down tables. Every once in a while she would glance over at the low rumble of laughter from the stranger. Everything said by the others, from their rough curses to their observations about life at sea, the streets of New York, or the people they knew, brought a fresh round of laughter from him. He seemed to be thoroughly enjoying their company, which only reinforced her first impression. Definitely a con artist. Who else could find those three shiftless gamblers good company?

Before Ned Lancaster could hold up his empty glass, she was there, circling the table, anticipating the need to fill his glass before topping off the rest.

"That's my girl." Without thinking, Ned reached out to draw Lana close and then looked astonished when she gave his arm a loud whack with her empty tray.

"You've been warned, Ned. Next time it'll be your head. A third time"—she pulled the dagger from its place of concealment at her waist—"and it'll be your manhood." She flounced away while the men around the table roared with laughter.

As the workday came to an end, more men began drifting into the Blue Goose, until the tables were filled and a pall of smoke hung over their heads from a variety of pipes and cigars and the occasional rolled cigarette.

Lana moved efficiently from table to table, balancing trays filled with foaming glasses. As she squeezed between the crowds, some of the bolder men would reach out a hand to encircle her waist or pat her rump. She would stop in midstride, round on the offending fellow, and wallop him with her tray if it happened to be empty or give him a swat with the back of her hand. That was enough to warn most of them that she wasn't to be trifled with. Woe to the lad who didn't heed the warning and tried to touch her a second time. She would haul him up by the front of his shirt, swear at him in a mixture of Gaelic and English, and leave him standing in front of the entire roomful of jeering strangers with a warning to his manhood if he should forget his manners yet again.

Watching from his place at the table, Stone's eyes narrowed as yet another drunk caused Lana to round on him like a spitting cat.

"You son of a fat hog! Brainless, mealy mouthed twit! Shall I lay you out like the worthless slug you are?" Her voice carried through the length of the room, her curses causing the crowd to go silent.

Stone looked around the table. "Shouldn't the owner of the tavern put a stop to that?"

Across the table Ned chuckled. "When you've been here long enough you'll understand. A lot of the regulars actually encourage newcomers to behave in such a bold fashion, just to watch the display of fireworks that are certain to follow."

"They're setting the girl up?"

Toomy nodded. "Our girl, Lana Dunleavy, once her temper flares out of control, puts on the best show in town. Have you ever heard more inventive curses?"

Stump McGraw tossed aside two cards and waited for more to be dealt. "Wilbur Hasting has owned the Blue Goose long enough to know that men will be men. And men with the fire of liquor in their bellies are even more so. But don't worry about the lass. Our Lana needs no help to keep the drunks in line. I know she's slender as a willow, and her head barely reaches most men's shoulders, but there's nothing helpless about her." Warming to his story, he tilted his chair back. "I once saw her stand up to a drunken sailor who stood a head over every other man in the place. I think the poor lout foolishly believed his size alone would cow the lass. With one deadly swipe of her dagger, Lana opened his arm from shoulder to wrist. It took four of his mates to carry him to his ship, where he no doubt spent the rest of his journey in sickbay, wishing he'd paid heed to the pretty little lass's warning."

" 'Tis a true tale," Toomy put in. "For I was here that night and saw it with my own eyes."

"As did I. Ale!" Ned Lancaster lifted his empty tumbler, and Lana hurried to the bar to fetch another pitcher.

As she circled the table, topping off their glasses, she could feel the stranger watching her with interest. Up close she realized he hadn't shaved, and there was a shadow of whiskers darkening his chin. The pull of those smoky eyes had her throat going dry.

"What in hell . . . ?"

At Ned's outburst, she glanced down in time to see that she'd overfilled his glass and the ale was spilling onto his lap.

"Sorry." She tossed him the rag she carried over one arm.

"Sorry's not good enough, Lana. Have you lost your good sense?"

"I was—" *Distracted,* she thought, but aloud she merely added, "Careless, I suppose."

"More than careless." Ned mopped at the liquid and then tossed the rag to the floor. "The least you can do is pay for my drink."

That had her chin coming up like a prizefighter. She worked too hard for her money, and half of all she earned went to Siobhan and Colin. "I will in a pig's . . ."

"I'll buy your drink, Ned." The stranger's softly spoken words had the others around the table looking over at him.

"Not necessary, Stone." Ned held up a hand. "It's Lana's fault. She'll pay."

"I said I'd see to it." The stranger was still smiling, but there was a hint of steel in his tone now.

Ned studied the man a moment and then glanced at the

pile of money in front of him before giving a shrug. "Whatever you say, Stone."

The stranger handed Lana a coin and then picked up his cards.

The others followed suit, returning their attention to the game.

Lana pocketed the money, and the incident was forgotten as she was soon dancing from table to table, wondering how soon Verna Lee, Wilbur's niece, would be in to give her a hand with the crowd.

When she paused at the bar for another pitcher, she glanced across the room to Ned's table. At that same instant, the stranger looked up and caught her eye. Even from so great a distance, she could see that he was smiling.

"Here you go, Lana." Wilbur set two heavy pitchers on the tray and turned away.

As she hefted the tray and started around the room, she found herself wondering at the quiet way the man named Stone had diffused the awkward situation. Without raising his voice, without using any force whatever, he'd commanded attention as well as respect from men who would just as soon fight as eat.

That, she supposed, was what made for a great con artist. Which was why, the next time he smiled at her, she'd look the other way. It didn't matter how much that rogue smile made her heart flutter. The last thing she needed was the complication of a charming lowlife.

STONE FOUND HIMSELF chuckling at the name the others had given him. He supposed it suited him well enough. It had happened as soon as Ned Lancaster had asked where he came from.

Nowhere. Everywhere. A rolling stone.

As the game broke up and the others drifted to the bar or to their homes for the night, he pocketed his winnings and stepped outside the Blue Goose. Walking along the wharf, he took a cigar from his pocket, held a match to the tip, and drew deeply until a wreath of smoke circled his head.

Right from the start he'd seen through Ned's little game. The poor bloke was as transparent as glass. At least twice Ned had him beat but had tossed in his cards, allowing his opponent to claim the win. It was all a setup. Tonight they'd played for a few paltry dollars, and Ned had seen to it that their guest went away a winner. Next time they'd demand a rematch, and would play for much higher stakes. Of course, next time, they wouldn't toss aside a winning hand. He chuckled. Not that he intended to give them a next time. They'd need to look somewhere else for a sucker. He'd had his fun. Time to move on.

He paused to stare at the bobbing lanterns of dozens of boats in the harbor. New York was such an amazing, vibrant place. With its ebb and flow of humanity from every corner of the world, it was young and raw and unpretentious. And here he was, feeling the same way, and lucky to be in the middle of it all.

He'd had fun tonight. He'd enjoyed the bawdy stories, the raucous laughter. Best of all, he'd been thoroughly entertained by the lass. Now there was a woman. Not just beautiful, but with a mind of her own and a temper that was a joy to behold. In fact, everything about her had dazzled him. From that glorious mane of midnight hair, falling all loose and tangled, to those eyes that were neither green nor blue, but turquoise jewels that could freeze a man at twenty paces with just one look. A tiny thing, though there was nothing frail about her. If anything, she more resembled a hurricane roaring through the Blue Goose than a mere woman serving drinks.

Lana, the men had called her. His smile grew as he tossed his cigar into the foaming waters. In that faded gown of mud-brown, her hair a wild and glorious tangle of curls, and skin as flawless as fine porcelain, she was breathtaking. And with that quiet dignity, more regal than any queen.

He'd really intended to move on to the next game. He rarely allowed himself to spend more than a single night in any of the taverns that dotted the streets of New York. But he was intrigued enough that he might not be able to stay away. After all, what was the harm in it? For as long as it amused him, for as long as the girl held his interest, why shouldn't he become a regular at this den of iniquity?

By heaven, why not indeed?

Having made the decision, he chuckled aloud for the sheer joy of it.

TWO

———◆◆◆———

"WHAT'S WRONG, COLIN?" Lana knelt to gather the lad close, unmindful of the fact that the hem of her gown had drifted down around her to sweep the fifth in the street.

Ever since they'd left the tenement, Colin had been unusually quiet.

"Da was shouting at Mum." The boy rubbed at his eyes with dirty fists.

"He didn't . . . ?" She stopped, alarmed at what she'd almost asked. She must never plant such a thought in the lad's mind. The violence in his life was already far too real. Choosing her words carefully, she held him a little away and started again. "Did your da do anything more than yell?"

"I don't know. Mum pushed me out in the hall and told me to wait for you over at Mrs. Genovese's rooms. But I could hear them. Da was cursing. He wanted the money Mum got paid for doing Mrs. Schumacher's laundry. And Mum was . . ." His lower lip trembled. His voice dropped to a whisper. "She was crying, I think."

"Mothers do that sometimes." Lana gathered the lad close and hugged him fiercely and then forced a brightness to her tone she wasn't feeling. "I think we'll visit the park today. We both need to see green grass and pretty flowers."

"Will we do sums?"

She touched a hand to the slate in her pocket, feeling relieved at the fact that she'd managed to divert his attention and calm his fears. "We will. And then if there's time, I'll tell you about a new land I read about. It's called Australia, and there are animals there that are found nowhere else in the world."

"What are they called?"

"I don't know all of them. But there's a giant, rabbitlike creature called a kangaroo. And an oversize mouse called a koala."

"Do you have pictures?"

She shook her head. "I don't, no. But I'll describe them to you and you can draw them. You've a good mind, Colin. When you grow up, you'll make your mum and your Auntie Lana so proud."

"When we're done with our stories and sums, will you take me for a ride on the carousel?"

"I will indeed. For I love it as much as you."

"And after that, will you buy me an apple?"

"Now what do you think?" Laughing, she stood and caught his hand.

"I think you'll buy me the grandest apple in all of New York."

"That I will, love."

Swinging hands as though they hadn't a care in the world, they danced along the street until they came to Central Park, where ducks swam in sparkling streams and flowers grew in wild profusion. And best of all, where poor immigrants were free to walk alongside grand ladies and gentlemen. It was a reminder that the life they led here, though harsh, was better than the one they'd left on the far side of the ocean.

THE EVER-PRESENT PALL of smoke hung over the patrons of the Blue Goose. Lana was quick to notice that Stone was at his usual table, playing poker with Stump, Toomy, and Ned. He'd been back so often since that first time she'd begun to expect him.

Not that she was watching for him, she thought with a wave of annoyance. She didn't care one way or another if Stone wanted to waste his time doing nothing more strenuous than play cards every day of his life. Just another con, he was, and she had no time for the likes of him.

The regulars had all begun to accept him as one of their own, sharing jokes as well as pitchers of ale. By their own admission, it was hard not to like the man, even though he won at poker more often than he lost. There was just something about the way he listened respectfully to their every word, as though he couldn't get enough of their salty tales of life at sea. He laughed easily at their jokes and always seemed to have one of his own to share.

Though he and Lana had exchanged less than a dozen words, she was aware of him watching her at times, while the cards were being shuffled and dealt, or when she paused beside him to top off his tumbler of ale. Those smoky eyes seemed full of secrets. And when she was forced to put one of the drunks in his place, she'd begun to notice that Stone watched with more than a little interest. Once she thought she'd seen him start to shove back his chair, as though about to come to her aid. Seconds later, when she'd sent the drunken lout hobbling toward the door, cursing loudly and holding a handkerchief to his bloody wrist, she realized she'd only imagined it. A look in Stone's direction assured her that he was completely absorbed in the cards and hadn't given her a thought.

"Stop your woolgathering, girl." Wilbur's voice had her head coming up sharply. "I pay you to see to the customers, not daydream."

She hurried to the bar and accepted a tray loaded with foamy pitchers of ale. As she rounded the tables, filling glasses, she saw Wilbur's niece, Verna Lee, arrive and pause to look around at the men with that hungry, wolfish look she always wore.

Lana wasn't surprised to see her. Though Verna Lee was always late the rest of the week, she could be counted on to arrive early every Friday. The laborers would be getting off work soon, eager to spend their weekly pay. Verna Lee wanted to be first in line to get all she could before it was spent on cards and whiskey.

The girl reminded Lana of a dumpling—a pale, un-cooked lump of dough, with a brain to match. Her breasts were pendulous mounds of white flesh, always spilling over the neckline of something sheer and revealing. Verna Lee was the only female Lana knew who never bothered to wear a chemise beneath her gown. It was, she'd told Lana, just one more thing she'd have to remove anyway. The same went for drawers and petticoats, because they blurred the outline of her round bottom, which she believed the men particularly enjoyed seeing and touching through her sheer gown.

When Lana had first begun working at the Blue Goose, she'd wondered why the owner's niece spent so much time in the outhouse beside the tavern. It was only after several weeks that she'd caught on. The tips Lana made were a mere drop in the bucket to the money Verna Lee earned every Friday, taking the men, one at a time, to the small outhouse that stood beside the tavern and giving them as she termed it, "a quick ride to paradise." Her uncle had to be aware of what was going on, but he was always willing to look away whenever Verna Lee strolled out the door, arm in arm with one of the customers. For all Lana knew, the girl might have an arrangement with her uncle to share her earnings, because he was the one who provided her with the means and the men.

As the tavern began filling up with thirsty customers eager to spend their pay, Lana had no time to give Verna Lee a thought. There were trays to be carried, glasses to be filled, and greedy hands to be slapped whenever they happened to make contact with any part of her body.

"Lana, my sweet." Ned Lancaster's voice could be heard above the din. "Have pity on this parched crew, and fetch us some ale."

This brought a frown from Wilbur behind the bar, who shoved a tray at Lana just as his niece led another lamb to the outhouse.

"NO MORE FOR me." As Ned lifted a pitcher of ale toward his glass, Stone picked up his money and shoved away from the table. "I've had enough. I'll say good night to you now."

Ned eyed the money disappearing into his pocket. "I hope you'll give us a chance to win some of that back another time."

"Of course." Stone smiled, putting the others at ease. "I'm not a greedy man. How about tomorrow?"

"I'll be here," Ned said quickly. "How about you, Stump?"

The old man nodded.

"Wouldn't miss it." This from fat Toomy Davis, who was busy filling his glass to the brim.

Stone glanced around at the few stragglers left in the Blue Goose. Lana was nowhere to be seen, and he supposed she'd gone home for the night, leaving Wilbur and his niece to close up.

Stepping outside, he walked to the wharf and reached for the cigar in his pocket. In the darkness he sensed rather than saw a figure nearby. Stepping closer, he recognized Lana, standing with her head lifted, staring intently at the moon.

She hadn't yet heard him, and he took this moment to study her. Her gown was the same dull brown she'd worn all week in the tavern, topped by a ragged shawl draped around her shoulders to ward off the chill. Her hair hadn't seen a brush in hours and was a mass of tangles spilling down her back. In profile she had a tiny nose, a strong chin, and dark lashes framing eyes fixed on the sky.

He was more accustomed to seeing her dashing about the crowded room, filling glasses, mopping up spills, and admonishing in a mixture of English and Gaelic any man bold enough to invite her anger. Like a leaf caught in a summer storm, she seemed always to be a blur of motion. But here, encased in moonlight, as still as a shadow, she more resembled some ethereal creature of myth and legend. She was, in fact, so lovely she took his breath away.

Sensing his presence behind her, she turned, and her hand came to her throat in a gesture of surprise. "I thought I was alone."

"Sorry. I didn't mean to startle you. I didn't expect to find you here. I thought, after the night you'd put in at the Blue Goose, that you'd be eager to get home."

She smiled then, and he watched the way the moonlight sparkled in her eyes. "I am home. I sleep there." She pointed to the back door of the tavern. "Wilbur lets me rent the storage room."

"You have no home? No family?"

She shook her head, sending her dark curls dancing.

Because he wanted to reach up and touch her hair, he busied himself with the cigar in his hand, holding a match to the tip. Light flared briefly, and he watched her eyes as he drew deeply before tossing the match aside.

She studied the way the tiny flame sizzled and died as it hit the water. It kept her from staring up at him. He was so tall. Much taller than she'd thought. It was, she realized, the first time they'd stood face to face. Always before, he'd been seated at the table drinking and playing cards. "What are you doing out here?"

He exhaled a cloud of smoke. "Late at night, when the world is sleeping, I like to watch the boats in the harbor."

"Do you?" Her lips curved in the darkness and her voice softened. "So do I. I find myself wondering where they've been and where they're going. I play little games with myself, pretending that I'm the captain, ordering the crew to make ready for a grand sea voyage."

He could listen to that soft, lilting brogue for hours. "If you were captain of the ship, where would you go?"

"All around the world." She thought a moment before adding, "I'd see London and Paris and Venice. Oh, I'd climb mountains and swim in rivers that haven't even been charted on maps yet. I'd hide behind veils in Constantinople and visit the colorful bazaars. I'd drink tea on a plantation in India and ride elephants. I'd soar high in the sky in one of those giant balloons. I'd—" She stopped, suddenly aware of all she'd revealed. "I must sound foolish."

"Not at all. How do you know all those things?"

"I don't know anything. You're laughing at me."

"Is that what you think?" He shook his head. "I'd never laugh at you, Lana. You have a fine mind. I'm amazed at the variety of things that interest you. Most women I know spend their time thinking about how they look or how to get a man to give them what they want."

She shot him a sideways glance. "Just what sort of women do you know? I'd think a woman would rather get what she wants by herself, without asking a man for help getting it."

That had him throwing back his head and roaring with laughter. "I'd expect no less from you. And you're right. I believe I've been spending far too much time with the wrong kind of women."

He moved closer and, because he wanted so badly to just look at her, he turned his attention to the boats, their lanterns casting golden ribbons of light on the black water. His tone softened. Lowered. "If it's any consolation, I think you'd make a great sea captain."

He did look at her then, full in the face. "I think you'd be good at anything you tried."

He could read the surprise in her eyes—and the pleasure. And though it was a simple thing, he took extraordinary delight in knowing that he'd been the one to put the smile back in those eyes.

What happened next seemed the most natural thing in the world. Without giving a thought to what he was doing, he flicked the cigar away and closed his hands over her upper arms, dragging her close.

He saw the way her eyes widened in surprise.

Before she had time to protest, he lowered his mouth to hers and kissed her, long and slow and deep. When she tried to pull back, he took the kiss deeper, until he felt her gradual acceptance.

He hadn't intended any of this, but now that he was holding her, kissing her, it seemed the most natural thing in the world. Even after so many hours in a smoky, foul-smelling tavern, she tasted as clean, as fresh as a hilltop meadow. There was so much goodness here. So much innocence.

He could feel himself sinking into her, into all that sweetness, and wanting more. Wanting all. A man could get lost in someone like this, and never care about finding his way back.

"Lana." He whispered her name against her mouth, loving the sound of it.

"Stop this. You must stop." She pushed free of his arms and wondered at the tightness in her throat. Each word was an effort. "You know me well enough to be aware of what I do to men who dare to touch me. Now step away from me before you feel the sting of my dagger."

Instead of doing as she asked, he merely smiled. The look of it, at once sweet and dangerous, teasing and tempting, had a tiny ribbon of need curling along her spine.

"I think, Lana, that even your famous threat to my manhood won't be enough to keep me from kissing you again." His hand closed around her upper arms, and he drew her close. Against her temple he whispered, "God in heaven, I have to taste your lips one last time or die trying."

His mouth covered hers in a kiss so hot, so hungry, they could both feel the heat igniting between them.

Lana's body was on fire where his hands were touching her—a fire so hot she wondered that her bones didn't simply melt. Without realizing it, she reached up and wrapped her arms around his neck, afraid that if she didn't hold on tightly, she would slip, boneless and pliant, to the ground.

When a soft sigh escaped her mouth, signaling her surrender, Stone felt his pulse speed up until he wondered that he could still breathe. He couldn't recall the last time a simple kiss had him so fully engaged. Their mouths met, again and yet again, with all the flash and fury of a summer storm.

The thought of taking her, here and now, had his blood flowing like lava through his veins.

It would be so easy. So very easy. The door to her room was just steps away. The thought of it taunted him, and he could feel his willpower beginning to crumble. Then he heard the little moan of fear that told him he'd taken her too far, too fast. His conscience got the better of him as he allowed himself one final, lingering kiss before his head came up and he stood there, drawing in a ragged breath and cautioning himself to step back. When he finally did, he continued to keep his hands at her shoulders, as much for himself as for her. He simply wasn't ready to break all contact.

"Sorry." He managed a weak smile. "Not about the kiss, mind you." He drew in a deep breath before adding, "But I didn't mean to offend you. I'll say good night now, Lana."

She turned blindly toward the door of her room and prayed her legs would hold her until she was safely inside. As she yanked open the door and stepped in, she saw him turn away. Pushing the door shut, she latched it and then leaned against it, listening to the sound of his receding footsteps.

When she was certain that he'd gone, she crossed in the darkness to her tiny bed and sank down, still vibrating with need.

She'd been kissed a few times, but never like that. Stone's kiss had left her stunned and reeling. In truth, she was actually dizzy from it.

What had just happened out there? For the first time in her young life, she'd been completely overtaken by an urge unlike anything she'd ever known. Even when she'd told him to stop, she hadn't meant it. She'd wanted him to go on kissing her. That knowledge shamed her.

Was this how Siobhan had felt in Billy's arms? Had she allowed one moment of weakness to lead her into a life of such hardship?

Lana would have to be very careful to guard her heart. She'd worked too hard, endured too much, to give herself willingly to a low-life gambler.

She curled up in a tight ball and drew up the blanket, trying to erase the feel of his mouth on hers. But it was impossible. All she could taste was Stone. All she could feel was the heat of his touch. In her mind's eye, she could see those smoky eyes burning into hers. Could feel those big hands moving over her, igniting fires along her spine.

Even now, hating what he was, she found herself wanting him. And wishing with all her heart that she could be more like Verna Lee, for just this one night, so she wouldn't have had to send him away.

That must make her wicked indeed.

THREE

"SIOBHAN." LANA WAS startled to find her friend sitting in the middle of the tiny cramped apartment that was filled to overflowing with baskets of dirty laundry.

She'd become accustomed to finding Siobhan standing over a washboard, knuckles raw, stringing the clothes out the window as quickly as they'd been scrubbed clean.

One glance at her friend's red-rimmed eyes had her reaching a hand to Siobhan's forehead. "What's wrong? Are you sick?"

The young woman's forehead was cool to the touch, but her eyes had a feverish, sickly look to them.

Siobhan's voice sounded raw and wounded. "Maybe Colin could wait for you across the hall in Mrs. Genovese's rooms."

Lana turned to the lad and motioned him to do as his mother asked. As soon as the door closed behind him, Lana took Siobhan's hand. "Now tell me what's wrong."

"Oh, Lana. I'm . . ." Her lips trembled, and tears welled

up, spilling down her cheeks. "There's another babe on the way."

"So." Lana's lips pursed, considering her words carefully, even while her mind turned over this shocking news. "It isn't the end of the world, Siobhan. Maybe now Billy will get himself a proper job. What has he said?"

"I haven't told him."

Lana's eyes widened. "But why? You don't think you can keep a thing like this from him for long, do you?"

"I have to. He'll leave me if he finds out."

"Siobhan . . ."

"Listen to me, Lana. This isn't easy to say aloud, but I've known for a long time now. Billy doesn't love me. He's told me more than once that he only married me because of Colin. If he finds out there's to be another, he'll walk out and leave us all destitute. I don't know what I'd do if Billy left us."

"You'd be no worse off than you are now. It's you who keeps the lot of you in food as it is." Lana stared around at the baskets of other people's foul-smelling laundry. "Look what you do, just to keep body and soul together. And Billy drinks half of everything you earn."

"That may be. But I don't think the landlord would let us stay if there wasn't a man here."

Lana knew the truth of that. If the landlord didn't order them out, the other women in the neighboring rooms would. A woman alone was considered no better than the women who worked the streets and a threat to all decent mothers struggling to raise their children in this new land.

"Oh, Lana. What'll I do?"

Lana's mind raced ahead, considering possibilities. Hadn't she been saving every penny of her earnings and calculating what it would take to move her friend and the lad out of their miserable existence? But she was nowhere near ready for such a step.

"Keep your secret a bit longer. Unless you get too sick to do the laundry, Billy won't guess for a month or more. In the meantime, I'll search for a better-paying job. That way, if he does leave you, I'll have enough saved to get a place where we can live together."

"Oh, Lana." Siobhan burst into tears. "I can't let you waste your life taking care of us."

"That's what friends do. Besides, you and Colin are my family. There's nobody I'd rather be with."

That had Siobhan crying even harder. Through her tears, she managed to say haltingly, "What would I do without you?"

Lana held her until the tears had run their course. Reaching into her pocket, she withdrew some money. "Here. Take Colin to the fruit vendor. Buy two apples, and walk to the park." When Siobhan started to protest, she shook her head. "You need fruit now, too. If not for yourself, then for the babe you're carrying. And while you're gone, I'll get as much of this laundry done as I can." While her friend paused in the doorway, she bent to the scrubbing board. Over her shoulder she said, "If I'm not here when you return, you'll know it's because I had to get back to work."

Still, Siobhan remained in the doorway. "I love you, Lana."

She looked up. "I love you, too." She smiled. "Now go and get some sunshine in the park while you can."

LANA STARED AROUND at the patrons of the Blue Goose. Seeing Stump and Toomy alone at a corner table, her heart sank. Ever since that kiss in the moonlight, Stone hadn't been back.

Not that she wanted to see him, she told herself firmly. Actually, he was doing them both a favor. The last thing she'd wanted was to get involved with a con more interested in his own pleasures than settling into a proper life, with a proper job. Look what that had done to her best friend.

Obviously, that kiss had meant much more to her than to Stone. He'd already moved on to greener pastures.

She pushed all thought of him from her mind and looked around to see Wilbur Hasting glowering at her as he wiped down the bar. Taking a tray of ale, she made her way to the table, where she paused beside Toomy.

The big man looked up and, seeing the worried look in her eyes instead of the usual glint of humor, closed a hand over hers. "Hey now. Where's that big bright smile I've come to expect? What's bothering you, lass?"

She shrugged. "I need money, Toomy."

He laughed. "Don't we all, lass? Don't we all. Isn't Wilbur paying you enough?"

"He is, yes. He's always been fair with me. But it isn't enough. I have a friend who needs help. I need to find a job that pays more than this."

Toomy lifted the glass, drained it, and then held it out for her to refill before saying softly, "My cousin got a job as a maid in a rich man's home. She said the pay's decent, and she doesn't have to worry about paying rent anymore."

Lana's eyes widened. "Why not?"

"She lives there. So do the others who work there."

"In the rich man's house?"

He nodded.

Lana glanced toward Wilbur and lowered her voice to a whisper. "Would you be knowing how she went about getting such a job?"

"Not sure." He scratched his head. "A friend of hers worked there and told her they were hiring. She used the friend's name when she went to apply, and she was hired on the spot. Don't know much more than that, but if you're interested, lass, I could tell you where she's working."

"Would a person be needing references for such a job?"

He shrugged. "Not that I know of. Will I write down

my cousin's name and the name of the family she works for?"

Lana withdrew the slate from her pocket and watched as Toomy printed several names in crude letters before passing it back to her.

"Thank you." She slipped the slate into her pocket. "I'd be grateful if you didn't say anything about this just yet."

"I understand." The fat man winked. "Wilbur won't be happy about losing someone as dependable as you. Good luck, Lana."

Luck, she thought with a sigh. She'd need more than that if she hoped to make good on her promise to Siobhan.

LANA STARED AT the magnificent mansion standing four stories tall behind an ornate fence. A curving drive circled from the street to the front door. In the middle of the circle stood a statue of the Greek god Apollo, whom Lana recognized from one of the many books she'd devoured. At Apollo's feet was a fountain of water spilling into a basin.

As Lana watched, a fine carriage swept past her and stopped at the foot of wide stone steps that led to a pillared porch. The front door was opened by a uniformed man who accepted an armload of packages from the driver before escorting a lady inside.

Lana's jaw had dropped as she'd made her way along this stretch of Fifth Avenue across from Central Park known as Millionaire's Row. The row of mansions ran from east Seventieth Street between Madison and Lexington Avenues. In the years she'd lived in New York City, this was her first occasion to get so close, and each mansion was more spectacular than the last. Some were Gothic in style, others Greek, and some, like this one, more resembled an Italian villa than an American residence. She felt as though she'd stumbled into some mythical kingdom and half expected to see kings and queens rolling past in liveried carriages.

Lana knew enough to make her way around to the back door. Only invited guests entered through the front doors of such fine places as this.

As she climbed the steps, she smoothed the skirt of her gown. She'd been up since dawn, ironing the wrinkles from her best dress. She'd twisted her hair into a neat knot at her nape and pinned a tidy hat over it to anchor it in place. Now she forced a smile to her lips and tensed at the sound of approaching footsteps.

The door was opened by a scowling woman who was surely as tall as a man. She wore a prim black gown. Her dark hair was pinned back, revealing a face devoid of color, except for her eyes, which were as dark as a blackbird's. They peered at Lana without blinking.

"What brings you to this door?" The voice was cold, the tone curt.

Lana swallowed loudly and wondered if the woman heard it. "I was told you were hiring."

"Not likely. And certainly not someone so skinny she'd blow away in a stiff wind." The woman looked her up and down. "You're wasting my time."

Before she could close the door in Lana's face, there was the sound of breaking glass and a woman's high-pitched shriek that reminded Lana of a banshee. Before Lana could flee, a huge, round woman dashed up behind the one in the doorway, dragging a terrified young girl by the hair. With a furious hiss of anger, the girl was tossed through the open doorway, where she sprawled down the rough stone steps and sat in the grass, struggling to compose herself.

"What's this?" the tall woman asked.

"This lazy, no-good, useless scum dropped a stack of plates. An entire stack of 'em."

"My hands were wet," the girl cried, but no one seemed to notice.

"Now there's broken glass all over my clean kitchen floor. And who's to clean it up, I ask?"

Lana straightened her shoulders. "I'll do it."

The two women barely flicked a glance at her.

"I'm stronger than I look," Lana added quickly. "I'm neat and tidy, and I can clean anything."

"Irish." Hearing her brogue, the tall woman's voice held a faint note of scorn. "Like that one." She pointed toward the girl who was now getting to her knees as though in a daze. "How long have you been in this country?"

"Five years."

That seemed to please the woman. "At least you're not straight off the boat." She looked at the fat woman, who was still scowling at the girl she'd tossed out the door. When there was no objection, the taller one stood aside. "Come in."

To the girl in the grass she called, "Take off that dress. Now that you no longer work here, it doesn't belong to you."

"What about my things?"

"Oh, they'll be right along. It won't take but a minute to be rid of you and all that belongs to you."

As Lana started through the doorway, the girl in the grass sneered, "You'll be sorry. No matter how hard you try, there's no pleasing that fat, old biddy."

Lana felt a chill at the words, but she chose to ignore them as she stepped inside. She couldn't help but stare at the fine, big wooden cupboards and the sturdy table and chairs.

The fat woman waddled away, leaving Lana with the taller one.

"This is the servants' kitchen. They eat here after the VanEndel family has finished dining."

Lana had read the name on the slate. But now, hearing it spoken aloud, she felt a little thrill. Gustav VanEndel was one of New York's most famous industrialists, though she couldn't say what that meant. She had no idea how he made his money. His wife, Evelyn, was a society legend.

Their pictures were always in the paper, photographed attending fancy dinner parties and society balls.

The realization that she was standing in the VanEndel house filled her with awe.

She could only wonder what the dining room looked like if this fine big room was a servants' kitchen. It was bigger than any room she'd ever seen. Bigger even than the entire Blue Goose.

"As you just heard, Cook needs help in the kitchen. Someone to wash the dishes, the pots and pans, and the floors. She'll not tolerate any laziness. If she finds you slacking off, you'll be on the street like the last one. Is that clear?"

Lana nodded. "It is, yes."

The woman winced, as though the mere sound of that brogue grated on her nerves. "You'll not be allowed in the family quarters. That's only for trusted employees who've been with the VanEndel family for years. If you're found in there, you'll be dismissed at once. You'll be expected to work every day when the family is in residence, except for three hours on Sunday mornings. When the VanEndel family is away, you may take an additional hour on Monday afternoons. As for accommodations, you'll sleep in an upstairs room with five other girls, as you'll often be working late into the night, cleaning up after the VanEndel's dinner parties." She paused. "Do you have any questions?"

Lana fought to keep her tone even. "When would I start?"

"Now. Cook wants the broken glass swept away. After that, I expect you'll need to retrieve your belongings. You can return in the morning."

Lana blinked, unable to take it all in. Was that it? Had she just been hired to work in this fine, big mansion? "Show me to the kitchen, and I'll have the floor clean. Tomorrow I'll be back."

The woman nodded. "My name is Swanson. Cook starts her day at dawn. Follow me."

She led the way to the big, steamy kitchen, where the cook had already returned to the stove. She was stirring something in a huge black kettle. The smell of soup simmering and bread baking in the oven had Lana's mouth watering.

The floor was littered with broken plates and shards of glass.

Picking up a broom, Lana swept the floor clean of all debris.

While she worked, a young girl in a maid's uniform hurried past her, carrying a shabby valise, which the cook took from her hands and tossed out the back door with a final barrage of insults.

Lana felt a wave of sympathy for the poor girl who'd had the misfortune to incur the wrath of the cook. Still, had it not been for her incredible timing, Lana would be the one leaving without a job.

A short time later, when the kitchen had been restored to order, Lana danced down the steps, her mind in turmoil. She had a job as a servant in the VanEndel's fine big mansion on Fifth Avenue. She started tomorrow. That left time for one last long visit with Siobhan and Colin. And tonight she would say good-bye to Wilbur Hasting and all the men at the Blue Goose.

Though she warned herself not to think beyond that, her mind refused to cooperate. She found herself dwelling on the possibility that the handsome, mysterious Stone might be there to say good-bye.

HE WASN'T THERE. All evening, as Lana dashed about, dispensing glasses of ale and whiskey, she found herself glancing toward Ned Lancaster's table, hoping to see that rogue smile and those smoky eyes staring back at her.

It wasn't to be. By the time the night was winding down and the gamblers were playing their last hand of poker, Lana had to accept the fact that Stone wasn't coming. And if he should return another time, he wouldn't even know where she'd gone.

Catching herself daydreaming, her chin came up and she gave a quick toss of her head. She'd been granted her wish then, hadn't she? She wouldn't have to give another thought to getting involved with a lazy, shiftless con.

It was better this way. She'd grown soft and dreamy. Now it was time to face some hard, cold truths. Life from this day forward would be different. She'd known that as soon as she'd left the dreary tenement earlier today.

Her visit with Siobhan and Colin had been filled with tension. Siobhan fretted that she couldn't hide the changes in her body from Billy much longer. She could barely lift her head from the cot this morning, and that had sent Billy into a black rage.

Even worse than seeing Siobhan's fears was the scene with Colin when Lana had told him she wouldn't be able to see him for a week. They'd spent every afternoon together from the time of his birth five years earlier, and it was, she knew, a lifeline for the lad, as well as for his mother. Without someone to take him out into the fresh air, Colin would have to be cooped up all day with his mother in their cramped, foul-smelling apartment. Who would buy him apples? Worse, who would feed his dreams?

"It's only for a little while, Colin. Only until I've saved enough money to bring you and your mum to live with me. And then, what a grand life we'll share."

Even as she'd spoken the words, she'd prayed it was so. There was a slim chance that Billy would accept another baby. There was an even better chance that, no matter what, Siobhan wouldn't find the courage to leave Billy unless he deserted her and Colin, leaving them alone and desperate. The very thought of it filled Lana with sorrow.

Enough sadness, she told herself. Tomorrow was a new day. A new job. A new life. Now she could concentrate on saving every dollar to prepare for the future. She would, she vowed, give little Colin the life she'd never had.

"You're really leaving?" Wilbur's words had her turning toward the bar.

"I am, yes. I'm sorry there wasn't time to give you warning, but I'm sure Verna Lee can do my job."

"She's a lazy girl. There's no way she'll do all you've done, but I'm hoping the thought of earning more money will give my brother's girl some ambition." His head came up, and he looked beyond her with a sudden spark of interest. "Well now. I figured you'd found a new game in some other part of town."

Lana turned and found herself pinned by a pair of familiar smoky eyes.

Stone continued staring at her, his mouth curved into a hint of humor and danger, while addressing the tavern owner. "There's no other game quite like this one, Wilbur. Besides, the Blue Goose is beginning to feel like home."

The tavern owner was already shoving a glass of ale toward Lana. "Show the man to his table, and be quick about it."

Stone followed her. As they approached the table, the others paused in their game to look up and call out greetings.

"I figured you'd had enough of our money." Ned Lancaster laid down his hand and began scooping up the dollar bills littering the middle of the table.

"Is there ever enough?" Stone settled himself into his usual seat and accepted the glass from Lana's hand.

She jerked back as his fingers brushed hers. Before she could turn away he winked, and she felt her heart give a quick, hard bounce.

So much for ignoring Stone. Her mind might be willing, but her heart was another matter altogether. Her only salvation was that the night was nearly at an end. That knowledge gave her little comfort.

As the crowd thinned, Lana busied herself loading trays with empty glasses and depositing them at the bar before scrubbing the wooden tables until they gleamed.

She was still scrubbing when Ned's game ended with a few muttered curses and a low rumble of laughter. She didn't need to look over to know who'd won the money. She would recognize Stone's triumphant peals of laughter anywhere.

As the men headed toward the door, she heard Ned's good-natured jibe. "We'd better see you tomorrow night. We deserve a chance to win our money back."

"I'm always happy to oblige." He tucked the dollar bills into his pocket and shook hands all round.

When the others were gone, he lingered a moment, watching her. "If you're ready to go, Lana, I'll walk you to your room." He stepped closer, keeping his voice low so Wilbur, busy at the bar, wouldn't overhear. "We could watch the boats in the harbor if you'd like."

Oh, she was tempted. More than he'd ever know. But she couldn't afford to be foolish now. Not when her life was about to take such a turn.

"Sorry." She kept her face averted, afraid he'd see the lie in her eyes. "I've too much work to do yet."

"I'm sorry, too. I'll say good night, then. I guess I'll see you tomorrow, Lana."

"Good night." She waited until she was certain he was at the door before lifting her head and turning toward him.

He'd paused in the doorway and was staring intently at her. The shock of it sent a jolt through her system, and she took hold of the edge of the table to steady herself.

"Sweet dreams, Lana."

Those were his last words to her as he sauntered off into the night.

She swallowed back the regret that was welling up, threatening to choke her. She had to fight an almost over-powering impulse to go after him. The thought of it teased and tempted her.

She could have walked with him in the moonlight. Maybe he would have kissed her again. She would have had the memory of that to warm her through the long, lonely nights that loomed in her future. Instead, driven by her damnable common sense, she'd chosen to keep the truth from him.

The thought of Stone coming back tomorrow night, expecting to see her, only to learn that she'd left the Blue Goose forever, had her fighting tears.

Coward, she berated herself. Because of her fear of getting hurt the way Siobhan had been, she had passed up her last chance to be with the most handsome, intriguing man she'd ever known.

It hurt. Oh, how it hurt. But it was better this way. Of course it was, she told herself as she bent to yet another table, scrubbing with such vehemence her knuckles bled from the effort.

FOUR

———◆◆◆———

"AT LEAST YOU'RE prompt." Swanson opened the back door at Lana's first knock. "A good thing, too. Cook's in a snit over the horrible condition of her kitchen."

Lana barely had time to glance at the dirty dishes piled up everywhere, as well as a sink full of blackened pots and pans, as she was led through the kitchen.

"First, I'll show you where you'll sleep." The housekeeper led the way up the back stairs of the mansion to the top floor.

The stuffy attic room was vacant, the young women who slept there apparently already at work in various sections of the house.

Swanson pointed to a cot in the farthest corner of the room. "That's your bed."

Lana suppressed the groan that sprang to her lips and nodded toward a pale gray gown and crisp white apron lying across the cot. "Am I to put that on now?"

The housekeeper nodded and watched as Lana removed her dress and stepped into the uniform. The sleeves hung over Lana's wrists, and the hem fell over her shoes. Even tying the apron as snugly as possible didn't hide the fact that it was made for a much larger woman.

Swanson gave a sigh. "I see it's too big for you, but it will have to do until the seamstress can make one over to fit. I'll get her started on it right away. It wouldn't do for Mr. and Mrs. VanEndel to return from Europe and find one of their staff looking like this. They'd be horrified." She turned and opened a narrow closet. Inside were six small cubicles. "You can put your things there."

Lana started to open her small satchel, but the housekeeper gave a vigorous shake of her head. "You can empty that later. There's no time to waste. Cook is threatening to commandeer half the household staff and drag them off to her kitchen."

Lana stashed the bag and her gown in the empty cubicle, closing the door before following the woman down the stairs.

In the kitchen, she was given a brief tour of the many cabinets and supplies. She'd never seen so many stacks of dishes, all matching, and gleaming silver that would take an entire staff of servants days to polish. There were cupboards with every size of pot and pan, kettle, and tin. How, Lana wondered, could one family find use for all these? There were drawers crammed with spotless linen towels and others containing neatly folded table linens—none of which, Swanson explained, were ever to be used in the formal dining room. There was fine imported lace for that and embroidered linen.

The housekeeper pointed to several kettles of water heating on the stove, and the huge basin in the sink. "Once you've set this place to rights, Cook will tell you what to do next. See that you do everything she asks without question." She barely paused for breath before saying, "Cook inspects these cupboards daily and reports to me. If she should find a speck of dirt on the dishes, or a trace of grease in a pot or pan, you'll be reprimanded. Three such reprimands and you'll be gone like those before you. Is that understood?"

"Yes, ma'am." Lana began rolling up the sleeves of her uniform.

Swanson watched her a moment before motioning toward a step-stool. "You'll need that to reach the higher cupboards. Take care that you don't trip over that hem while putting away the dishes."

"I'll see to it." Lana wasn't likely to forget the scene she'd witnessed with the last servant. It was indelibly etched in her mind. She had no intention of ending up on the streets.

With a swish of starched skirts and petticoats, the housekeeper was gone, leaving Lana to tackle the mess. With such a daunting task, there was no time to dwell on the life she'd left behind, or to give a single thought to what she'd gotten herself into.

"WELL." THE FAT cook stared around the spotless kitchen with her beady little eyes, pausing to run a hand over the countertop. "Did you go to the laundry as I asked and fetch clean towels?"

"I did, yes." Lana nodded toward the drawers, but Cook was already striding over to see for herself. Lifting out a stack of neatly folded towels, she looked them over, replaced them, and then carefully examined the table linens before closing the drawer.

"I'll just take a look at those pots and pans."

Lana stood across the room and waited as Cook ran a plump finger around the rim of each and every pot and lifted several to the sunlight, searching for spots.

If the woman had a name, Lana hadn't heard it. Everyone referred to her as "Cook," and she'd made no attempt to offer another. But then, Lana realized, she was also without a name in this place. Cook called her "Girl." Mrs. Swanson called her "You there." She supposed it was better than being cursed.

"Will you be wanting anything else cleaned?"

Cook replaced the pot and straightened. Without even glancing up, she said, "That's all for now. Go take your supper with the others. See that you're down here by dawn, girl."

"Yes, ma'am." Lana made her way to the servants' kitchen, where only recently she'd set the table and laid out the meal prepared for them.

When she entered, the room was already filled with a blur of strangers, filling their plates from a side table and taking their places around the long harvest table.

"You'd be the new kitchen help." The girl filling her plate from a steaming kettle was tall and reed-thin, with the biggest hands Lana had ever seen.

It was well past dusk, and after more than ten hours of nonstop work in the steamy kitchen, Lana could feel her energy draining. Her legs felt shaky. Her arms were aching from slinging so many heavy pots. In fact, her entire body ached. "I am, yes."

"Irish." The girl exchanged a look with several others. "I'm surprised Swanson would hire you."

"She had no choice. Cook tossed the other girl out the door and was in need of a replacement."

"Happens a lot." The tall girl helped herself to a thick slice of bread and spread it with butter. "In the time I've been here, there've been at least half a dozen new girls hired in the kitchen. None of them lasted more than a few weeks."

"Quit trying to scare the new hire, Johnny." A pretty little blonde took a seat across the table.

"Johnny?"

At Lana's arched brow, the tall girl gave a grin and snagged an empty chair. "My father wanted a son. I was the sixth daughter, and last, according to my mother, so she named me after him." She motioned toward the blonde girl. "And this is Swede."

"Not my name, of course," the girl corrected. "But it's all I've ever been called here. I'm betting you'll be known as 'Irish.' "

Before Lana could answer, one of the other women asked, "How was your first day on the job, Irish?"

"It was all right." Lana filled her plate and found an empty seat at the end of the table.

"At least you haven't been fired." The woman grinned at the others around the table. "Working for Cook, that's something. Some of the help didn't even last until the end of their first day."

Lana glanced around the table, but the others were too busy eating to take the time to join in the conversation. They merely nodded as they continued eating.

"Would one of you be related to a man named Toomy?"

The others glanced around and then returned their attention to their food. There was, Lana noted, a plump girl with corkscrew curls at the other end of the table, shoveling food into her mouth and barely taking time to chew before shoveling more. Beside her was an older woman who paused to bless herself before cutting her meat. All were dressed alike, in the dull gray dress and white bib apron that was the VanEndel uniform. Though their hair was supposed to be secured off their faces with a white lace dust-cap, most of them had long ago given up trying to keep their hair in place. Curly or straight, red or blond or dark, it fell in damp strands around their faces while they mechanically ate their fill.

"That may have been the girl you replaced," Johnny said with a grin.

Lana's heart sank, and she found herself fervently hoping Johnny was wrong. If it hadn't been for the kindness of

Toomy, she wouldn't have this job. Still, she hadn't been the cause of his niece's misfortune, only the beneficiary of it.

"Do you always eat this late?" Lana asked between bites.

Swede gave a snort of derision. "Sometimes it's midnight before we get time to eat. Swanson rules this house with an iron fist. I think she enjoys the power, though some say she has no choice but to take the orders set out by Mrs. VanEndel. No matter who makes the rules, we have no choice but to do as we're told, or find a new place to work."

"Thinking about complaining, Irish?" Johnny asked.

When Lana gave a quick shake of her head, the tall girl laughed. "Good. The last girl to complain wasn't just tossed out on the street, she was told that her name would be circulated to the other households around town as a troublemaker. So there she was, alone, unable to find work, and facing the sad news that none of the other rich families in New York would hire her either." Johnny drained a glass of milk, wiping her mouth with her sleeve.

Seeing it, Lana was reminded of another who always did that.

While the others continued eating, Lana fell silent, her thoughts on little Colin. She might not be able to be with him as often as before, but she had made a difference in his life, and she would do so again. She was determined to save every dollar she earned until she had enough to lift Colin and Siobhan out of their miserable existence.

"Don't talk much, do you?" Johnny broke into Lana's thoughts.

She merely shrugged and looked up at the clanging of a bell. She'd heard that same sound all through the day, but there had been no one to ask about it.

"What is that ringing?"

"The VanEndels use it to summon one of the upstairs maids."

"Upstairs maids?"

"Those who serve in the family's private rooms." Johnny's voice lowered. "You'd think, with the Mr. and Mrs. away, we wouldn't have to hear it as much. But with Wilton home alone, it's even worse."

"Wilton?"

"The VanEndel's son. He and his friends have the run of the house with his parents gone, and he's leading the servants on a merry chase."

At the mention of his name, the others had fallen silent. Sensing a distinct chill in their mood, Lana kept the rest of her questions to herself.

When the meal ended, she followed the example of the others, carrying her dishes to the sink, washing them, and carefully putting them away before climbing the back stairs to the attic room. There, she stripped off her uniform and slipped into a cotton nightshift.

Swede blew out the candle, leaving the room in darkness.

As Lana settled herself on the hard cot, she glanced toward the high, narrow window across the room. In her mind she was once again in the orphanage in her homeland, forced to live by the strict rules set by others. Was that why she had so eagerly embraced her little room on the wharf?

At least there she'd lived by her own rules and had been free to come and go as she pleased. It had been such a comfort to lie in her bed and stare out the window, watching the darkened sky come alive with light from the moon and stars. The ocean scents and the slap of water against the wharf had been her nighttime lullaby. Here there was only darkness, and the vague outline of five other cots, and the stifling heat of the attic closing in around her, making every breath an effort.

She found herself yearning for her room behind the Blue Goose and aching for the freedom to skip across town and spend a carefree morning with Colin.

Was he missing her? Was someone telling him grand stories and buying him an apple at the fruit vendor's? Was he ever taken for a ride on the carousel or allowed to race across the green grass of Central Park?

Be patient, Colin, she thought with a sense of desperation. *Soon. Very soon, I'll have a morning free, and I'll hold you and hug you and kiss you until I've had my fill of baby kisses. Oh, how I wish it could be right now, this minute.*

Turning her face into the pillow, she wept silent, scalding tears until sleep finally overtook her.

"WHERE HAVE YOU been, Auntie Lana?" As soon as the door to their cramped apartment was opened and Colin saw her standing in the doorway, he flew into her arms and wrapped his chubby hands around her neck, clinging tightly.

"Have you forgotten? I've a new job. It keeps me awfully busy. But I'm here now." She hugged him fiercely, pressing kisses to his cheeks, his hair, the tip of his nose.

Finally, setting him down, she held him a little away. "Oh, let me look at you, lad."

His skin looked pale. He'd lost the color in his cheeks, and there were circles under his eyes. Such sad, old little eyes.

When she looked at his mother, the pallor was even more pronounced. Instead of the rounded hips and swollen breasts she'd expected to see, Siobhan appeared thinner than ever. Beneath the faded dress, there was no sign of her condition. She seemed to be a shadow of her former self.

"Are you . . . all right?"

"I'm fine. We're both fine." Her friend seemed to take a long time drying her hands on a linen towel. All the while, she kept her gaze averted.

"And Billy?"

"He . . . went off with some friends. To a game, I think."

It took Lana a moment to realize that Siobhan meant a card game. "He's playing poker on a Sunday morning?"

The young woman sank down on a chipped kitchen chair. "The game actually started last night. Billy said, if it went well and he was winning, he probably wouldn't get home until sometime today."

"I see." Lana forced a smile to her lips. "Then I say it's the perfect time for the three of us to walk to the park."

"You go." Siobhan remained seated. "I'll stay here and rest."

Lana caught her hand. "Come with us. The sunshine will do you good." Before her friend could argue, she withdrew her shawl and wrapped it around Siobhan's shoulders. "And while Colin and I ride the carousel, you can lie in the grass and snatch some sleep in the fresh air. On the way back, we'll buy apples from the vendor, and you can tell me all about your week."

Looping her arm through her friend's, with her other hand holding tightly to Colin's, she led them out of the dreary tenement room and into the sunlight of the warm summer morning.

She could have used some rest herself. It was difficult falling asleep in the heat of the attic, with so many bodies close around her. But this was better than any nap. Just being with Siobhan and Colin had her spirits lifting considerably. The tedious work she was forced to do hour after hour at the VanEndel mansion was forgotten, as was the sound of those incessant bells. The strict rules were for later. For now, there was only sunshine and friendship.

The sound of their laughter as they left the tenement behind and joined the throngs in Central Park meant even more to Lana than the coin in her pocket. Oh, it was so good to be free, even if it was for a brief time.

An hour later, after kissing them good-bye on the stoop and tucking an extra apple into Colin's pocket, she dashed along the streets and arrived breathless at the servants' entrance, ready for another week of drudgery.

Not drudgery, she reminded herself. She was working. Working toward a goal. Soon she would have enough money saved to make a home for Siobhan and Colin. When that day came, they would be together forever. And no one, no one in this world, she vowed, would ever separate them again.

FIVE

"FINISHED ALL THE tasks I left for you?" Cook waddled around the kitchen, opening drawers and cupboards, examining the linens and dishes, the pots and pans.

"I did, yes."

If the fat woman noticed the way the kitchen sparkled, she never mentioned it. If she was pleased to see that the countertops, the floors, even the windows, were spotless, she didn't bother to convey her thoughts to the girl responsible.

The interminable days and nights had slid past in a blur of hard work. Lana had learned to expect no words of praise from the cook or the housekeeper, no matter how diligently she labored. The work they meted out was to be done without question. Though good work was neither rewarded nor praised, sloppy work was punished swiftly and efficiently. The turnover of servants in the VanEndel house was the main topic of conversation among the staff.

Cook motioned toward a pile of sodden rags spilling over the edge of an empty bucket. "Take those to the laundry, and bring back clean linens."

"Yes, ma'am." Lana resisted the urge to press a hand to the small of her back. She'd been bent over scrubbing the floor for the past hour. And before that, she'd been on a stepstool, washing windows. But the last thing she wanted was to give any hint of weakness. As Cook was fond of pointing out to all the staff, there were dozens of women waiting to take the place of anyone dissatisfied with the conditions of their employment here.

With a grunt Lana lifted the heavy pile of rags and staggered out of the kitchen. Through the open doorway she could see Swede outside on her hands and knees, scrubbing the paved courtyard that led to the wide, curving steps up to the door. *Poor Swede,* Lana thought with a rush of feeling. She'd heard that the girl, one of the few who'd been here long enough to work as an upstairs housemaid, had been reprimanded for spending too much time gossiping instead of doing her chores. As punishment, Swanson had ordered her outside to scrub the entrance. It was hard, punishing work, and Lana had no doubt the girl's knuckles would be raw and bloody by the time the job was finished to the housekeeper's satisfaction.

All week the household had become a beehive of activity, when word had reached them that the VanEndels would be returning from Europe by week's end. Rugs had to be taken outside and beaten to freshen the rooms gone unused for several months. Curtains had been washed and hung in the sunshine while windows were scrubbed clean. Mattresses had been turned and fresh linens added to the master suites on the second floor. Cook had been in a frenzy, ordering Mr. VanEndel's favorite foods from the market and nearby farms and planning a special dinner for the homecoming. The gardener was busy filling the rooms with fresh bouquets.

The VanEndel son, Wilton, on the other hand, had been, according to those servants who worked above stairs, more demanding than ever. There had been both men and women invited to his private suite for all-night parties. It was whispered that the women were not his society friends, but rather, actresses and street women, brought in to amuse him and his friends. Though Lana was scandalized, the others appeared to take such behavior in stride. It was, they'd hinted, typical behavior by the son and heir to the VanEndel fortune.

Lana hurried off to the laundry, breathing in the sharp smell of disinfectant as she stepped inside. Two girls stood on either side of a round tub feeding dripping articles into a roller that squeezed the moisture from the fabric. Once squeezed, the clothes were tossed into large wicker baskets. Four more girls carried the filled baskets outside and hung the items to dry. On sunny days such as this, the work was pleasant enough. When the days turned raw and wintry, these same girls would be shivering from the cold as they removed stiff, frozen bed linens from the lines.

Lana set aside the bucket of rags before greeting the young women. With little more than a smile and a wave, they continued their work. It occurred to Lana that Swede's punishment had had the desired effect on the rest of the staff. For the next few days at least, Swanson would be assured of an efficient workforce, especially now that the VanEndels would be in residence. No one wanted to be the next to spend hours on their hands and knees, shoveling horse-droppings and shining up the grand entry.

Lana picked up a basket of fresh linens and started down the hall. As she passed a small storeroom off the pantry, she heard a muffled sound. Thinking it was Cook, she continued on. Before she'd taken more than a couple steps, she heard it again. This time she thought it sounded more like a woman's cry before it was abruptly cut off in midscream.

"Cook?" Sweet heaven. Had the fat woman tripped?

Juggling the basket, Lana managed to turn the knob and yank open the door. Inside she could see Swede lying on the floor, her clothes in disarray, with something on top of her. Peering around the pile of linens that obscured her view, Lana let out a gasp.

Not something.

Someone!

A man, she realized, with his body pinning Swede to the floor. One of his hands was over the girl's mouth, while his other hand fumbled under her skirt and petticoat. He was so intent upon his dark deed, he never even bothered to look up.

Lana reacted instinctively, swinging the basket against his head as hard as she could. The force of the movement knocked the basket from her hands and it tumbled to the floor, sending a cloud of towels spilling everywhere. With a vicious oath, the man rolled to one side and clutched his head while towels drifted down, encasing him in a white cocoon.

Using that moment of distraction, Lana reached down and grasped Swede's hand, yanking her to her feet. The poor girl stumbled, and Lana was forced to drag her out the door before slamming it in the man's face. When the door started to open outward, she dug in her heels and used all her weight to hold it shut.

"Help me," she pleaded.

Though stunned and reeling, Swede joined her weight to Lana's and they managed to hold the door closed.

They could hear the man's voice spewing a string of violent oaths while his fists pounded on the closed door.

"Damn you! You'll pay for this." The voice lifted in a blaze of fury.

"Quick. Bring me that serving cart," Lana whispered frantically.

When Swede rolled the cart over, Lana tipped it on its side and jammed it against the closed door.

While the pounding continued, Lana grabbed Swede's hand, and the two ran away without a backward glance.

In the kitchen, Lana paused to catch her breath. Beside her, Swede dropped to the floor and began to weep.

"There now." Lana patted the girl's bowed head. "You're safe. That monster wouldn't dare show himself here." She glanced around and snatched up a butcher knife, brandishing it like a sword. "I'll find Swanson and ask her to summon the police."

"The police? Oh no. You mustn't." That had Swede crying all the harder.

"Hush now. They'll keep you safe. I'll tell them what I saw."

"You don't understand." The girl hiccupped and used the hem of her apron to stem the flow of tears.

"I do. You want no scandal brought to the door of your employer. But a beast like that needs to be put away where he can't hurt an innocent girl again." Lana got to her feet. "I'll fetch Cook or Swanson. They'll know what to do."

"No. Please." Swede caught the hem of Lana's skirt and tugged fiercely to keep her from turning away.

Lana was surprised at the girl's vehemence. "Are you suggesting that we let such a deed go unpunished?" She paused, studying the girl more closely. "You didn't invite that man's advances, did you?"

"Of course not." Swede gave a firm shake of her head, sending blond curls dancing. "But you can't tell the police."

"And why not?"

"Because." The girl's lips trembled, and the tears started afresh. "That monster lives here. He is Wilton VanEndel."

"That was . . . ?"

Swede nodded. "He seems desperate to do as he pleases for this one last day of freedom before his parents return."

"But this . . ." Lana fought for control. "What he did is evil."

"It isn't his first time. He's done this before to . . . other girls who worked here."

"You can't mean this. Why wouldn't the girls go to his parents?"

"Some have. But all they got for their efforts was to be sent packing." Swede blew her nose. "Do you think people like the VanEndels want to hear that their son forces himself on servants?"

"He must be stopped."

"Not by me." Swede clutched Lana's hands. "And not by you, Irish. Not if you value your job."

Lana shook her head. "I doubt I'll have a job once this . . . this Wilton fellow tells his parents what I did."

"He won't tell them. He may be spoiled and willful and malicious, but he isn't stupid. He'll never admit to something like this. He knows his parents are willing to overlook his faults, choosing to blame others whenever his behavior takes things too far. Once, in fact, he forced himself on a young servant who was too afraid to tell. When she found herself with his child, she went to his parents. Wilton accused her of lying to get their money. She was coldly dismissed and left to fend for herself on the mean streets, without a job, without a family." Swede took a deep breath. "That's why you can't go to his parents. You're safe here in the kitchen. It's the one place Wilton would never bother to enter. Right now, he doesn't know you. Nor does he even know it was one of the servants who stopped him. He was too busy . . ." She shivered and lowered her face to her hands. "He was too busy trying to force me to even see who prevented it."

"Are you all right? Did he . . . ?" Lana couldn't bring herself to speak the words.

"Thanks to you, I'm all right." The girl sniffed. "At least for now. But he won't give up. In fact, he'll be more determined than ever, now that someone's thwarted his efforts."

"Then you can't return to the upstairs work. If you do, you know he'll be waiting for you."

"I know. But what else can I do? Irish, I need this job."

They both looked up as Cook waddled into the kitchen, followed by Swanson. They came to an abrupt halt at the sight of the two servants kneeling on the floor. For a moment neither woman spoke.

Moving past them, the housekeeper remarked, "It seems Wilton VanEndel stumbled into a storeroom by mistake and somehow a serving cart became upended, locking him in."

Lana glanced at Swede before turning to the older woman. "You saw him there?"

"Indeed. Looking for some clean linens, from the look of him. He must have bumped into an entire stack and was still wearing them."

Cook fixed Lana with a piercing stare. "Speaking of linens, I believe I sent you to the laundry to fetch some. See that you bring them now."

When Lana hesitated, the housekeeper interrupted. "We'll keep Swede here with us. I'm thinking she might want to share a cup of tea now that she's finished her chores for the day."

Cook nodded. "A fine idea." She stared hard at Lana. "Go on with you now, girl."

As Lana hurried away she heard Swanson's voice, low and urgent, and Swede's answering tones, soft and halting, sounding dangerously like cries.

As Lana made her way to the laundry, she found herself looking over her shoulder, jumping at every shadow. She'd thought men like Wilton only sought their sport in taverns, with women like Verna Lee. Even the wealthy and privileged, she realized now, were to be feared. Perhaps more so. For who would believe a poor servant if she were to accuse a millionaire's son of such despicable behavior?

LANA LAY IN her bed, listening to the soft snoring around her. Sitting up, she stared at Swede's bed, now empty. The girl had been gone by the time Lana had returned from the laundry. No explanation had been given. She was simply there one minute and gone the next. Her meager belongings had been removed from the closet. Her uniform had already been laundered and starched and hung in the tiny cubicle, awaiting her replacement.

There had been whispers over supper. Some said she'd run off to meet a lover. Others said she'd accepted a better job. Lana had been sorely tempted to tell them what she knew, but she'd wisely kept her thoughts to herself, choosing to trust no one. Was it any wonder most of the servants working here chose not to reveal their true names? It was far better, she decided, to remain simply "Irish" or "Girl." If she found herself in Swede's position, at least the ugly rumors wouldn't follow her through her lifetime.

Had Swanson and Cook arranged Swede's employ in another household? Or had they simply sent her packing with nothing but the clothes on her back? On the one hand, she was happy for Swede. She'd avoided Wilton's revenge. But on the other hand, she would be forced, through no fault of her own, to start over in another place, no doubt under conditions far worse from the ones she'd encountered here at the VanEndel house.

Lana rolled to her side, willing sleep to steal over her and put an end to her worrisome thoughts. She needed to be fresh in the morning. Judging by the tension she'd sensed in Swanson and Cook, the pending arrival of the wealthy owners of this mansion was sending everyone into a panic. She had no doubt that from this day forward, her workload would be doubled.

SIX

"WHAT'S THIS? SWANSON, come look at this smudge. I want the maid who cleaned this room dismissed at once."

Lana lifted her head at the strange woman's voice and knew at once it must be Evelyn VanEndel. Ever since the return of the VanEndels, the household staff operated at a frenzied pace. The lady of the house, it would seem, was a demanding taskmistress, finding smudges on the banister, dust on the mantel, or complaining that her morning chocolate was not hot enough to suit her discriminating pallet. For each infraction, one of the servants' heads would roll. The turnover of staff had everyone on edge.

It fell to Swanson to bear the unpleasant duty of executioner, carrying out her employer's harsh directions or risk her own employment.

Gustav VanEndel, plump, bewhiskered, and mild-mannered, seemed oblivious to his wife's complaints, leaving the management of the household completely to her discretion. After coffee with his wife, Mr. VanEndel took his breakfast in the dining room at precisely seven each morning before leaving for his office. His only interest lay in making money—piles of it, according to the whispers among the staff. Once the man of the house was gone for the day, the servants steeled themselves to find a way to please his demanding wife. Mrs. VanEndel insisted upon breakfast in her suite, followed by a leisurely bath and then an afternoon with friends. There were teas in the garden or lunch at one of the many charity functions of which Evelyn VanEndel was chairman. Each evening brought a new flurry of activity as both Mr. and Mrs. VanEndel prepared for the theater or dinner at one of the many famous restaurants in the city.

At least once a week the VanEndels' picture would appear in the society column of the *New York News and Dispatch,* smiling at the camera as they dined or danced or attended yet another dinner. After the housekeeper and cook had read the newspaper and tossed it aside, it was surreptitiously passed from servant to servant, as they devoured all the details of their employers' latest activity. Those who couldn't read were content to look at the pictures.

Lana studied the grainy photo in the paper. "She looks pretty enough."

"And why not?" Johnny paused in the kitchen to pour a glass of water. "She has a woman to do her hair. Another to do her nails. Another to alter all her dresses so they hide any imperfections."

"Does she have any?"

Johnny laughed. "Not to hear her. She looks in the mirror and sees perfection." She pointed to the photograph. "I'll bet all the old fools seeing this think she's some sort of angel for all her charity work."

Lana picked up the newspaper. "I think it's grand that she visits orphanages and raises money for police widows."

"While she fires the poor servant who didn't make her chocolate hot enough."

Lana shrugged. "It's her house, Johnny. She has the right to make the rules."

The tall girl leaned close, aware that she could be overheard if someone passed by. "If you ask me, she does those charity things so others will approve of her. If she were really an angel, she'd devote some time to looking at what needs to be done right here in her own house."

Lana shot her a look. "You mean Wilton?"

"I heard he found Swede working at the Carnegie's."

Lana's eyes went wide. "Did he . . . hurt her?"

The girl shrugged. "Nobody knows. She never showed up for work since, and nobody has seen her."

"Maybe she saw Wilton and ran away."

"Maybe." Johnny started toward the door. "Or maybe when he was through with her, she was too afraid to stay."

When she was alone, Lana fought to push aside the little fear that hovered at the edges of her mind. To keep from thinking about Swede, she began to read the society column written by a reporter named Farley Fairchild. When she finished that, she devoured the newspaper from front page to last, willing as many of the big, fancy words to memory as possible. While the rest of the servants looked only at the pictures, Lana forced herself to read every word, especially those she didn't know. She was hungry to learn all she could.

When she was finished, she looked again at the happy VanEndels, smiling for the camera. These photos were the only view Lana had actually had of her employers. As lowly kitchen help, she had never been privileged to see them, nor did she expect to. They had no need to set foot in this part of the house, because they expected Swanson to carry out their requests without question and deal with less-pleasant details of housekeeping.

All the frenzy that had gone on before was nothing compared to what was happening this week. The VanEndels were throwing a dinner party. And not just any dinner party, Swanson had explained as she'd hired half a dozen caterers to assist Cook. All the top names on the Social Register had been invited, along with one very special guest, as well.

While touring Europe, Mr. and Mrs. VanEndel had met the Queen of England, and though the queen herself couldn't be here, a cousin of hers would be the guest of honor.

Swanson was quite beside herself, seeing to all the last-minute details.

Cook rushed in, slightly out of breath, and deposited a pile of towels on the countertop before turning to Lana, who was now elbow-deep in hot water. "When you finish those pots and pans, come to the dining room."

Though Lana knew where the dining room was, she'd never before been allowed inside. Her chores kept her exclusively consigned to the kitchen and laundry.

After putting away the clean dishes, she made her way to the dining room and stopped in midstride to stare in open-mouth surprise. The room was bigger than any she had yet seen and was bustling with activity. The gardener was directing the placement of huge urns brimming with ivy on either side of a marble fireplace surround. Swanson was calling commands to the girls from laundry who'd been pressed into service to polish silver.

The big room was dominated by a table that could have easily seated thirty or more guests. The table and chairs were mahogany, polished to a high sheen. Standing in the middle of the table, on several thicknesses of towels, two housemaids were carefully washing every facet of the crystal chandeliers hanging above. Another servant was busy dressing a mahogany sideboard in shimmery lace. To one side stood a silver tray holding an ornate coffee and tea service. On another tray stood a crystal punchbowl and dozens of matching cups.

The windows of the dining room looked out over late summer gardens of perfectly manicured boxwood and colorful annuals interspersed with stone benches and marble fountains. Several young men carried ladders around the outside, carefully washing the windows under Swanson's watchful eye.

Cook nodded toward a serving cart laden with fine china. "Take these to the kitchen, and see that they're washed and dried. I'll be in to examine them when I've finished here."

Lana's head was swimming. She had never dreamed of such luxury. How much money would it take to acquire all this?

As she rolled the cart from the room and down the hall, she found herself wishing she could have stayed longer to drink it all in. And to think that there were a dozen or more such rooms in this grand house. Were all of them as lavish as the one she'd just left? It didn't seem possible, and yet she was certain it was so.

She carefully washed and dried the fine china, laying it out on layers of thick towels for Cook's inspection. When the older woman finally waddled into the kitchen, she was muttering to herself.

Distracted, she examined the dishes and gave a nod of approval. "You can take these back to the dining room. Leave them on the serving cart. One of the others will set the table."

"Yes, ma'am." Lana eagerly returned to the dining room and stared around at the changes that had been made.

Already a lace cloth had been added to the table, as well as low bowls of white roses. Their fragrance perfumed the air.

Lana lingered a moment, studying the painting on the far wall, of a seascape that reminded her of Ireland. A tidy cottage on a patch of green land. Foamy sea hurling itself upon a stretch of sandy beach. A lone woman staring out to sea, and far beyond, a tiny fishing boat.

She felt her heart contract, and the yearning was so strong, she was forced to press a hand to her mouth to keep from crying out.

"You there. Irish." Swanson's voice had her head coming up sharply.

"Yes, ma'am. I didn't mean to dally." Lana turned toward the door.

"Wait." The woman hurried over and looked her up and down.

Lana thought about smoothing the skirt of her uniform but kept her hands behind her back. After her first week on the job, the seamstress had made two dresses and aprons to fit her so she would have a clean one each day. "I put on a fresh gown and apron just this morning, ma'am, but I've been busy in the kitchen since dawn. I'm sorry if I've soiled . . ."

The housekeeper lifted a hand to silence her. "You'll have to do."

"Do?"

"I'll let Cook know that you won't be working in the kitchen tonight. She has enough help down there. I have need of you in the parlor."

"Parlor?" Lana knew she was parroting the woman's words, but they made no sense. "I'm afraid I don't know where it is."

"I'll show you when it's time. For now, change into a fresh dress and apron, and see that your hair is tidy."

"My hair . . ." She lifted a hand but then lowered it to her side. "Yes, ma'am."

"Hurry. Change now. There isn't much time. When you're ready, come to the kitchen."

Thoroughly confused, Lana hurried to the laundry to fetch her clean dress and apron and then climbed the back stairs to the attic room, where she found several other servants changing their clothes and tidying their hair.

"Going to serve at the dinner party, are you?" Johnny asked.

"Serve?" Lana looked stricken. "Swanson never told me."

"If she told you to change, it's because she wants you to look good in front of all those fancy guests. My bet is you'll be serving, along with the rest of us. I'll be accepting the guests' wraps at the front door," she added importantly.

Though Lana's hands were sweating, she followed the other girls from the room and down the stairs to the kitchen, where Swanson, in a fresh black gown, her hair in a perfect knot at her nape, was waiting.

Some of the girls were led to the dining room and told what they would do. The rest were taken to the parlor.

The housekeeper handed Lana a silver tray. "You will mingle and serve champagne to the guests in this room."

"Mingle?"

"Walk. Very slowly and carefully. If there are too many people, just stand out of the way. You are not to intrude upon any guests who are conversing. Do you understand?"

Lana nodded and felt her throat go dry. "I don't belong here, ma'am. I'd be better in the kitchen."

"I know that." Swanson's eyes narrowed. "But I have no choice. Just see that you don't drop anything or spill anything on the guests."

Lana felt her heartbeat begin to accelerate. "But I . . ."

"Not a word. Just do your job, girl."

"Yes, ma'am." Lana lowered her eyes and stared hard at the floor while the housekeeper gave the others their list of duties.

Before Lana had time to consider the implication of what she was about to do, the first guests were arriving, and she could do nothing more than stand perfectly still, her hands frozen on the silver tray, and watch as the dizzying scene began to unfold very quickly before her eyes.

No one wanted to arrive first or last, and so they came in a sea of people, setting a frantic pace for the staff that was forced to rush about, trying desperately to keep up. With a clatter of carriage wheels, they swept up the long, curving drive and were assisted up the wide, stone steps to the foyer, where they handed their wraps to the waiting serving girls.

The women were in elegant, colorful gowns, their hair dressed with combs and jeweled pins, and the most amazing array of jewels at their throats and earlobes. Men in fine dark suits and stiff, starched shirts greeted one another like old, lost friends, while their eyes, Lana noted, kept shifting to others around the room, as if seeking escape.

". . . was telling my broker just this morning"—the man speaking idly lifted a tulip of champagne from Lana's tray without even glancing at her—"that price is no object. I want to own controlling interest in the company."

". . . was wearing the most hideous rubies at the theater last night." The young woman, who couldn't have been much older than Lana, smiled knowingly at the older woman, dripping in ropes of pearls, before turning to her escort. "Will you fetch me a drink, darling?"

The man beside her helped himself to two glasses from Lana's tray and handed them off to the women before taking one for himself.

Lana took a halting step and paused beside a cluster of people until her tray was empty. Looking around, she saw Swanson nodding toward a serving table in the corner of the room. At once she turned and made her way there, waiting while another servant filled her tray with fresh glasses of champagne, before moving on.

For nearly an hour she slowly circled the room, hearing snatches of conversation as the guests sipped champagne and nibbled from trays of cavier and tiny points of toast with salmon.

"Now that Evelyn and Gustav were invited to Kensington Palace, we'll never hear the end of it." A fat dowager in mauve satin gown and upswept silver hair adorned with pearl combs accepted a tulip glass from the portly gentleman beside her.

"But just think. If they hadn't been, we'd have never had this opportunity to meet royalty." The pretty young woman beside her opened a paper fan and used it to cool her face.

"I can't believe we're actually going to meet a cousin to the Queen of England. I told Harold that this was one dinner party I simply couldn't miss."

At a flurry of activity in the foyer, the guests glanced expectantly toward the doorway. Lana took that moment to hurry back to refill her tray.

Evelyn VanEndel stepped into the room, clearly enjoying the fact that her guests had fallen silent, with all eyes on her and the handsome man beside her.

Looping her arm through his, she led him toward the first group of guests. "Jeslin Jeremy Jordan Hanover, Duke of Umberland, may I present some friends of mine. This is Judge Harold Farmer, of the New York Supreme Court, and his wife, Eunice. Harvey Freeman, whose family is in lumber. And Lloyd Carpenter, who was the chief architect for the Landover Building, which you said you so admired when you first arrived in our country."

Like the rest of the company in the parlor, Lana watched with interest, though she couldn't actually see Mrs. VanEndel or her guest, who were obscured by the crowd that had circled around them.

"How good to meet you."

The voice, though British, sounded familiar to Lana's ears. She strained to see the man's face.

"Should I call you sir, or duke?" one of the women asked with a breathy laugh.

"Here in your country, I much prefer Jesse."

"Jesse."

Lana could hear the sighs from half a dozen women as the introductions continued.

"Would you have some champagne?" Evelyn VanEndel motioned for Lana to step closer.

At last Lana could see the woman who had only been a picture in the newspaper. Like a queen, she wore a tiara in her soft brown hair. The jewels twinkled in the light of hundreds of candles. She was a pretty woman, with small, even features. Her brown eyes were alive with excitement. Her slight frame was enhanced by a gown of pale peach satin with a full skirt gathered here and there with darker peach velvet ribbons. At her throat was a diamond necklace that must have cost a king's ransom.

Lana felt a hand at her back and realized that Swanson was shoving her forward.

As the sea of bodies parted, Lana stepped timidly toward the hostess and her guest of honor.

In that instant, she was only vaguely aware of someone reaching for a glass from her tray. She could hear the snatches of words being spoken all around her as though a buzzing of a great hive of bees. But the only thing Lana could see was the man, dressed in a perfectly tailored dark suit and crisp starched shirt, at his throat a tri-colored ribbon bearing the royal crest. He was speaking to his hostess, his comment making Evelyn VanEndel smile and blush. Though Lana was unaware of the words, that stiff, upper-lip British tone was so utterly perfect, so regal, it left no doubt that the man speaking could be none other than English royalty.

She felt a rush of horror as the realization dawned.

The man that all of New York's society had turned out to welcome, the man over whom these people were fawning like silly fools, was none other than the actor and con she knew as Stone.

SEVEN

❖━◆━❖

AND WHAT AN amazing actor, Lana thought. Even when Stone caught her eye and realized that she was staring at him with her jaw dropped, he didn't so much as pause or even draw a breath. Instead, with a wicked smile, he helped himself to a glass from her tray. And winked.

Winked.

The sight of it was so shocking she nearly bobbled the tray. The nerve of this gambler. He was so sure of himself, so confident she wouldn't reveal his identity, he wasn't at all perturbed at seeing her here.

As soon as she'd managed to regain her composure, she shot him a look of outrage before turning away.

What was he up to? Was he here to steal the silver? She wouldn't put it past him. He'd always seemed to have plenty of money for the games at the Blue Goose. Still, stealing money didn't seem to suit him, especially because he was such a good gambler. A man that lucky at cards didn't need to steal.

She chanced a quick glance at him across the room,

surrounded by adoring females, and it struck her with such force, she had to take hold of the edge of the table. Of course. Why should he risk stealing, when he could simply charm all the money he wanted out of those foolish society women?

That would be his game, she thought with a rush of righteous anger. Oh yes. She had him figured out now.

She picked up her tray and began circling the room again, always keeping an eye on the guest of honor. She wanted to stay as far away from Stone or . . . what had he called himself? . . . Jesse? She wanted to stay as far away from this liar as she could. It just wouldn't be wise to have anyone guess that she knew him in his other life. Some might even believe they were a team, and that she'd hired on here just to aid him in his scurrilous scheme.

She felt a hand on her arm and nearly jumped out of her skin before realizing it was Swanson.

"Can you sew, girl?"

Lana stared at her blankly.

"Are you deaf? Can you ply needle and thread?"

"I can, yes."

"Good." The housekeeper took the tray from her and handed it to one of the other servants. "Follow me."

Puzzled, Lana trailed the housekeeper to a lovely, rose-colored room off the hallway. Inside, a young woman was seated on a satin bench, with several other young women standing and sitting on matching benches scattered around the room. This was, Lana realized, a feminine sitting room, used by the guests to repair their hair or simply to escape for a few moments of gossip.

Swanson handed Lana a sewing kit. "Miss Enid Morgenthall caught her heel in the hem of her gown. It needs to be repaired quickly, and our seamstress wasn't readily available. See to it."

"Yes, ma'am." Kneeling at the young woman's feet, Lana examined the tear and was grateful to find that it was a simple pulled seam.

Threading a needle, she began to sew, loving the way the silky fabric felt against her fingers. How grand it would be, she thought, to be able to wear something so fine as this. Not that she ever would. But what a grand thing to contemplate, all the same.

While she worked, the women sipped champagne and fiddled with jeweled hair clips in front of the mirrored vanity. They seemed to spend an inordinate amount of time studying their reflection in the looking glass. And why not? They all looked as lovely as fairy princesses.

One of the young women giggled behind her hand. "Isn't the Duke of Umberland the most handsome man you've ever seen?"

Enid Morganthall's voice was a squeaky, high-pitched whine that had Lana wincing. "And so wealthy. Evelyn VanEndel told me in confidence that he's one of the wealthiest men in England."

"You don't say?"

"Who knows?" another said in a breathy whisper. "He's in the line of succession, so he could one day sit on the throne of England."

Enid crossed one foot over the other, causing Lana to hiss in surprise as she pricked her finger. "He can sit on my throne any day."

Enid's words brought gales of laughter from the others.

"I certainly wouldn't toss him out of my bed." A dark-haired, dark-eyed woman in a slender column of champagne satin drained her glass and got to her feet.

"You won't have the chance." Enid patted her hair and tucked an errant curl behind her ear. "I saw the way the duke was looking at me. If all goes well tonight, I believe I just may permit him to seduce me."

Some feigned surprise, while others merely laughed aloud.

The dark-haired woman merely smiled. "What a grand idea, Enid. But while you're here being tended to, I think

I'll just go out there and keep our poor duke company. We
wouldn't want him to get lonely now, would we?"

"Annie Davis." Enid fidgeted, and Lana looked up as
the needle was yanked once more from her fingers.

"I told you." The woman slanted her friend a look. "It's
Anya now. Anya Davis. See that you don't forget."

"I'm not forgetting the fact that when we were in
school, before your father made that fortune in sugar im-
ports, you were just plain Annie."

"But Anya sounds so much better, don't you think?"
With a little cat smile she added, "Take your time, Enid.
Little Anya is only too happy to keep our duke company."

As she sauntered out of the room, Enid stomped her
foot in annoyance. Glancing down at Lana's bent head, she
asked, "Are you almost finished?"

"Yes, ma'am." Lana bit off the end of the thread. Finished or not, she knew better than to keep this impatient female waiting another minute, or she was apt to dash out of
here dragging along a needle and thread, with Lana's fingers still attached.

"Good." Enid got to her feet and hurried across the
room, with the others trailing behind her.

Lana returned the needle and thread to the sewing kit
and got slowly to her feet, pressing a hand to the small of
her back. She'd wanted to warn Miss Morganthall that the
seam might not hold but had thought better of it when she
realized that the young woman would no doubt rather find
herself naked in the middle of the VanEndel parlor than
lose her chance to snag the very handsome, very wealthy
scoundrel she'd set her sights on.

If only, Lana thought with a weary shake of her head,
they knew the truth about the phony Duke of Umberland.

To Lana, the evening seemed endless. Throughout the
tedious meal she was busy removing the dishes from the

table and setting them on a serving cart, before rolling the
cart to the kitchen where it was emptied into one of the
many basins of steamy water. After several such trips her
hair defied the dustcap, turning to corkscrews that dripped
over one eye and curled around her cheeks, earning her several dark looks from Swanson.

Stone, she noted, never seemed to run out of clever
things to say. And while he held court at table, the company around him hung on his every word. Especially the
women. They smiled and blushed and hid behind their nap-
kins when he turned the full force of his smile on them.

When the meal ended, their hostess suggested they take
their desserts in another room. Lana breathed a sigh of relief.
At least now she would no longer have to watch this clever
actor ply his craft on all those unsuspecting innocents.

"You there." Swanson stepped into the kitchen and motioned to Lana, who was busy emptying yet another serving cart. "Fetch that tray and follow me."

Lana dutifully followed the housekeeper into a large
open ballroom. Small round tables had been set up around
the perimeter, flanked by gilt chairs. In the middle of each
table a candle flickered, and beside it, a crystal bowl in
which floated a single white gardenia. Lana had never seen
such a pretty sight. The wonderful fragrance of all those
flowers perfumed the air, while the men and women in their
elegant clothes looked like the kings and queens of her day-
dreams.

Lana's tray was laden with after-dinner liquors in tiny, elegant glasses, and she was told to begin serving the guests.

While the women chose a variety of sweets and pastries,
the gentlemen helped themselves to cordials and brandy.
Several of them stepped out onto the terrace to enjoy a fine
cigar. Stone, Lana noted, was among them. She studied the
way his shoulders strained the perfectly tailored jacket as
he bent forward slightly, accepting a light from one of the

other men. He straightened and emitted a puff of smoke before turning his head slightly, catching her eye.

"I'll have one of those," the other man said, and Lana had no choice but to approach with her tray.

Stone waited until his companion snagged a glass of brandy and stepped away.

He touched a finger to the rim of a glass while keeping his gaze steady on hers. "So this is where you've been. I missed you at the Blue Goose, Lana."

Why did he have to speak to her in that low, intimate tone she remembered from the docks? She resented the quick little thrill and then the slow curl of heat along her spine.

To cover the unwanted feelings, she lifted her chin like a prizefighter. "I'm sure Verna Lee kept you from feeling lonely."

The smile warmed his eyes as well as his voice. "She's a very generous girl, Lana, and willing to share her gifts with one and all, but she isn't you. I get no pleasure watching Verna Lee the way I enjoyed watching you."

"Here you are." Evelyn VanEndel stepped from the shadows. "My husband was hoping you would join him for a drink before returning to the ballroom."

"It would be my pleasure." Without missing a beat, Jesse lifted a glass from Lana's tray and turned away dismissively, allowing his hostess to lead him across the terrace.

Lana stayed where she was, watching as he joined a cluster of guests who were soon laughing at something clever he'd said. Within minutes, the other guests had gathered around him, like moths to a flame.

Lana returned to the ballroom and walked from table to table, dispensing drinks without any trace of emotion. For these few moments she found herself grateful that she was all but invisible to these people. If they were to but look into her eyes, they would see the sheen of tears there, for

she wanted, more than anything, to give in to the desire to
weep, though she hadn't a clue as to why.

"GOOD RIDDANCE." COOK closed the door on the last
of the caterers and their assistants and looked around at the
mess they'd left behind. Every dish, every glass, every pot
and pan owned by the VanEndels was stacked around the
counters, spilling their congealed sauces onto the floor.

"See to this, girl." Cook sank down onto a chair and
helped herself to a plate of pastries.

Lana filled a basin with hot water from the stove before
rolling her sleeves above the elbows.

"I'll give Mrs. VanEndel this much." Cook's words were
muffled around a mouthful of pastry. "She knows all the
best people."

Lana rinsed each plate before setting them on a layer of
towels to drain. "You mean Miss Morganthall?"

Cook gave a snort of derision. "That one. If her daddy
didn't have more money than Mrs. VanEndel, she wouldn't
be allowed in the door. As for her friend, Anya, I've heard
she's shopping around for a title to buy, if she can't find one
to marry. And speaking of marrying a title, what about that
English duke? The one all the ladies were fawning over.
From what I've heard, if enough of those English royals
were to die, he could be king."

Lana set down a plate with a clatter and began to dry the
dishes.

Cook pushed aside the sweets and picked up her tea.
"I'd wager the VanEndels spent more on this party trying to
impress that English duke than you and I and the lot of us
together would earn in a year."

Lana looked over. "Why do you suppose they do it?"

"To show off to their society friends."

"You mean it was all for show?"

The older woman shrugged. "Isn't that what all this is for? Mrs. VanEndel's tea parties, her luncheons, even her charities are to make her friends notice her. And after tonight, with an English duke as guest of honor, I'm thinking they'll all sit up and take notice." Cook got wearily to her feet. "I'm going to bed now, girl. See that you set this place to rights before turning in."

"I will."

As the cook waddled away, Lana was deep in thought.

It had been the most amazing night. She'd never seen such luxury as she'd witnessed tonight. The elegant rooms with their fancy furniture, and guests dressed like royalty. Enough food to feed the entire city. Champagne in pretty glasses. And Stone, looking more handsome than any man in the room.

She'd been forced to watch him dance with every woman at the dinner party. He was as smooth on the dance floor as he was everywhere else this night. And from the smug little smile on Enid's face, it would appear that he had agreed to escort her home.

Though it hurt to think of him seducing that silly, shallow woman, Lana couldn't help but admire his style. She'd give him this. He was as cunning as a fox, even if he did have the morals of an alley cat.

She was well rid of that obnoxious actor. And the heaviness in her heart was nothing more than the result of the long, tedious hours she'd worked this day.

EIGHT

"SWANSON SAID MRS. VanEndel was pleased at the success of her dinner party last night." While she spoke, Cook moved around the room, running a finger over the wooden cutting table, then around the rims of several pots and pans. Satisfied that the kitchen was cleaned to her specifications, she turned. "Because she has the entire day given over to one of her charities, the staff is to be given the morning off."

"Today?" Lana's eyes lit with pleasure.

"As soon as you've prepared Mrs. VanEndel's chocolate, you're free to go."

"Thank you, ma'am." Lana was so excited, she almost hugged the old woman before catching herself and turning away.

An hour later she was dashing through the streets of New York, listening to the chorus of voices in a dozen different dialects, hearing the clatter of horse-drawn wagons and carts rolling along the streets, feeling like a bird that had just been turned free of its cage. With coin jingling in her pocket, she hurried past the old fruit vendor. She couldn't wait to watch Colin's eyes while he mulled the difficult choice of which apple to buy.

Her footsteps were light as air. Oh, how she'd missed the wee lad and her Siobhan. She couldn't wait to see how they were doing.

Would the expected babe be showing by now? Not by much, she thought. But soon. Very soon. Lana thought about the money tucked away in a corner of her satchel in the attic room at the VanEndel mansion. By her calculations, there was enough to pay the rent on a clean, small apartment. She couldn't wait to see Siobhan's eyes when she gave her the news.

She paused at the foot of the steps and glanced around, breathing in the smells of garlic and grease, charred meat, and burned bread. Her ears were assaulted by the cries of babies, their scolding mothers, and the shouts and curses of their men. Flies swarmed around horse droppings and rotting garbage.

How had Siobhan survived all these long years in such a place? No matter, Lana thought as she bounded up the steps. From this day on, Siobhan and Colin could begin to make plans for their new life, far away from the sights and sounds and smells of the tenement.

"Siobhan. Colin." Lana paused outside the closed door of their apartment and rapped loudly.

From inside she could hear a baby cry. A baby? But that was impossible. It was much too soon for that.

"Siobhan! Colin!" Lana knocked louder and heard the door of the apartment behind her being thrust open.

Before she even turned, she recognized the familiar voice of Mrs. Genovese. "They're not in there."

"Not here?" Lana's brows furrowed as she studied the woman. "Where did they go?"

"Your friend, the young mother, she is dead."

"Dead?" Lana's hand shot out, steadying herself against the wall. "What . . . ? How . . . ?"

"I didn't see it with my own eyes, but I heard from others that your friend was run over by a horse and cart."

"Run over?" Lana licked her lips, which had gone dry as dust. "Colin?"

"They said she pushed the bambino out of the way just in time."

"He's alive. Oh, thank heaven." Lana could feel her legs beginning to tremble and wondered that she could still stand. "Where did his father take him?"

"You should know about the father." Mrs. Genovese's eyes grew hard. "I'm thinking he may have driven the cart that ran down your friend deliberately, though I couldn't say for certain."

Lana went very still. "Why would you think that, Mrs. Genovese?"

The woman shrugged. "Maybe he thought he would be free."

"Free?"

"I heard them fighting, the morning of the accident. A bigger fight than usual, when your friend told him about the expected bambino."

So Siobhan's secret was actually known by all of them. She should have expected as much.

"And you think . . ." Lana couldn't finish her thought aloud. It was too horrible to imagine. Was Billy capable of such a thing? A runaway carriage. Confusion in the street. A chance to be free to make a new life.

"Where is Billy now?"

"After your friend was struck down, the horse and cart went careening down the street. At the corner, it collided with another cart, and by the time the drivers were pulled from beneath their carts, both were dead."

"Dead. Billy is dead as well?" Lana's heart was beginning to break into pieces. "What about Colin? Where is he now?"

"The police took the bambino to the East Side Orphan Asylum."

"An asylum?" The very words had her numb with panic.

Seeing her dazed expression, the Italian woman reached out a hand. "You come inside, I give you a drink of water."

Lana backed away. "No, thank you just the same, Mrs. Genovese. I have to go to this place and rescue little Colin."

"He is a good boy," the woman said softly. "My Giovanni said he was a smart one. And your friend, she was a good mama."

Was. The word was like a knife to Lana's heart. "Thank you." She turned away quickly to hide the rush of tears. "Thank you for being a good neighbor to them, Mrs. Genovese."

"I tried," Mrs. Genovese called after her, "but it wasn't enough."

I tried, but it wasn't enough.

The woman's words echoed through Lana's mind.

Oh, Siobhan. I tried, too. I'm sorry. So sorry that it wasn't nearly enough. And far too late.

THE EAST SIDE Orphan Asylum was as bleak and forbidding as the tenements that had been built around it—a gray stone monster, soaring four stories into the air, with a dozen steps leading to the door. The upper windows were narrow and dingy, and in one of them, Lana could make out a face pressed to the pane. The sight of it had her stomach clenching.

She remembered. Had spent years in such a place. Knew intimately the feeling of dread and hopelessness that each new day brought. The cheerless existence. The dour, joyless people who seemed to take such satisfaction in enforcing the rules and reminding the children how fortunate they were to have whatever meager comforts were given them.

She knocked and felt the gloom spread as the door was opened, and the smell of the place assaulted her. That same smell. A mixture of foul, fetid air, unwashed bodies, and urine-soaked pallets.

The woman was plump and pink-skinned, her hair a tidy knot, her gown and apron spotless. "Can I help you, miss?"

Lana swallowed twice before finding her voice. "I'm here to inquire about Colin O'Malley. Would you know if he's here?"

"Are you family?"

"I'm a friend of his mother. Could I see him, please?"

"I'm afraid it isn't possible to see any of the children today." The woman's voice lowered. "This is a very important day for all of us. The Ladies' Aid Society, patrons of the East Side Orphan Asylum, are here today, along with some of the city's most important officials. The mayor is here. Can you imagine? And the chief of police. Why, even Farley Fairchild from the *New York News and Dispatch* is here to write about it. Perhaps if you come back tomorrow . . ." She was closing the door as she said it.

"Wait. I just need to know if Colin is . . . all right."

The woman looked her up and down as though she were daft. "We pride ourselves on the care we give those unfortunate orphans. All of our children are fine. Especially on such a day as this. Now if you'll excuse me . . ."

Before Lana could say another word, the door was closed firmly in her face.

As she descended the steps, Lana felt the need to breathe deeply. But even the fresh summer breeze ruffling the hem of her gown couldn't clear her lungs of the smell of the orphanage, a smell that had been branded into her very soul.

When she reached the bottom of the steps, Lana paused and turned toward the forbidding facade, willing little

Colin to be standing there, arms outstretched, waiting for her. The door remained firmly closed. Again she turned and this time forced herself to walk away.

With every step, she felt her heart growing heavier in her chest. All her fine dreams and plans for the future were now just empty promises.

"I'll be back, Colin." She spoke the words aloud, as much for herself as for the lad. "Don't give up, nor will I. I gave my word to your mum that you'd never be alone. I mean to keep it."

"You're back early." Cook looked up from her plate of roast beef and mashed potatoes as Lana stepped into the kitchen.

"I . . . I finished my personal chores and thought I'd see if you needed me."

"I can always use some help." Cook continued shoveling food into her mouth. "You can start on those pots and pans. I've prepared a simple supper for the staff because the Mr. and Mrs. will be out tonight."

Lana filled a kettle with water and placed it on the burner, then added more coal to the stove until the water was soon boiling.

"You can make me a cup of tea before you start the dishes," Cook said over a mouthful of potatoes.

As Lana filled a cup, she added, "Make one for yourself, girl."

Lana was so startled by the woman's words, she nearly bobbled the kettle before gathering her wits.

When she brought the two steaming cups to the table, Cook pointed with her fork. "Sit."

Lana sat across from her and sipped her tea.

"Something go wrong today?" Cook speared her with a look.

"I had news of a friend's . . ." She couldn't speak the word. To say it out loud would make it real. She wasn't ready to face the finality of it. ". . . of a friend's troubles."

"We've all got them. Wouldn't be alive if we didn't have trouble." Cook mopped up the last of her food with a piece of freshly baked bread and then shoved the plate away. "Best to put aside your friend's troubles and get on with life, girl."

"Yes, ma'am." Lana took another sip, burning her tongue. Getting to her feet, she pushed away from the table. "Thank you for the tea. Now I'd better see to those pots and pans."

Cook sat at the table and watched as Lana tackled her work. Minutes later the older woman waddled out of the room, leaving Lana to her chores.

For the rest of the day, Lana went through the motions, helping Cook serve in the staff dining room, cleaning the kitchen afterward, and falling into bed around midnight. When the soft snoring alerted her that the others were fast asleep, Lana allowed herself at last to think about all that had happened this day.

It didn't seem possible that Siobhan was really dead. Sweet, dreamy Siobhan. Whenever Lana thought about her childhood, she thought about Siobhan. The two had shared secrets, had shared pain, had even shared a pallet on the cold floor when the younger girl was frightened or troubled. And when hunger drove them to steal from Mother Superior's private cupboard, they had shared food. Lana couldn't imagine her life without Siobhan.

With his mother dead, Colin was now a prisoner in . . . that place. The memories of her own time spent in a foundling home were too painful, too vivid, to even imagine wee Colin living through the same horror.

Those two were Lana's whole life. Without them, she felt as though she'd lost her compass. Adrift in a storm. Without Siobhan and Colin, she had no history left. No family. Nowhere to go. The realization was a shock to her system. For all these years, she had made these two special people the center of her life. They were her only life. And now that life had been snatched away, and she was alone.

Wasn't that how Colin must be feeling, too? Alone in a frightening world, with nobody to care about him?

These thoughts were too painful. She couldn't bear them. Siobhan was really gone, and they would never laugh again. Never tell each other the secrets of their hearts.

The finality of it struck Lana with all the force of a blow to the midsection. With a cry of pain, she rolled into a ball and jammed a fist against her mouth to muffle the sound as she began to sob. Great gulping sobs wracked her slender body and seemed to pour forth from her very soul.

She had failed them both. Failed Siobhan, and because of it, her friend was dead. If only she'd acted immediately to get her away from Billy's fury, sweet Siobhan might still be alive. She'd failed Colin, as well, consigning him to a fate worse than death.

In the darkness of the night, as she wept bitter tears, Lana had never felt so desperately alone, so utterly useless. Not when her da died, leaving them destitute. Not when her mum died and the authorities had carried her, kicking and screaming, to the foundling home. Those times were nothing compared with this. She'd failed the two people who mattered the most to her. Failed them.

But as night slid silently toward morning, a light of hope began to glimmer in her mind.

She could do nothing to bring Siobhan back, but at least she could keep the promise she'd made to her friend.

She had saved enough money to rent a room. She was young and strong and willing to do whatever it took to raise Colin.

She would visit the East Side Orphan Asylum again.

And this time, she would see the lad who owned her heart and make arrangements to take him home with her.

Home. If she couldn't provide it for Siobhan, at least she would make it a reality for the lad.

It was her last thought before sleep claimed her.

NINE

"I MAGINE THAT." EVEN before Lana opened the kitchen door and stepped inside she heard Cook's voice, an octave higher than usual, as though in awe and wonder.

"Lucky little boy." Swanson was standing beside Cook.

Both women were huddled close, staring at something on the table.

"Do you think she meant it?" Cook turned to the housekeeper with a sly grin.

"I find it unimaginable." Swanson's voice lowered. "I can't imagine young Wilton welcoming a rival for his father's vast fortune, can you?"

The two women shared a knowing laugh.

They looked up at Lana. Aware that she was listening, the housekeeper handed her a plate of freshly baked scones. "Take these upstairs to Mrs. VanEndel's suite."

Lana's eyes widened. "The living quarters?"

"That's what I said. And be quick about it."

"But I'm not allowed . . ."

"Just set these on the table in the upper sitting room and leave without a word." The housekeeper returned her attention to whatever it was that held her fascination.

Lana climbed the stairs, wondering how to discover which of the many rooms above stairs would be the lady's bedchambers. After passing several closed doors, she spied double doors standing open. Inside was a setting as lovely as anything she'd ever seen. A pale sofa was positioned before a marble fireplace. In an alcove, on a table set for two, was a vase of fresh flowers. On a silver tray rested a coffee service. Steam rose from one of the cups.

Lana stepped closer and set down the plate of scones.

As she turned, she could hear a man's voice raised in anger. "What in heaven's name were you thinking?"

A woman's voice, low, cultured. "I'm afraid I got caught up in the moment. After all, the mayor was there, and all those dignitaries. Not to mention Farley Fairchild scribbling every word I spoke and a photographer to record the event. It wasn't until I read this morning's *News and Dispatch* that I realized that all of New York society will be reading about it as well."

"And expecting you to follow through." The man's voice was filled with scorn. "I won't have one of those Irish scum living under my roof."

"Do you think I like it any more than you? But I don't see how I can graciously decline now without looking like a fool."

Lana spotted the hem of a morning gown fluttering in the doorway between the bedroom and sitting room and spun away before hurrying down the stairs.

When she stepped into the kitchen, Cook motioned toward a basket of soiled kitchen linens. "Take those to the laundry, girl, and fetch fresh towels."

"Yes, ma'am." Lana hefted the basket to her hip and headed down the hall.

The laundry room was empty, and Lana caught sight of the women in the yard, removing dry items from the clothesline and replacing them with wet ones.

Leaving her basket of towels beside the washtub, Lana walked outside, enjoying the feel of morning sunlight on her face.

As she approached, she heard the lilt of voices as the servants enjoyed a bit of gossip while they worked.

"At least he'll be rich."

"He'll never have to wonder where his next meal is coming from."

"Won't even have to wash his own clothes."

One woman straightened and turned to face the others. "There's more to life than money. Can you imagine a sweet, innocent being turned into a spoiled, willful, malicious monster who actually believes he has the right to despoil another?"

The woman beside her touched a finger to her lips and whispered, "Hush now, Mollie. You never know who's listening."

The speaker put her hands on her hips. "We may not like to talk about it, but that's what was done to one here. Would you wish it for another? Do they have the right to turn yet another lad into a monster?"

The women fell silent.

Lana approached. "I'm here for fresh kitchen linens."

One of the women pointed to a full basket. "I've just taken them from the line. You can take them with you, as long as you don't mind folding them yourself."

"Thank you." Before lifting it Lana paused. "Who were you talking about?"

The woman seemed surprised by her question. "You haven't seen the Mrs. in Farley Fairchild's column in today's *News and Dispatch*?"

Lana shook her head.

"I don't know where the newspaper is now, but earlier today we passed it around. There's a photograph of Mrs. VanEndel taken yesterday at one of her charity events. It seems she has decided to adopt an orphan."

"An . . . orphan?"

"Some poor unfortunate immigrant."

Lana felt a trickle of ice along her spine. "Do you know the orphan's name?"

The woman shrugged. "Can't read. None of us can. Swanson was the one who read it to us."

With a feeling of dread, Lana picked up the basket of towels and hurried back to the kitchen. Cook was nowhere to be seen, but on the table was the newspaper, lying open just as she'd left it.

Lana dropped the basket and studied the grainy photograph of Evelyn VanEndel, wearing a fashionable day gown and bonnet, her face carefully composed into a smile for the photographer.

In her arms was a lad who could only be Colin.

For a moment Lana was frozen. Then she bent and quickly read the entire article from beginning to end.

Mrs. Evelyn VanEndel, one of New York's most ardent patrons of the East Side Orphan Asylum Ladies' Aid Society, told this reporter that she was so taken with this poor lad's blond curls and sad blue eyes that she decided on the spot to adopt him and give him all the things he has been denied.

Adopt Colin. The very words were an arrow through Lana's already-shattered heart. This couldn't be happening. It wasn't possible. But now that she'd read this, the words spoken by Swanson and Cook, and those spoken by the maids in the garden, made sense.

It was the words spoken by Evelyn VanEndel herself that had Lana paralyzed. This was happening, not because the woman had so much love in her heart to share with a sweet orphan, but rather because, now that her words had been captured in a newspaper account and read by half the city of New York, there was no way to graciously avoid it.

"I won't have Irish scum living under my roof."

Gustav VanEndel's words had Lana going very still. Irish scum?

She couldn't allow this to happen to sweet Colin. Not when she knew of a way to save them all from this horrid folly.

There was no time to waste.

Lana tore aside her apron, tossing it on the basket of towels.

She would simply go to the director of the orphanage and explain her friendship with Siobhan, her solemn vow to raise Colin as her own, and her intention to fulfill that vow immediately. Once the director was made aware of Lana's connection to Colin, of the love she bore for the lad and his now-dead mother, no person of authority would possibly stand in the way of doing the right thing.

LANA SMOOTHED THE skirt of her simple gray dress, wishing there'd been time to change into one of her own. She still wore the silly dustcap pinned to her hair, hair that had pried loose during her run of dozens of blocks. Instead of the usual prim knot, her hair now curled in a most annoying way around her neck and cheeks.

She was suddenly filled with so many doubts. She should have thought this through more carefully. Should have taken time to change so the director of the asylum would know that she was a lady and not just a housemaid. She should have prepared a speech. It was important that she make a fine impression, so the director would understand that she could take care of Colin the way his mother would have.

When the door to the orphanage opened, she took a deep breath and forced a smile to her lips. "I'm here to see the director."

"Yes, miss." It was the plump woman who had greeted her the previous morning. But now, her gown and apron were stained and dingy. Instead of the expectant smile, the woman was frowning. She looked, Lana thought as she followed along the narrow hallway, more frazzled than Lana herself.

They paused outside a closed door, and the woman knocked before poking her head inside. "There's someone to see you, Mrs. Linden."

The woman behind the desk was writing in a ledger. She looked up with a trace of annoyance. "Yes. What is it?"

Lana stepped around her guide. "I'm here about Colin O'Malley."

"You don't look like you work for a newspaper."

"I don't. No." Nerves had Lana's brogue deepening. "I'm here to talk about adopting him."

"I'm sure, now that his picture has appeared in the newspaper, there will be many interested in adopting him. But he's already spoken for." The director returned her attention to the ledger.

Lana walked to the desk, aware that the other woman was still waiting in the doorway, eager to watch and listen. "It's true that I saw his picture in the newspaper. But I was here yesterday, as well, long before that picture appeared. That lady can attest to my words."

The director glanced beyond Lana to the woman in the doorway, who quickly backed away.

The director frowned at Lana. "What is it you want?"

"As I said, I wish to adopt Colin. His mother was my dearest friend. I was with her when he was born and am as much his aunt as any blood relative."

Mrs. Linden gave her a long, slow appraisal. "By your appearance, it would seem that that you work as a housemaid."

"I do. Yes. I work in the VanEndel house."

"VanEndel. How . . . convenient." The director folded her hands atop her desk. "Does Mrs. VanEndel know you're here?"

"No. I've never met . . ." Lana licked her lips. "I came here because Colin needs me."

"I see. How do you plan on working and raising a child?"

"I've been saving my money. I have enough to rent a room and put food on the table."

"And when your savings run out?"

Lana could feel herself sweating. After running all those blocks, it felt too close in here. She glanced toward the window, wishing someone would open it. All the old feelings were coming back. The lack of fresh air. The lack of freedom. The feeling that she was nothing more than an insect, about to be squashed by this woman's shoe. "I know how to work hard. When I need to, I'll get another job."

"While raising a child?"

"I'll find a way to work at home if necessary. I love Colin. I would never do anything to harm him."

"I can assure you, you will not get that chance." The director shoved away from the desk. "You're a clever one, I'll give you that. Your little scheme to extort money from the VanEndels will not work."

"Scheme?" Lana could feel her face flaming. "You're mistaken. I love wee Colin. I would never do anything . . ."

"That's right, I'll see that you never do anything to that boy." Mrs. Linden looked beyond her to the woman in the doorway. "Martha, show this"—she looked Lana up and down as though she were the vilest creature ever born—"person to the door. And see that she isn't allowed inside again."

"Yes, ma'am." Martha reached for Lana's arm.

Lana wrenched herself free. "At least let me see Colin. I need to see for myself that he's all right."

"You will not see him. Not today, nor any day. Now leave, or I'll summon the authorities and tell them all about your little scheme to extort money from one of our city's finest patrons."

Lana felt a hand tugging on her arm and allowed herself to be led down the hallway toward the front door. When she was once more on the steps, she turned a tearful face to Martha. "At least tell me this. Is Colin being treated kindly?"

Martha stared hard at the floor. "I shouldn't be telling you anything. If Mrs. Linden thought I was talking to you . . ."

"Please," Lana whispered fiercely. "I love the lad like my own. Tell me how he is doing."

"The boy has stopped talking."

"Stopped . . ."

Martha put a finger to her mouth. "Mrs. Linden said it's a bid for attention and has ordered all of us who work with the children to ignore him."

"Are you saying that no one talks to him?"

The woman shrugged. "He refuses to eat, as well, miss. As our director said, it appears to be another bid for attention. Mrs. Linden has ordered everyone to ignore it. She insists that when he gets hungry enough, he'll eat. When he realizes that his little schemes won't work, he'll speak."

"How can you be so cruel? Do you have any idea what this poor lad has been through these past few days?" Tears sprang to Lana's eyes, and she blinked rapidly to stem the flow.

"Mrs. Linden said, though it seems cruel, the sooner the boy learns his lesson, the sooner he can adjust to the reality of his life as it is now."

The reality of his life. The very words caused Lana to wince in shared pain. "Couldn't I just see him?" She grabbed the woman's hand in both of hers. "Just for a moment?"

"I'd lose my job, miss." Martha glanced around uneasily.

"You really must go now." She pulled free and closed the door before Lana could say another word.

Lana stood a moment staring at the closed door, feeling her heart shattering into tiny pieces. If anything, the pain she felt now was even worse than the pain of losing Siobhan and a hundred times worse than when her own da and mum had died, forcing her into a life of misery in a foundling home. At least she'd been able to survive by her wits. But wee Colin was like his mum, shy and sweet and trusting, with no defenses against such cruelty. And who would look out for him, as she'd looked out for Siobhan?

As she stumbled blindly toward Fifth Avenue, Lana mulled over all she'd seen and heard.

An innocent like Colin would be so confused, thrust into an institution, his mum and da gone, and his only friend absent without any explanation. No wonder he'd stopped talking or eating.

She had to help him, and soon.

If she honestly believed that Colin would be happy with the VanEndels, it would ease her mind considerably. After all, they could give him things she could only dream of. Education. Fine clothes. A life of luxury. But could they give him the most important thing in the world? Would they love him? Lana thought about the words she'd overheard between Gustav and Evelyn VanEndel. It was all a ruse, to make themselves look good in front of their society friends. They had no thought of opening their hearts to a poor orphan.

Lana couldn't bear the thought of the child being raised by a series of disinterested servants who would view him as just another chore in their daily routine.

In truth, whether the VanEndels and their staff were good to Colin or not, how could anyone love him in the special way she did? She was his teacher, his auntie, his second mother. She had to save him from this nightmare. Not only for his sake, but for her own.

* * *

THE CLOSER LANA drew to the VanEndel mansion, the harder her heart began to pound. What had she been thinking, departing in such haste, without any explanation?

The truth was, she hadn't been thinking about anything except Colin. Now she would have to hope that when Cook heard her story, she would understand the importance of such an emergency and forgive her sudden departure.

As she rounded the house and started toward the back porch, she saw something fluttering on the ground. Not a bird, she realized as she drew nearer, but the dress she wore while working at the Blue Goose. It was one of two she owned. The other was lying nearby, pinned beneath her valise. Alongside lay her bonnet and shawl.

Understanding dawned in an instant.

With a cry, she bent to retrieve her belongings.

While she knelt in the grass stuffing her things into the valise, she heard the door open. Looking up, she saw Swanson at the top of the steps. Cook hovered behind her, hands on her hips, eyes narrowed in fury.

The housekeeper's voice was low with anger. "I'd expected no more from the likes of you."

"You don't understand. I had to . . ."

Swanson held up a hand. "Not a word. You're through here. Take your things and go."

"But it isn't what you think. I . . ."

"It is exactly as I thought. It's why I'll not hire another immigrant. Now go, girl. But first, you'll return that uniform, or I'll have you arrested for stealing."

She watched as Lana stripped away the gown and hurriedly slipped into her own soiled dress. Swanson bent down, retrieved the uniform, and turned, nearly bumping into the fat woman behind her.

Both women stepped apart and hurried inside before the door was firmly slammed shut.

For another stunned moment, Lana remained where she was, staring at the closed door and hearing the sound of it reverberating through her brain.

Like one in a trance, she picked up her valise and turned away.

As she moved past the big houses with their lovely sweeping lawns and big fancy carriages gliding along curving ribbons of driveways, she felt as she had when she'd escaped the foundling home that fateful day. She was once again homeless, without a job or a place to sleep. But then, she'd felt in control of her destiny. Now she felt empty, powerless. It was so much worse this time, she realized, because of Colin. How could she possibly hope to raise a lad when she had no job?

All her fine hopes and dreams of taking the lad with her and lavishing on him all the love that had been denied her in her childhood were now dashed. How could she persuade the director of the aslyum to release him to her care, when she couldn't even claim to have a means of supporting him?

She'd failed Colin.

Failed Siobhan.

Failed herself.

TEN

———◆—◆———

DARKNESS HAD SETTLED over the city. As Lana moved along the dingy streets with their row upon row of cramped houses and tenements, she could hear the sounds of tinny music, the occasional raucous laughter as doors burst open and the sudden hush of silence as they slammed closed. The smell of woodsmoke mingled with the scents of garlic and pepper, lamb and curry, beef, and chicken fat spilling onto hot coals.

Lana hadn't eaten since early in the morning, but the smell of food wafting on the air from doors and windows couldn't whet her appetite.

She'd found her money still hidden in a corner of her valise and knew she could afford a room, but the thought of spending the money on herself wasn't even tempting.

She'd been beaten down by life before, but this was the lowest point of her life. If she didn't find a way to pick herself up, there was someone far more important who would suffer. Her job didn't matter, nor did her life. But Colin deserved better. The thought of that frightened little boy burned like a beacon in the darkness of her mind. Still, how could a lowly unemployed housemaid hope to beat the VanEndel family? Only someone with wealth and privilege would have a chance of winning against them. With enough money, there wouldn't be a court in New York that would override her wishes.

With enough money. The words teased her. Taunted her. Mocked her.

She looked up to find herself striding along the wharf. Up ahead was the Blue Goose. Had she known she was headed in this direction? Not consciously, she thought. But perhaps unconsciously she'd needed something comforting. Something familiar.

Still, she didn't have the heart to go inside. She felt drained beyond belief. Battered by the storm raging inside.

She paused outside the door, listening to the high-pitched whine of Verna Lee's voice above the lower drone of male voices. Someone called for a refill. Wilbur shouted an order from the bar.

There was a low rumble of laughter from a corner of the room, and Lana felt a prickly sensation along the back of her neck. She would know that sound anywhere. Stone was here, playing cards with the regulars.

She hadn't seen him since that night at the VanEndel's. He'd looked so natural playing the part of a regal duke. Imagine Stone pretending to be related to English royalty. The thought had the corners of her lips twitching. He'd had not only the VanEndels, but all their high society guests, as well, falling over themselves to impress him. Impress Stone. A gambler. A lowly actor and con. If only they'd known how foolish they'd all been.

She went very still as a new thought intruded. Could an actor as believable as Stone teach her to act like that? With enough lessons, could she become an actress expert enough to pass herself off as royalty?

What would Evelyn VanEndel do if an elegant, high-born member of British royalty were to lay claim to Colin?

The very thought had Lana's breath coming hard and fast, her pulse racing.

What nonsense. She was no actor. She couldn't even lie without blushing. Still, if Stone could pull it off, why should she think she couldn't? With enough incentive, she could do it. Couldn't she do it for Colin?

The answer came instantly. For Colin, she would walk through fire or even rush into hell, if need be. For Colin, she would do whatever was necessary to save him.

She took a deep breath and, giving herself no time to think of the hundreds of arguments that were already whirling around in her mind, pushed open the door and strode inside.

Through the pall of smoke she saw him across the room, seated at the corner table. Toomy Davis was shuffling the cards. Stump McGraw was quaffing an ale. Ned Lancaster was saying something to Stone, something that had him laughing. He was still laughing when he looked up and saw her walking toward him.

Toomy shoved his three-hundred-pound frame out of the two chairs and got to his feet. "Lordy, look who's here. Lana Dunleavy, if you aren't looking prettier than ever." He gaped. "I guess this means you didn't get that job you were lookin' for."

"I did, yes. And I never had the chance to thank you, Toomy." She turned to Stone. "I need to talk to . . ."

"Came back to work, did you?" Wilbur Hasting ambled over, wiping the empty glass he was holding. "Figured one of these days you'd come to your senses and come back to the Blue Goose where you belong."

"Thank you, Wilbur. I'll talk to you about it later. But right now . . ." She turned back to Stone, who was watching her with that same careless grin. "I need to talk to you, Stone."

"You can talk in front of us, Lana." Stump winked at Ned Lancaster. "Can't she, Ned?"

"Of course you can, Lana, my sweet."

Her reaction was automatic, as though she'd never been away. "I'm not your sweet, Ned. And don't you forget it. Now . . ." She dropped her valise and closed her fists at her hips as she turned to face Stone. "I need to talk with you. Out back, if you don't mind."

"That's Verna Lee's territory."

At Ned's outburst, the others roared with laughter.

Lana shot him a look before picking up her valise and heading out the door. The suspense of not knowing whether or not Stone was following had her spine stiff as a board. Still, she refused to look back or slow her pace. Everything depended upon her firm resolve and her powers of persuasion, if she were to see this through.

Once outside, she gave a sigh of relief when she caught sight of Stone's tall figure stepping around the back of the saloon and blending into the shadows as he approached.

"All right." He held a match to the tip of a fresh cigar and drew on it while he studied her in that way that always caused her heart to do a funny little dip. "What's this about, Lana? I've lost a lot of money tonight and was hoping for a chance to win it back."

"I'm sorry, but this couldn't wait. I want you to teach me how to act like a titled Englishwoman."

"You . . ." He stared at her for so long he suddenly swore as the match burned his finger. Tossing it into the water, his eyes narrowed on her. "I think you'd better say that again."

"No need to playact with me, Stone. I knew the minute I saw you that first time here at the Blue Goose that you were an actor and a con."

A grin played at the corners of his mouth. "Did you?"

"I did. Yes." She nodded. "It's always there in the way you smile, so smug and satisfied with yourself. In your swagger when you walk. In the way you watch the other players at the table. I could see right off that you weren't like Ned's usual suckers."

He was staring holes through her, and she could feel the heat rising to her cheeks. "But I didn't realize just how good you were until I saw you at the VanEndel's. You talked better English than the king, I wager. And those fine clothes. I don't know where you bought them, but they looked every bit as fancy as all the others in the room. I saw the way Mrs. VanEndel looked at you. And all those rich ladies and gentlemen. Like you were one of them. Like you belonged."

"Lana . . ."

She shook her head. "You don't need to explain. I know. Because you're a really good actor. And that's what I need to learn. What I need you to teach me. Right away."

Intrigued, he arched a brow. "Why?" Now he took the time to really look at her. Despite the shadows of evening, he could see the red-rimmed eyes, the pallor of her cheeks, the slump of those thin shoulders. Though he wanted to catch hold of her and draw her close, he kept his hands to himself. "What's happened, Lana? Did someone hurt you?"

When she held her silence, his tone lowered persuasively. "If I'm going to trust you with my secrets, I think you ought to do the same. Now tell me, Lana. What happened?"

Her breath came out on a long, drawn-out sigh. "Something awful. Something really terrible. And if I can't persuade the VanEndels and everybody else that I'm a grand, high-born lady, I'd just rather die."

He chuckled. "You're much too young and sweet to want to die."

"Stop that."

"Stop what?" He drew on his cigar and blew out a stream of smoke.

"All that actor sweet-talk. This is serious business, Stone, and I need you to agree to help me. You see, a life hangs in the balance."

"A life?" Now he was all business. "Yours?"

She gave a shake of her head, sending corkscrew curls dancing. "There's a wee lad, Colin, born to my best friend, Siobhan. I was there when he was born, and that makes me the closest thing he has to family. Siobhan and I grew up in a foundling home, and I made her a solemn promise that if anything ever happened to her, I would raise Colin like my own. Now she and her husband are dead, and Colin is in the East Side Orphan Asylum. The director won't let me see him, or comfort him, because I'm nothing but an immigrant and a housemaid. What's worse, Mrs. VanEndel agreed publicly to adopt Colin, and now she's stuck with that promise, and even though she wants to back out, she won't. So I have to prove to everyone that I'm even richer and more high-born than Mrs. VanEndel, or I'll lose Colin forever. And you're the only one who can help me."

Stone's rogue smile had faded during her long-winded narrative. His tone became as solemn as hers. "I can see that this means a great deal to you, Lana. But are you really sure the boy would be better off with you? Think about all the things the VanEndel money can give him. A fine education. A life of ease. These are things you can never provide."

"But . . ."

He held up a hand to silence her objections. "It's a fine thing that you want to keep a promise to a dead friend. But what can you give the boy that the VanEndels can't?"

"I love the lad with all my heart. That's something they can never claim."

"You may think that, but you can't be certain of it. Maybe, once they take him into their home, they'll come to care about him the way you do."

"They've already closed their hearts to him. I overheard Mrs. VanEndel telling her husband that she doesn't really want Colin, but now that all of New York has read about her offer, there's no way she can back out. As for Mr. VanEndel, he called Colin Irish scum, and his wife agreed with him."

"I see. You heard this from their own mouths." He paused, trying to digest all she'd said before giving a sigh. "Listen to me, Lana. There are some things you need to know before we go on."

"No. You're the one who needs to listen." She dug into her valise and held out a handful of money. "This is what I've saved so far. It's yours, Stone, all of it, as long as you agree to teach me how to act like you."

His head came up sharply. "I know how hard you have to work for your money. Does it mean this much to you that you'd give me your life savings, just to keep a promise? Just to learn to act like a . . . lady of title and means?"

"It means everything to me." She thrust the money toward him. "Take it. It's all yours."

When he hesitated, she looked away, toward the boats on the water. Her tone was wistful. "I know I'm not clever and sly like Verna Lee. Or as smooth and polished as you. I'm plain and awkward, and maybe a little too honest to ever be as good an actor as you, but I'm willing to work at it."

His tone softened. "You're serious, aren't you, Lana? This is something you're determined to do."

"I am, yes. It's not just what I want; it's what I must do. I have to succeed. I couldn't bear to let Colin exist in a place without love, for I've been there. I'm desperate, you see. And desperate times call for desperate measures. So if I must spend all I have to learn to be an actor and con, if I must learn to lie and cheat and pass myself off as something I'm not, I'll do it, if only you'll agree to teach me all you can."

Stone leaned a hip against a rock that formed part of the sea wall, mulling all she'd said. He was silent for so long, Lana could hardly breathe.

At last he tossed aside his cigar and turned to her. She

could see the roguish gleam in his eyes, signaling that his wicked humor had returned.

"If I agree to this, you'll promise to do whatever I tell you."

"I will. I promise." She thrust her money into his hand.

He looked at it before tucking it into a pocket. "You'll need the right clothes. You'll have to learn how to walk; how to talk without the brogue; and how to pass yourself off as a living, breathing member of English royalty."

"You could ask me to walk naked through Central Park, and I'll not complain."

"So you say now. Don't forget that you'll need to devote all your time to this new path you've chosen."

"All my time? But I've just given you my money. You heard Wilbur. He's willing to give me my old job back. I could work nights, and you could teach me during the day."

"You'll need to devote all your time to this, Lana. Both days and nights."

"But what will I do for money? The little I've given you can't possibly buy my clothes and pay for a room."

"Let me worry about your clothes. As for a place to stay, you can stay with me. I'm currently holed up in a place on Fifth Avenue."

Her eyes went wide. "How can an actor and con afford a house on Fifth Avenue?"

"As you said yourself, I'm the best. I happen to have very generous benefactors." He smiled. "And very clever associates, who will help me transform you into a fine lady."

"Associates?" She studied him with a look of suspicion.

"People who will coach you in the proper way to speak, to walk, to wear fine clothes and jewels."

She shot him an incredulous look. "Would your associates happen to be actors and con artists like you? Or maybe worse? Could they be women who ply their trade on the streets?"

He put a hand to his heart. "I'm shocked, I tell you. Shocked and appalled, that you would think such things of me and my . . . associates." He gave her a level look. "Having second thoughts, Lana? Don't tell me you're afraid."

It wasn't in her nature to lie. "What if I am?"

"Thinking of changing your mind?"

She lifted her chin like a prizefighter. "I just don't know how I'm supposed to survive without a job or the means of earning my own way."

Stone gave a careless shrug of his shoulders. "If we're to succeed, you'll just have to put those worries aside and let me do my job. Are you willing to trust me to turn you into a believable member of royalty?"

He could see the way her mind was mulling the problems and decided to play his trump card. "Let me put it this way, Lana. What's more important to you? Honesty? A prim and proper lifestyle? Or winning custody of your beloved Colin?"

He could see the pain in her eyes and knew he'd hit his mark. He much preferred her this way, ready to stand and fight. At least she wasn't close to tears now, though he'd been afraid that's what she was about to do when he'd first met her out here. He didn't think he could bear seeing her cry. This strange, tough little female seemed to have some sort of power over him. With one smile or the hint of a single tear, she had a way of wrapping herself around his heart and tugging.

Picking up her valise, he put a hand under her elbow and steered her away from the Blue Goose.

"Aren't you going to say good night to your friends?"

He merely smiled. "I think not. I was losing anyway."

And it looked like his luck had just changed dramatically, he thought as he hailed a carriage. What a lark this could be.

He helped Lana up to the seat and settled himself beside her before giving the driver directions.

As he sat back, he could feel the way she held herself stiffly beside him and knew she was fighting a battle with nerves. But to her credit, she didn't bolt and run, even when their carriage slowed and turned up the wide, curving driveway that led to one of the biggest, most impressive mansions on Fifth Avenue.

ELEVEN

———◆◈◆———

LANA KNEW HER mouth was open as Stone helped her from the carriage. An older gentleman, perfectly groomed, his white hair combed neatly off his face, back ramrod straight, reached into the carriage and retrieved her valise.

"Withers, this is Miss Lana Dunleavy. She will be staying with us a while."

The man showed absolutely no emotion as he nodded slightly. "Miss Dunleavy. Welcome." He glanced at her shabby bag in his hand. "Will there be any other baggage?"

"None."

"Very good, sir."

The man stood to one side, waiting for them to precede him up the steps.

She leaned close. "A man servant? Is he yours?"

"He comes with the house."

"Ah." She nodded in understanding. "To see you don't filch the silver or help yourself to any other valuables."

Stone merely grinned. "Something like that."

Lana stared in absolute amazement at lantern light

playing over an elaborate fountain spilling water into a basin of green-and-gold–veined marble. Wide stone steps led to an ornate door that was opened before they had climbed the first step. If possible, she thought, this house was even grander than the VanEndel mansion.

Jesse leaned close to whisper with a grin, "It's humble, but it's home. At least for now. Oh, and one more thing. Here in this place, you'll refer to me as Jesse. Jesse Jordan."

"Another of your lies, Stone?"

"I prefer the word *con* to *lie*. See that you don't forget. Here my name is Jesse. Stone was fine at the Blue Goose. The men there thought of me as a rolling stone. Here in Millionaire's Row, Stone just wouldn't do now, would it?"

A tall, thin woman stood in a pool of light spilling through the open doorway. Her gown was the color of ripe plums. Her hair, coal black threaded with silver strands, was plaited on top of her head like a coronet. She wore a fringed shawl around her shoulders. The gown, the shawl, the hair, all added to her exotic beauty.

"You're early." She smiled as Jesse assisted Lana up the steps and into the sweeping foyer. "I wasn't expecting you for hours."

Her voice was dramatically low, and to Lana's ears, intriguingly foreign.

"I had a bit of an emergency." Jesse went on to say something in a language Lana didn't understand, and the woman answered him in kind before turning to Lana.

If she noticed the soiled gown, the shabby boots, the wild tangle of dark hair, she gave no indication as she bowed slightly. "I am Maria Escobar, the housekeeper here."

"You've a lovely place." Lana nearly sighed before she caught herself. "My name is Lana Dunleavy."

Maria started toward the stairs. "If you will follow me, Miss Dunleavy, I'll show you to your suite of rooms."

When Lana turned to Jesse, he merely smiled. "I'll be along in a while."

Maria led the way up a curving staircase to the second floor. Opening double doors, she stepped back, allowing Lana to precede her into the luxurious suite of rooms. The first was a sitting room, with a Persian rug in brilliant shades of sapphire and turquoise making a splash of color against the walls of muted pearl. Two white sofas mounded with jewel-toned pillows flanked either side of a magnificent marble fireplace.

"I'll send someone up to start a fire as soon as I've seen to your comfort, Miss Dunleavy." Maria opened another set of doors to reveal the most beautiful bedroom Lana had ever seen. A huge bed covered in white satin dominated the room. To one side was an ornate gilt dressing table and satin-covered chair. Beside it stood a tall mirror framed in gold. Across the room was a white satin chaise set before yet another fireplace, this one in white and gold marble.

While Lana stared in astonishment at her surroundings, Maria opened a door to reveal a bathroom, with a porcelain basin set atop a gilt and white vanity, and situated in front of a third fireplace, a round gilt porcelain tub. Lana had never seen the likes of such a room in her life. It was as different from the outhouse at the Blue Goose as day was to night. It was, quite simply, beyond anything she could have imagined. But then, everything she had seen so far was like nothing she had ever experienced.

"I'll have water brought up immediately for your bath, Miss Dunleavy." Maria pointed to the valise, which had been set on a table in an alcove. "And when you've changed, I'll send someone to fetch you to enjoy refreshments in the parlor."

Lana was too overcome to find her voice.

Before she could get her wits about her, the housekeeper was gone, leaving her alone to stare about in wonder.

Who could afford to own such a magnificent home? And why would he allow the likes of Stone . . . Jesse to live here?

It occurred to Lana that she had chosen well in her quest to win custody of Colin. Stone, or Jesse Jordan as he called himself here, must surely be the finest actor in all the world to persuade someone of wealth and substance that he was fit to be trusted to live in such a manner as this.

Now if only he could prove to be as excellent a teacher as he was an actor.

She had no time to pursue her thoughts. The door opened, and several servants entered, each carrying a bucket of warm water, which they poured into the round tub.

When they left, one of the servants remained.

At Lana's questioning look she merely smiled. "I was told to stay and assist you in your bath, miss."

Flustered by all the attention, Lana gave a quick shake of her head. "Thank you, but I'd prefer my privacy."

"As you wish, miss." The girl turned to leave and then paused and added, "If you should require anything at all, you need only pull that cord."

Lana stared at the white velvet cord hanging beside the wash basin and thought about the countless times she'd heard the annoying sound of a bell pealing in the VanEndel house, summoning a servant to the private quarters above stairs. Unless she should find herself in an impossible situation, there was no chance she would ever inflict such a thing on a servant in this household.

"Thank you. What is your name?"

"Rosa, miss. Maria Escobar is my aunt."

"You look like her." Lana extended her hand. "My name is Lana."

The girl stared at her hand, then up into her eyes, and offered a timid handshake. "Shall I return to help you dress?"

"No, thank you. I'll be fine on my own."

On my own. Lana thought how appropriate those words were. Didn't they describe her perfectly?

She stripped off her scuffed boots and shabby cotton hose, her dress, her chemise and drawers, and touched a toe to the steaming water. Assured that it wasn't too hot, she stepped into the tub and settled herself comfortably.

She picked up the soap and inhaled, astonished that it smelled exactly like lilacs in springtime. How was that possible? After staring at it for a long, silent moment, she tentatively began to soap herself. Oh, how wicked she felt, luxuriating in this fine tub, lathering her body, her hair, and then ducking beneath the water to rinse clean before coming up for air. Never in her life had she done something so decadent. It didn't seem right somehow, that she should be spoiling herself like this, while poor Colin was right now sleeping on a hard, cold floor, with nothing but a thin blanket to ward off the night's chill.

She'd expected that thought to nudge her out of this lethargy, but her tired body simply refused. And so she remained in the warm scented water for the longest time, eyes closed, breathing slowly and deeply, as though in a trance.

"Do you think you can handle all this, Maria?" Jesse accepted a tumbler of Scotch whisky from one of the servants before turning to the housekeeper.

"It would be my pleasure to assist the young lady."

"Don't be so quick to agree. This could prove to be a bit sticky. You'll have to dance around her questions. And knowing how her mind works, there will be at least a hundred, I assure you."

The older woman smiled. "I have always enjoyed a challenge."

"I thought perhaps Nadia could handle the seamstress duties. As I'm sure you're aware, Lana will need an entire wardrobe."

The woman's eyes lit with pleasure. "Of course. A brilliant choice. And Colette could teach the young miss to walk like a lady."

"I hadn't thought of that." Jesse grinned. "She'll definitely need to learn to slow down and walk like a lady. She always seems to be running. Have you noticed?"

"Indeed."

The butler cleared his throat. "You mentioned a speech teacher. What do you think of Ian Hyde-Smythe?"

"The bookkeeper?"

Maria nodded in agreement. "He'd be perfect for the job. He's handsome, charming, literate."

"And a bit of a dandy." Jesse frowned, seeing an image in his mind that didn't please him in the least. Still, someone had to work with Lana to overcome that brogue. "I suppose Ian will have to do, as long as he can be trusted to keep his mouth shut."

Maria nodded. "Shall I fetch the young miss now?"

Jesse handed his drink to the butler and turned toward the door. "I'll do it."

As he climbed the stairs, he was still frowning. What in hell had he taken on? Why hadn't he just walked away when he'd had the chance?

Not too late, he reminded himself. He could still back out. Now that she'd enjoyed a hot bath, it would be a simple matter to feed her, tell her he'd had a change of heart, tuck her money into her valise, and send her on her way. He'd even have the driver take her back to the Blue Goose, so she could boast to all her friends about her taste of the good life.

Yes, by heaven. That's what he'd do. Tough luck about her sad story, but if he could put an end to this nonsense, he could get on with his own bit of playacting. After all, wasn't that why he'd come to New York in the first place? This was all getting too complicated, and complications always took the fun out of things.

He paused outside the double doors and knocked. When he heard no response he knocked again, calling out, "Lana? Are you decent?"

His words were met with silence.

Perplexed, he pushed open the door and called out more loudly, "Lana? Are you in here?"

Good Lord, had she panicked and run? He didn't know whether to be alarmed or relieved at that thought. He walked through the empty sitting room and into the bedroom, which proved to be equally empty.

He pushed open the door to the bathroom and stared around in amazement.

Wet clothes were hanging everywhere. A threadbare dress draped over the vanity. Chemise and drawers swinging from the washstand. A nightshift flapping from the mantel, being dried by the heat of the fire.

Lana, barefoot, wearing the frayed gown she'd always worn while working in the Blue Goose, was on her hands and knees scrubbing the floor, which was swimming with soapy water.

"What are you doing?"

At the sound of his voice, she looked up with a start. Her wet hair spilled in ropes of wet tangles around her face. "I'm cleaning up the mess I made."

"There's no need to do that here. There are servants to see to it."

"I couldn't. After all, 'tis my mess."

"So I can see. What is all this?" He swept an arm to indicate the wet clothes.

"I couldn't bear to let all that hot water and that grand-smelling soap go to waste. So I thought I'd wash all my clothes while I was at it."

"Very thorough. It appears you've washed . . . everything."

Seeing his gaze sweep over her undergarments, she turned several shades of red before snatching them down from their perch and clutching them to her chest.

With her back to him she said, "I'll thank you to leave this room."

He couldn't keep the warmth of laughter from his tone. "In a moment." He stepped closer and touched a hand to her arm. "Lana, look at me."

"I'll not." She shrugged free of his touch. "You're laughing at me."

"Maybe I am, just a little."

When she continued to avert her face, he ever so gently turned her toward him. "Did you come here to learn how to be an actress?"

She avoided his eyes. "You know I did."

He tipped up her chin. "Then the first lesson is this: you must be willing to trust me."

"I do."

"Do you?" He paused a beat, before adding, "If you are to pass yourself off as a titled Englishwoman, you must think like one. There are servants to see to your needs. You must permit them to do their job, so you can learn to do yours."

"But I saw how selfish and demanding the VanEndel family was, and how reviled they were by their own servants."

He smiled. "I didn't say you must become vain, or arrogant, or self-centered. But to play a part, a good actor must always think like the person he portrays."

"Like you, portraying a duke?"

He was standing so close, Lana could see the little laugh lines around his eyes. In fact, she thought with a jolt, she could see herself reflected in his eyes. It was a most unsettling realization.

"Quite right. Now." He took a step back as though suddenly realizing that he was far too close and she was wearing far too little. "You might want to put on your boots and come downstairs with me. Maria has prepared some refreshments." He paused as a thought had him grinning. "That is, if you haven't soaked your boots in the bath along with the rest of your belongings."

"You're laughing at me again."

"I am. Forgive me, Lana. I'll learn to temper this nasty humor of mine."

"Not likely. Now go. Leave me to my privacy."

"A high-born lady never uses that tone of voice, Miss Dunleavy."

"You can turn me into a lady tomorrow. For tonight, I'll use whatever tone I please. Now leave me before I forget my manners."

She waited until he'd left the room before retrieving her good gown from the fireplace, where it had thankfully dried. After hurriedly dressing, she slipped her feet into her boots. Without the benefit of stockings, they were uncomfortable, but she had no choice. Nor, she thought with a trace of embarrassment, did she have any undergarments, because hers were still too wet.

She felt decidedly wicked wearing nothing but the thin gown. Is this how Verna Lee felt? The thought had her face flaming.

When she stepped into her sitting room, Jesse was standing by the fireplace, staring pensively into the flames. When he caught sight of her, he looked her up and down for a long moment. The color on her cheeks grew in direct proportion to his lingering look. Could he tell, just by looking, that she wore no chemise or drawers?

To cover her feelings she blurted, "What sort of actor can talk himself into a mansion as grand as this? Just what sort of con are you running?"

He shot her a dangerous look. "I agreed to teach you how to act like an English noblewoman. But I didn't agree to answer any and all questions. There are some things that are better left alone, Lana." A rogue smile slowly curved his lips, and he found himself actually beginning to enjoy this challenge. "We may as well continue your lessons. A gentleman always offers his arm to a lady." He took her hand and placed it on his sleeve. "And a lady always accepts his assistance."

"But I . . ."

He lay his hand over hers to keep her from pulling away. His tone was deceptively soft. "Even if the lady knows she can do just fine without his help."

Lana clamped her mouth shut on the argument she'd been about to make.

Without a word, they walked from the room and down the long curving staircase.

Lana felt the spiral of heat that tingled through her fingertips and snaked along her spine, leaving her uncomfortably warm. It wasn't his touch, she warned herself. Or the nearness of him.

Of course not. She was too wise to ever permit herself to be careless around an actor like Stone . . . Jesse.

It was, she told herself firmly, the knowledge that, right or wrong, she was now committed to see this charade through to its ending, however satisfying or disappointing the outcome.

She would not give up until Colin was hers. That was why she was here, wasn't it? To that end, she would do whatever was needed, even if it meant allowing Jesse Jordan to turn her into a con like him.

TWELVE

———◆———

"Ah. Here you are." Maria looked up as Jesse and Lana entered the library. "I thought this would be more comfortable for you than the formal parlor, Miss Dunleavy." The housekeeper left several servants to finish setting out an assortment of covered dishes on a small, round table set with fine lace in front of the fire. China and crystal gleamed in the firelight.

"You went to so much trouble." Lana thought about the work that had gone into the VanEndel's dinner party and found herself wishing fervently that she hadn't created additional work for these weary servants.

"It was our pleasure. Would you like me to stay and serve?"

Jesse shook his head. "It's late. You and the others may retire now. I'm sure Lana and I can serve ourselves."

Maria signaled the servants to leave before pouring sparkling liquid into two fluted glasses and placing them on a silver tray.

Turning away she called, "I will say good night, then. I hope you find your suite of rooms comfortable, Miss Dunleavy."

"Thank you, Maria. They're beyond anything I could have ever dreamed."

When the housekeeper was gone, Lana looked around with a shake of her head. "I didn't think anything could be prettier than the rooms I was given above stairs. But this." She spread her hands to indicate the mahogany bookshelves that lined three walls, filled from floor to ceiling with leather-bound tomes. "Look at this. So many books. Do you think the owner of this house has actually read any of them?"

"Quite a few, I'd wager." Jesse handed her a glass and helped himself to the other. "He strikes me as a man with a curious mind."

"Who is he?"

"I'm afraid that will have to remain my little secret."

Deflated, Lana studied the glass in her hand. "What is this?"

"Champagne."

She gave a gasp of surprise. "I couldn't possibly drink this."

"And why not?"

"It wouldn't be right. What if the owner should find out?"

Jesse smiled. "My orders were to make myself at home while I was here."

"Maybe so, but the owner knows nothing about me."

"Then we'll keep this our little secret." He touched the rim of his glass to hers. "Here's to secrets. And playacting."

She sighed. "I suppose it's all right, because it's only for a little while. And it's for a very good reason."

"Right you are. Well then." Jesse winked. "I'm sure we'll be forgiven all manner of sins, as long as our intentions are noble."

Her chin came up a fraction. "There you go, laughing at me again."

She sipped the champagne and felt the little bubbles explode on her tongue. Surprised, and more than a little pleased, she took another sip, and could feel the way it slid, smooth as silk, down her throat. "I never dreamed champagne tasted like this. It . . . tickles." Delighted, she sipped again and turned toward the table. "I've never seen such a pretty thing. All that silver and crystal gleaming in the firelight."

Jesse studied Lana. The table setting wasn't the only thing gleaming. Despite the shabby gown and the worn boots, she looked more charming than any of the society women had looked at the VanEndel's, in their finest gowns and elegant hair styles. There was an honesty, a sweet shyness, that was so appealing. But it wasn't just her artful innocence. There was a sensual quality about her as well. That glorious tangle of curls, spilling damply around the face of an angel, and the smell of her, as sweet as spring flowers, added just a hint of the temptress.

He held out a chair. "Because Maria went to so much trouble, why don't we sit and have something to eat."

As she took her seat, she felt the back of his hand brush her hair and was forced to absorb the most incredible tingle along her spine.

Jesse took the chair across from her and studied the way she looked in candlelight. All that fine, fair skin and those jewel eyes, watching him with such trust. And then there was that spill of coal black hair. The mere touch of it had caused his throat to go dry.

He drained his glass and refilled it before topping off hers. He lifted the lid from a silver serving platter to reveal slices of rare roast beef swimming in a rich burgundy sauce. He spooned some onto each of their plates. Uncovering several more serving dishes, he added breast of quail, potatoes mashed with onions and turnips, and crusty rolls still warm from the oven.

Lana looked down at her plate. "I couldn't possibly eat all this."

"And why not?"

She laughed. "Because I've never had the chance to eat this much in my life. If I should try it now, I'd most likely fall ill."

"We wouldn't want that to happen." He lay a hand over hers and was once again jolted by the heat.

He saw the way her eyes went wide and knew she felt it, too. That knowledge had him keeping his hand on hers a moment longer, as though to tempt the fates.

She could see the humor lurking in his eyes, in the slight upturn of his lips. When she tried to pull her hand away, she felt his grasp tighten.

Annoyed that he was having fun at her expense, she gave him an icy look. "If you don't mind, I need that hand to eat."

"But I do mind. You have two hands. I don't see why you're not willing to share one."

"I should think after your time spent at the Blue Goose you'd know what I do to men who dare to touch me."

"Is a simple hand on yours so repugnant to you, Lana?"

"It is if I didn't invite it there."

"Ah. I see. So if I wait for your invitation, there'll be no problem?"

"None at all." She took in a long, slow breath when he lifted his hand from hers. "And if you're willing to wait until hell freezes over, you'll have such an invitation."

At that he threw back his head and gave a growl of laughter.

"Am I always so amusing?"

"You are indeed, Lana." He picked up his fork. "Let's enjoy our meal."

"What about my lessons?"

He couldn't suppress another grin. "I should think morning would be soon enough for that."

He watched as she tasted each of the foods on her plate, letting them linger on her tongue before chewing and swallowing. With the first taste she paused and then smiled. With each succeeding taste her smile grew.

She was such a delight to watch. As open, as honest as a child. By the time her plate was half empty, she was actually humming with pleasure.

She glanced over. "You're not eating."

Surprised, he realized he'd been too intent on watching her to give a thought to his food. Now, as he moved things around his plate, he continued to watch her.

This little female had the strangest effect on him. From the beginning he'd been drawn to her, though he couldn't say why. But because she amused him, why shouldn't he simply accept the challenge she'd offered him? After all, he'd never been able to resist a challenge. Besides, it would be a grand lark. He'd have some fun with her, turning the simple little immigrant into a lady, and afterward they'd have a laugh about it.

Where was the harm in that?

And if she should succeed in gaining custody of the orphan, all the better, though he had his doubts that even the finest actor in the world could beat New York society in their own corrupt courts.

"You're so quiet, Stone." She set down her fork. "What are you thinking?"

Caught by surprise, he sat back and studied her. "You can't afford mistakes. Here, my name isn't Stone, but Jesse. Don't forget again. And I was thinking that we have our work cut out for us. Which is why I've arranged for a number of my . . . associates to tutor you."

"You mean other actors and cons?"

"Exactly. And I'll remind you, Lana, that you're to ask them no questions about the work they do here."

"Why not?"

"Secrets, dear Lana. Remember? You asked to learn from the best, and you shall. But you'll do so with no questions asked. That's my rule."

Annoyed at his tone, she lifted her glass and drained it in one long swallow.

"Another rule. Champagne is meant to be sipped, not swallowed down like a mug of tea."

Stung, she glared at him. "I'm thirsty."

"No matter. Next time, you'll sip."

"But . . ."

He lifted a hand. "The hour is late. I believe we're both too weary for this. I suggest we go up to our rooms. We can continue the lessons in the morning."

"You're truly going to teach me?" She flushed and stared down at her plate. "I was afraid you were going to feed me and send me on my way."

He shoved away from the table, ignoring the wave of guilt that swept over him. Was this little witch a mind reader?

Offering his hand he said, "My word on it, Lana. I'll do my best to turn you into a fine lady."

"Thank you." She accepted his handshake. "And I'll do my best to learn all that you have to teach me."

He looked down at that small hand in his and felt something twist deep inside.

With a frown, he placed her hand on his sleeve. This time she didn't resist. Together they moved down the hallway and climbed the stairs to the second floor.

When they reached the door to her suite of rooms, he opened the door and then stood aside, allowing her to move past him.

She paused on the threshold and turned to him. "Good night, St— Jesse."

"Lana. Sleep well."

He'd fully intended to bid her good night and take his leave. But she was looking up at him with that sweet, trusting smile, and before he knew what he was doing, his arms were around her and his mouth brushed hers in the softest of kisses.

He heard her quick intake of breath and felt the way she started to resist. Instinctively, his arms tightened, gathering her even closer, while his mouth moved over hers, teasing, coaxing a response. In some small corner of his mind he knew this was wrong. He should step away, but the heat between them was already too intense.

With a hiss of anger, she pushed free of his arms and sucked air into her lungs. When she managed to catch her breath, she pulled the knife from her waist. "You know better than to try such a thing with me."

Her eyes were narrow slits, and he could see the tiny points of flame that warned him he'd pushed her too far.

When she lifted her arm and took aim, he closed his fingers around her wrist. "I mean you no harm. Drop it, you little fool."

"You're the fool, to think you can trifle with me."

She was stronger than she looked, and Jesse was forced to press her back against the wall, using all his strength to hold her still while twisting her wrist until the knife clattered to the floor.

Her breath was coming hard and fast as she cursed him in a mixture of Gaelic and English. "You miserable, despicable son of a lecherous toad. Do you think, because I've accepted your offer to live here, that I owe you something more than money in return?"

"You owe me nothing." Taking no chances, he kept her pinned to the wall while he kicked the knife across the room.

When he finally released her, he shot her a dangerous grin. "It seems another lesson is in order. A high-born lady may use whatever means is at her disposal to protect her honor, but she must never permit such naughty words to cross her lips."

"May you burn in . . ."

He touched a finger to her mouth. "You simply must find another way to express anger, Miss Dunleavy. That litany, though colorful, just will not do for a high-born lady."

Before she could say a word, he leaned forward and brushed his mouth over hers and whispered against her pursed lips, "This one isn't a lesson, Lana. No business, just pure pleasure."

Just as quickly he stepped back and strode from the room and down the hall, giving her no time to react.

Much to his amusement, the sound of her curses followed him all the way to his room.

Once inside he closed the door and crossed to the window, looking down at the gardens glistening in the moonlight.

He'd told Maria he wanted to help a young woman in need of some tutoring, so she could claim an orphan who owned her heart, and that was true. It was also true that he loved nothing better than a challenge. But there was something else going on here, and he wasn't certain he wanted to probe it too deeply.

For now he would help Lana gain custody of the boy, and while he was at it, pull a clever con on the pompous New Yorkers and their revered Social Register.

The fact that she intrigued him, and had since he'd first seen her rushing around like a little whirlwind in the Blue Goose, had nothing to do with it.

And if, in the silence of his heart, he admitted that he'd wanted her then, and wanted her now, it changed nothing.

He'd keep his word and turn her into a fine, titled lady. And when it was over, they'd all have a good laugh over their little prank, and each would go their merry way alone.

Alone.

That was the way he liked it. That was the way it would remain, no matter how tempting the lips or how sweet the promise.

THIRTEEN

———◆◆◆———

"GOOD MORNING, MISS." Rosa cheerfully called out a greeting while drawing open the draperies.

Lana lay perfectly still, trying to gather her wits. She'd been so emotionally drained, she could only vaguely recall falling into bed the previous night. And then that soft, soft feather bed with its sumptuous linens, down pillows, and satin comforter had closed around her like warm, loving arms, taking her instantly into sleep.

Her life had always been one of hard work and few simple pleasures. She'd never known luxury. It would be so easy to grow accustomed to such living. It occurred to her that she would have to guard her heart against such a thing. When this playacting was finished, and she and Colin moved on, she couldn't afford to be lazy or soft.

"Your chocolate, miss." Rosa plumped up the pillows and helped Lana sit up in bed before placing a tray over her lap.

"I'm to drink this in bed?"

"It is the way it is done, miss." Rosa moved to the vanity.

"When you are fortified, I will help you dress before going below stairs."

"For my lessons?"

"For your morning meal, miss."

"I must fortify myself before eating?"

Rosa put a hand to her mouth to stifle a giggle at the absurdity that had just been pointed out to her. "It is the way of it."

"What foolishness." Lana drained the cup in one long swallow before swinging her legs to the floor and getting to her feet.

Her dress had been carefully ironed and was now draped over a chaise. Her undergarments, too, had been neatly pressed and looked better than they had when Lana had first made them out of some old castoffs.

"Did you do all this while I slept, Rosa?"

"I did, miss. But because you had already washed everything, all I needed to do was iron them and lay them out for the morning."

"I didn't mean to make more work for you, Rosa."

"I don't mind. Really."

When Lana was dressed, the little maid indicated the dressing table. Lana sat and watched in the looking glass as her hair was arranged in a most becoming fashion, with each side caught up and twisted at the back of her head and anchored by a pretty comb, leaving long ringlets to spill down her back.

Lana studied her image with new interest. "How did you learn to weave such magic?"

"It is a simple thing, especially when working on hair as lovely as yours, miss."

Lana grinned at the little maid. "In all my life I've never given a thought to my hair. Nor to the rest of myself, if truth be told." She walked to the door. "Will I see you below stairs?"

Rosa shook her head and began straightening the bed linens. "My chores will keep me here through the morning, miss. But I shall see you later, when you come up for a midday rest."

"Rest? What folly."

"I'm told that Maria has set up a strenuous round of lessons, miss."

"How could lessons be as tiring as the work I've done?" Lana was still laughing as she made her way down the stairs.

Following the sound of voices, she paused in the doorway of a lovely, sun-drenched room set with a table as large as the one she'd seen in the VanEndel's dining room. A sideboard was set with trays of silver serving dishes from which steam was seeping from beneath the lids.

Jesse looked up from a corner of the room, where he had been conversing with Maria in a foreign language.

"You're to leave nothing to chance."

The housekeeper nodded. "I'll see to everything."

"Fine." He turned to greet Lana. "Good morning."

Lana nodded, afraid to trust her voice. That scene from the previous night was etched too clearly in her mind. Her last coherent thought before sleep overtook her had been that she would keep her distance from this clever con artist while learning all she could from him.

"Good morning, Miss Dunleavy." Maria hurried over. "I hope you slept well."

Lana avoided looking at Jesse. "I can't remember ever sleeping so soundly. Or in such comfort. Thank you."

"You need not thank me. It is my job to see to your comfort. I hope you are hungry."

Lana was surprised, after all she'd eaten the night before, to realize she was ravenous. "I suppose I could eat something."

"Come. I will show you what Clara, our cook, has prepared, and you may make your selections."

Lana followed Maria, only too aware that Jesse was trailing behind her. She couldn't stifle a little gasp as the housekeeper lifted the lids on the various serving dishes to reveal eggs, both hard-boiled and coddled, crisp bacon, thinly sliced roast beef, biscuits and toast with both jam and marmalade, milk and tea, as well as more of the lovely chocolate which she'd enjoyed in bed.

Seeing it all, she gave a shake of her head. "I can't decide, Maria. It's all too much."

"Then you shall have some of each." The housekeeper lifted a hand when Lana started to protest. "Sit, Miss Dunleavy, and let one of the maids serve you."

When Lana turned away she bumped into Jesse and was startled by the wall of muscle she encountered. There appeared to be nothing soft or coddled about this man. Even his hands, reaching out to still her movements, were firm as they grasped her upper arms.

Such strength didn't come from holding a deck of cards. Obviously there were other things that occupied his time when he wasn't at the Blue Goose. Perhaps in his life of drifting he'd actually been forced to work from time to time. That may have been when he'd decided that accepting favors from wealthy women was much more satisfying than working a real job. Had that been when he'd decided to change his name as often as it suited him?

Feeling the heat of his touch, she stepped back. Instead of turning away, he moved beside her and held her chair.

She shot him a glance, and he muttered, "You'd better get used to it, Miss Dunleavy. It's the way a lady is treated by a gentleman."

"I'm sure you'd know all about such things."

"Indeed." When she was seated, he took the seat beside her. His voice was warm with humor. "Just tea for me, Maria."

"As you wish." The housekeeper motioned and a servant set a small pot of tea beside his plate.

"You're not eating?" Lana watched as a servant began filling her plate. So much food. How was she to manage all this?

"I'll have something later. I have several pressing appointments this morning."

Lana tried to hide her disappointment. "I thought we'd begin my lessons."

"And so you shall. I've found some very good teachers to work with you."

It occurred to Lana that he seemed considerably relieved to have turned the work over to someone else. Had he suffered his own pangs of conscience last night?

What nonsense, to assume a man like Jesse had a conscience.

"As you requested, Clara and I will see to her table manners. And then," Maria added, "the young miss must meet with Nadia."

"Of course." Jesse smiled. "Dear Nadia. You'll enjoy her company. Be sure to give her my love, Maria." He drained his cup of tea and pushed from the table.

His love. Those two words had Lana going very still. Was she about to meet someone important in Jesse's life? A mistress, perhaps? A future wife?

"Will you be taking your evening meal here tonight?" Maria called as he crossed the room.

He paused in the doorway, glanced at Lana, and gave a quick shake of his head. "I'm afraid not. I have dinner plans. In fact, I'll be quite busy for the next few days."

Lana felt her heart plummet and wondered at the way the sunlight seemed to fade from the room the minute he left. She chided herself for her gloomy thoughts. Not that she'd expected Jesse to spend his time with her. After all, she was merely a pupil, here to learn what he had already mastered. Why would he want to be here when he could be the center of attention at fancy dinner parties with silly, brainless women like Enid Morganthall and Anna-call-me-Anya Davis falling over themselves for his favors?

"You haven't eaten a thing, miss."

"I'm not hungry."

"That matters not the least." Maria opened a door and summoned someone. Minutes later a small, birdlike woman hurried over to the table and stood beside Lana's chair. She wore a pale gray gown, and over it, a spotless white apron.

"Miss Dunleavy, this is Clara Portland. She is not only one of the finest cooks in all of New York, but she is something of an expert on exotic foods. Because you will be encountering many foods you've never tasted, I thought Clara might help you become comfortable with them."

"Clara." Lana gave a sigh at the thought of having to learn new foods and how to eat them. "I'll be grateful for your help."

"Then we shall begin with this rule." The small woman reached over and removed the linen napkin that Lana had tucked into her bosom. "A lady never tucks her napkin."

"Then what does she do with it?"

"She lays it across her lap, like this." Clara settled the linen across Lana's lap and then pointed to the array of silverware. "You begin eating with the outermost fork of the setting." She watched as Lana picked up a fork. "Very good, miss."

When Lana picked up her knife in the other hand and began to cut her roast beef into small pieces, the cook gave a firm shake of her head. Hearing Lana's sigh of exasperation, she merely smiled. "If you were taking a meal with royalty, you could do almost anything and it would be tolerated. But here in New York, society matrons look down upon anything that is different. So you must cut your meat one bite at a time."

"But that will take forever."

Clara chuckled. "Indeed it will. But at a society dinner party, what else is there to do, after all, but cut one's meat and eat slowly? It will be far more entertaining than the conversation, I assure you."

When the cook and housekeeper shared a smile, Lana bit back whatever she'd been about to say and did as she was instructed.

While she ate, Clara settled herself at the table beside Lana. "As I said, with royalty, almost anything is tolerated, because they know that foreign guests follow their own customs. When I cooked for the princess royal, one of her guests from a foreign land wanted to offer her his highest compliment, so when the lovely meal was finished, he very loudly belched."

That had Lana's eyes going wide. "You . . . actually cooked for a princess?"

"Actually I was cook for the Duke of Argyll. After he wed the princess, I remained in their employ until she asked to send for her own cook. Since I then had nowhere to go, I made my way to America, and here I am."

A likely story, Lana thought. Why would a cook for royalty end up cooking for an actor in America? But she held her silence and asked the obvious question. "What did the princess royal do when her guest belched?"

"Knowing it was meant as a compliment, she did the same."

Now Lana was certain the woman was making up the entire story. She couldn't imagine a princess doing such a thing.

"If that were to happen to one of New York's society hostesses, she would no doubt be horrified and have the guest's name removed from her list. You see, Miss Dunleavy, the society matrons in this land are as yet unsure of their social standing and have no tolerance for anyone who is different." The cook smiled. "I'm sure in a hundred years or so they will learn to accept those who are not like them.

But for now, it is my duty to teach you how to become like them."

Lana asked no more questions and merely endured the cook's monologue as she made her way through the heaping plate of food that had been set before her. Though her appetite had fled along with her sunny nature, she forced herself to sample each new thing and follow Clara's instructions on the proper way of eating each one.

If she continued eating like this, she would soon need to let out the seams of her only good dress.

"AH. SUCH A fine, lithe young body. Stand. No fidgiting. Turn when I say. Now. *Nyet.* Not now. *Dah.* Now."

The woman, who had been introduced as Nadia, was speaking in a never-ending mixture of Russian and badly mangled English while kneeling on the floor with a pincushion in one hand and a measuring stick in the other.

Lana was standing on a small stool, wearing nothing but her chemise and cotton drawers and stockings, trying not to flinch under the older woman's piercing stare.

At least she knew now that if Jesse loved this woman, it was like a mother, and not like a lover. Her face and neck, beneath the elegant gown of black wool, revealed wrinkle upon wrinkle. But though her face showed the ravages of a life fully lived, her eyes were as bright and curious as a child's.

Maria stood back, watching and repeating the orders when they were mispronounced.

Nadia looked over at the housekeeper. "How many gowns you need?"

"A complete wardrobe, from day dresses to evening things, as well as undergarments, shawls, a coat, matching bonnets, shoes, and boots." Maria paused for breath.

"For that, I'll need to hire an assistant."

"Of course. Perhaps more than one."

Nadia's brow lifted. "Bringing assistants here will cost money."

Maria merely nodded.

"Here?" Lana looked from one woman to the other.

"*Dah*. I live here. I work here."

"In this house?"

"Where else?"

Lana's mind was reeling, wondering how many other actors lived here as well. There were perhaps half a dozen bedrooms on this floor, though she had no idea if they were empty or occupied.

Satisfied with her measurements, Nadia got to her feet and began laying out fabrics across Lana's bed.

There were watered silks, jewel-toned satins, and shimmering velvets. There were fur pelts and bolts of softest wool. There were samples of handmade lace and exquisite bead work. An entire basket was brimming with colorful spools of ribbon and bits of yarn that had been worked into intricate designs.

Maria drew Lana closer. "What appeals to you, Miss Dunleavy?"

"It's all so lovely." Lana couldn't bring herself to touch anything, afraid she might soil it.

"This for a day dress." Nadia scooped a pale ivory wool and held it up to Lana. "With that dark hair and goat skin . . ."

"Goat?" Lana looked startled.

"Goat's milk. Milk skin." Nadia seemed unaware of her mangled words or of the young woman's reaction. "And this." She fingered a pale pink watered silk. "For evening, this I think." She lifted a deep ruby velvet, studied it a moment against Lana's face, and nodded. "*Dah*. And a cape of the same velvet, lined in . . ." She tossed aside several pelts until she found the one she was looking for. "*Dah*. This." She held up a white ermine pelt. "With kidskin boots. I make one like this for the Tsarina."

"Tsarina?"

"Marie. Daughter of Tsar Alexander of Russia.

"You . . . sewed for the Tsarina of Russia?"

"*Dah*. Lovely lady. Her husband is son of the queen, you know."

"Queen Victoria of England?"

"Is there another?" Nadia warmed to her task, holding up this fabric and that, tossing some in one pile, some in another.

She was too busy to take note of the confusion in Lana's eyes. "This I think. *Dah. Nyet*. Not this. But this. This also." Like a woman possessed, she continued on until she had gone through the entire mountain of fabrics and accessories.

Hours later she breezed out, after assuring Maria that the wardrobe for the young miss would be ready soon. Lana watched as Maria handed Nadia an envelope.

"Was that the money I gave Jesse?"

Maria shrugged. "I know not, Miss Dunleavy. I didn't open the envelope to see what was inside. I am merely the messenger. I do as I am told."

"But how could my meager savings possibly pay for a seamstress who had once sewed for the Tsarina of Russia? Not to mention two assistants and all those exotic fabrics?"

"I am not the one to ask, Miss Dunleavy. And now it is time for your lessons to begin."

As Lana followed the housekeeper, her mind whirled with questions. Had Nadia truly been a seamstress to Russian royalty? Impossible. No doubt she was just another actress playing a role. Of course, Lana thought with sudden clarity. An actor of Jesse's stature would surround himself with like-minded actors and slight-of-hand experts. Hadn't she expected as much? Oh, Nadia was good. Very good. As was Clara. All that talk of royal connections. Cooking for the princess royal. And Nadia, sewing for the Tsarina. The fact that Nadia spoke so quickly, making it impossible to follow her, was proof that she was an expert at her craft.

Perhaps she'd actually learned to sew by making costumes for her friends onstage.

Lana had a quick impression of bold harlots with painted lips and cheeks, wearing revealing gowns and sauntering across a stage while men cheered. Not that she had ever seen such a thing, but she'd heard the things Billy had told Siobhan about some of his friends and their lewd behavior. The streets of the city were a veritable kingdom of darkness, eager to lure the vulnerable into their web of vice.

Hadn't she become a willing victim?

Lana stepped inside a room Maria described as the solarium. The ceiling appeared to be made of stained glass, and sunlight spilled down over a floor made of gold-veined marble.

"Miss Dunleavy, this is Colette."

"Colette." Lana couldn't help but stare at the woman with dyed red hair and a scandalously low-necked dress that clung to every curve of her willowy body.

Standing before her was one of the very women she'd just been seeing in her mind. A perfect partner for a man like Jesse.

"Maria tells me I am to teach you how to walk like a lady." Her French accent was so thick, Lana had to pay close attention to every word.

From the looks of Colette, Lana wondered if she even knew any ladies, other than those who plied their trade on the streets after dark. She wisely kept her thoughts to herself.

"You will walk for me, please." Colette waved both hands. "Now. Now."

With a quick glance at Maria, Lana did as she was told.

"*Non. Non.*" There followed a stream of French words that meant nothing to Lana. Then in broken English the woman said, "You will watch me and then do the imitation."

With her hips undulating, Colette moved slowly across the room.

Lana was reminded of a swan moving across a pond of smooth-as-glass water. She didn't so much walk as glide. The hem of her revealing dress barely fluttered. Nothing above Colette's waist moved. Not her head, nor her torso. Though her hands were held loosely at her sides, they were as graceful as a dove's wings.

Lana knew her jaw had dropped. "How did you do that?"

"It is something I have perfected over the years as a ballerina in France. With enough effort, you can learn. Would you wish?"

"Oh, yes, please." Excitement had Lana's brogue deepening. Whatever thoughts she'd entertained about this woman were forgotten in an instant. "I very much wish it."

Colette clapped her hands in delight. "Then it shall be. We have much work to do. We begin now. Head up. Back straight. Hands at your sides."

Lana walked, stopped, turned, and at times dropped to the floor while Colette showed her exactly what she wanted her to do.

"You must move like the dancer. Each step effortless. You see?" As she spoke, Colette glided across the floor. "When first I met Bertie, he told me that it was my walk that seduced him."

"Bertie?"

Colette gave a slow, dreamy smile. "Others know him as the Prince of Wales. We met at a dinner party, and within weeks, had become lovers."

Lana was scandalized. "But everyone knows the Prince of Wales is married."

"This is true. But it is not a loving arrangement. Bertie swore to me he had never known happiness until he met me." Colette gave a long, sad sigh. "Those were the most amazing years. Dinners with England's most fascinating royals. Dancing until dawn. Traveling the Continent. Alas, his mother found out about me, and I soon found myself bound for America."

"The queen, Victoria, had you banished?"

"She reminded Bertie that she is queen and will not have her first-born, the first in line to the throne, living the life of an aging playboy. If it were not for my dear Jesse and his generous spirit, I would be living on the streets." Colette clapped her hands. "Enough of this sad talk. I am here to teach you to walk like a lady. Come. You will do as I do." Humming a little tune, she began to undulate around the room.

Lana had to choke back the laughter that bubbled just below the surface at the thought of imitating Colette. Yet despite this woman's bold image, and her admission of a life that was far from ordinary, there was something rather endearing about her. Perhaps, Lana thought, it was her openness. Lana had never before known a woman who was willing to reveal the most private of her life's details to a total stranger within minutes of their meeting.

Following her lead, Lana trailed slowly behind, allowing her hips to sway to the tune. In no time, her movements had become fluid, her walk sensuous.

Hours later, after Colette left to retire to her suite, Lana collapsed onto the floor of the solarium.

When Maria came searching for her, she found Lana with her head back, eyes closed, looking more exhausted than if she had worked as a kitchen maid for days on end.

"When Colette took her leave, she said you're an apt pupil, but she'll need to spend many more hours before you can take your place in society."

Your place in society. Those words played through Lana's mind as she made her way up the stairs to her room. How could a few dresses and a new walk change her from plain old Lana Dunleavy to a high-born woman who would be welcomed into New York society? How could she hope to fool not only the wealthy people of this city, but the officials who would determine Colin's future?

Jesse did it with all the ease of a seasoned actor.

With enough time and training, she would become an actor as well. Despite her fears at the task before her, she would cling to that knowledge and hope it was enough to see her through this dangerous charade. For if she failed to play it convincingly enough, she would lose Colin forever.

FOURTEEN

"ROSA TELLS ME you made up your bed linens before she could stop you." Maria's tone was accusing. "And that she found your undergarments freshly washed and hanging about the room when she arrived with your morning chocolate."

Lana avoided the housekeeper's eyes. "I don't want to make more work for her."

"It is her job, Miss Dunleavy."

Lana knew that whenever Maria used that formal tone, she was being rebuked. "I'm sorry. It's just that I've always had to work so hard, and I can't bear to cause others to do what I can do for myself."

"While you are here, Miss Dunleavy, you will allow the servants to serve." The housekeeper opened the door to the library and stood aside. "This is Ian Hyde-Smythe. He's here to tutor you in English. This is your student, Miss Lana Dunleavy."

Lana stood hesitantly in the doorway of the library, feeling awkward in her faded dress and scuffed boots, while the man standing beside the desk in his dark suit and neatly tied cravat was dressed as formally as the men she'd seen at the VanEndels' dinner party. "Do you live here, too?"

He smiled. "I'm afraid not, though I wouldn't object to such opulence. Actually I have my own place."

"I see. I don't understand why I need a tutor. I can already speak English."

"And very well, from the little I've heard so far." The man started toward her with a smile. "But I've been told to help you lose your brogue."

"Ah." She swallowed as he paused before her. He was perhaps as tall as Jesse, but where Jesse was darkly handsome, this man was fair as the sun, with pale hair and mustache, and laughing blue eyes. "Do I address you as Mr. Hyde or Mr. Smythe?"

That had his boyish smile growing. "It's Hyde-Smythe. All in one. A bit too formal, I think. I suggest you call me Ian, so long as I may call you Lana."

"That's my name."

"And a lovely name it is." Noting her shyness, he indicated the French doors that led to a terrace overlooking the gardens. "It seems a shame to stay indoors on such a day as this. Perhaps we could begin the lessons out there?"

Maria crossed the room and threw open the doors. "Shall I bring some refreshments out on the terrace?"

"Tea would be nice." Ian glanced at Lana. "Or would you prefer lemonade?"

"Tea is fine." She paused on the stone terrace, clasping her hands together. She'd never been to school, unless the harsh reading lessons taught with a hickory stick at the foundling home counted for anything. She had never had a session with a tutor in her life, except for the walking classes each afternoon with Colette. But this was different. This was a man, and though she had no doubt he was an actor like the others, the look of him, formal and elegant, had her feeling completely out of her element.

"Would you care to sit, Lana? Or would you prefer to walk in the gardens?"

"Do you mean to say we can walk during the lessons?"

"If you'd like." He put a hand beneath her elbow as she descended the three stone steps that led to the gardens.

As Lana made her way along the curving walkway between formal plantings of roses, Ian clasped his hands behind his back and moved along beside her. "Tell me a little about your life."

"There's little enough to tell. I've been in this country for five years now."

"Did you come alone or with family?"

"I have no family, but there was a friend." Her lower lip began to tremble. She couldn't speak Siobhan's name. It was too soon. Her feelings were too raw. There'd been no time to grieve before being thrust into this strange new situation. A situation of her own choosing, she thought with a twinge of guilt, but a strange one nonetheless.

Sensing her unease, Ian turned aside and pretended interest in a nearby fountain. "What brought you here to America?"

"Hope." She answered without even giving it a thought. "I knew there was a better life to be had than the one I was living in Ireland."

"And have you found it? Hope, I mean?"

She paused and took a moment to cup a lovely crimson rose in her hand, leaning close to inhale its perfume. "I have, yes. I suppose I'll always have hope."

She glanced over in time to see him wince. "What's wrong?"

"It's your brogue. I can see that I have my work cut out for me." He motioned toward the terrace, where Maria was overseeing several maids who were busy arranging a silver tea service on a small table. "Why don't we take our tea while we begin?"

Lana lowered her voice to avoid being overheard by the servants. "What's wrong with my brogue?"

"There's nothing wrong with it, if you're Irish. But to many wealthy people here in America, it has become a symbol of the working class."

"They know, just by hearing me speak, that I'm beneath them?"

"Not beneath them, Lana. But not one of them, either."

"And if I sound like you, what will I be?"

"Accepted." He smiled and held her chair before taking a seat across the table from her. "That's just the way of it. Even though most of the people here came from other countries that are disdainful of royalty, they've decided that they want to be thought of as regal. And there's nothing more regal to them than England's royal family. Victoria and Albert and their princely brood have become the model of social standing. So those of us with decidedly English accents are considered more acceptable in their eyes. I'm here to see that you take your rightful place in society, Lana." He lifted his cup in a toast. "With that in mind, let us begin."

"THANK YOU, ARTHUR." Jesse accepted a tumbler of whiskey from the manservant and glanced around the Manhattan Gentleman's Club. Spotting his prey holding court across the room, he deliberately took his time, stopping to chat at several tables along the way.

"Jesse. How good to see you here." A banker stood and offered his handshake before introducing his guest, one of New York's best-known newspaper publishers.

At a second table Jesse greeted a lumber baron bent in earnest conversation with one of Wall Street's financiers.

The two men beamed. "Always an honor to have the Duke of Umberland numbered among our company. I say, would you care to join us?"

"Thank you. But I'm joining friends." Jesse gave his most engaging smile before moving on yet again.

Long before he'd crossed the room, he could see his prey listening to his companion with only half an ear while watching his progress.

"Jesse." Richard Vanderbilt extended his hand. "How good of you to join me." He turned to his friend. "You know Gustav VanEndel."

"Of course."

"Our table is over here." Vanderbilt led the way, with the other two following.

Soon they were exchanging small talk about the cost of land in Manhattan, speculation about whether the square mile of electric lights would soon catch on across the city, and whether or not to buy stock in the old Edison General Electric, which, now that J.P. Morgan had merged with Thompson Houston, was to be known as General Electric.

"What do you think, Gustav?"

Jesse sat back, allowing the other two to carry the conversation, which they were only too happy to do. Each man tried to outdo the other with words of wisdom.

Richard Vanderbilt turned to Jesse. "You're quiet today."

"Sorry. A lot on my mind."

"Business or personal?"

Jesse frowned. "A little of both. I'm looking at a piece of land not too far from here."

"I hope you'll entertain the thought of accepting investors."

Jesse flashed one of his famous smiles. "You may be able to persuade me."

"Good." Vanderbilt rubbed his hands together. "And the personal?"

"News from home. My cousin will be arriving soon for a visit."

"Another eligible bachelor?" Gustav sipped his Scotch.

"Eligible, but hardly a bachelor. She's actually quite fetching."

"A lady. Excellent." Richard brightened. "She'll be here just time for the season. I'd like to be the first to extend an invitation for your fetching cousin to join us at our annual dinner party."

"Thank you. I know she'll be delighted."

When the meal ended, Jesse touched a linen napkin to his mouth and stood to follow his friends from the club.

As they descended the steps, he spotted Farley Fairchild in his usual spot across the street. Fairchild and his photographer, who routinely caught New York's most famous millionaires leaving the Manhattan Gentlemen's Club, had been ordered to keep a discreet distance.

Jesse shook hands with his friends and then started toward his carriage, which he'd arranged to have waiting across the street. Before he could climb up, the reporter, recognizing him from the VanEndel dinner party, dashed forward.

"The Duke of Umberland."

Jesse feigned a look of surprise. "Yes?"

"Farley Fairchild, with the *New York News and Dispatch.*"

"Of course." Jesse gave him a dazzling smile. "How are you?"

The reporter seemed amazed that British royalty would remember him. His tone became slightly breathless. "I wonder if you have any news you'd care to share with my readers, your grace."

"I'm afraid not." Jesse turned away and then seemed to think better of it and turned back. "But if you plan to cover the Vanderbilt dinner party next week, you'll have a chance to see my lovely cousin, coming to America for her first visit. Her name is Lady Alana Dunning Griffin Windsor, from Shrepshire, England."

"Is the lady traveling alone?"

"She is." Jesse lowered his voice. "Though I suspect when all the eligible bachelors in America get a chance to meet her, she won't be alone long."

When it came to appreciating the beauty of women, the two men shared a knowing smile that bridged all social, cultural, and financial boundaries.

His business completed, Jesse pulled himself into the carriage and signaled to the driver to leave.

"WHAT'S HAPPENING WITH the gowns?" Jesse looked more than a little weary as he accepted a cup of tea from one of the servants and turned to the housekeeper.

"Nadia has already provided half a dozen, along with shoes, bags, wraps, and cloaks. They are, as expected, exquisite."

"I never had a doubt." He sipped. "And Lana's voice, demeanor, and bearing?"

"She is making great strides. Colette calls her a quick study. Ian seems equally delighted with his pupil. In fact, he spends so much time here, extending the hour into three and four, that the young lady has had no time to rest in the afternoons."

Jesse's eyes narrowed. "Isn't young Hyde-Smythe taking his responsibility a bit too far?"

Maria's brows arched. "I thought you'd be pleased. I told him you'd left word that there was no time to waste."

"That's true enough, but . . ." Jesse's head came up sharply at the sound of feminine laughter filtering through the terrace doors. Setting down his cup and saucer with a clatter, he crossed the room and stood glowering at the sight that greeted him.

Lana was seated in a chair on the terrace. Ian stood behind her, one hand on her shoulder, the other pointing to something in an open book. At the rumble of masculine words, she turned and looked up into her tutor's face with a smile of pure pleasure.

Jesse wondered at the hard, tight knot of feeling in the pit of his stomach. Jealousy? Impossible. He'd never in his life been jealous of another. Nor would he begin now.

No, not jealousy, he reasoned, but annoyance, that someone in his employ should be wasting precious time on a book instead of working on Lana's accent.

That's what happened when he spent too much time letting others take charge of his affairs. Not that it could be avoided entirely, but he'd actually drawn out his time away to avoid close contact with Lana while her lessons were underway. That little scene at her bedroom door had shaken him to the core, and he was determined to keep his distance in the future. He couldn't afford to let personal pleasure get in the way of business.

Now look what he'd done by being an absent employer.

With a muttered oath, he yanked open the door and stormed onto the terrace.

Two heads turned at the sound. Seeing the murderous look in Jesse's eyes, Ian took a step back.

Jesse fought to keep his tone civil. "What are you two up to out here?"

"When I learned that Lana shares my love of books, I was so delighted, I thought I'd share mine with her." Ian glanced at Lana, and his smile returned. "This young lady has an amazing mind. I hope you don't object to the fact that we helped ourselves to some of the books on the library shelves. Having her read aloud was a fine way to help her learn to speak without feeling self-conscious."

"And the brogue?" Jesse's eyes remained hard.

"I believe we're making great progress." Ian lifted a hand. "Would you care to say something, Lana, to display your skill?"

"I would, yes." The brogue tumbled out before Lana had time to prepare herself. "I mean . . ." She struggled to speak the way Ian had so painstakingly been teaching her. But how could she think with Jesse looking at her like that?

Here he'd been absent for weeks, except for an occasional visit, leaving her in the hands of all these strangers, and now, instead of saying how nice she looked in her fine new gown, he was looking at her the way he'd looked at her the night he'd caught her on her hands and knees scrubbing the floor.

"It's all right." Ian prompted in a stage whisper. "Remember what I've taught you. Whenever you feel overwhelmed, take a moment to compose yourself and then start again."

Lana cleared her throat. "Ian has been ever so helpful in teaching me to speak slowly and enunciate clearly, as befits your cousin, Lady Alana Dunning Griffin Windsor." Pleased with her perfect imitation of his British accent, and the fact that she'd mastered the lie they'd concocted about her relationship to Jesse, she added, "And the books he's been sharing with me have been grand. In the past few days, we've been to France and England and even Australia. Did you know that kangaroos are capable of hopping clear over a man's head? And they carry their wee ones in a pouch?"

Jesse glared at Ian while addressing his words to Lana. "A discussion about the penal colony should make absolutely fascinating conversation around the table at the Vanderbilt dinner party this weekend."

"This weekend?" Her voice turned to a high-pitched squeak. "But I couldn't possibly. I'm not ready." She turned to Ian. "Tell him I'm not ready for this."

"Yes, tell me, Ian, whether or not my money has been well spent." Jesse's tone was pure ice.

Ian's chin came up. "It would have been better to give us a few more weeks together."

"I don't dictate when New York's society leaders will want to invite me to dine." Jesse continued glaring at Lana while addressing his words to her tutor. "This dinner will be the most important social event of the year. Acceptance by the Vanderbilts will assure inclusion in future invitations. Being New York's wealthiest family, they've become the one to emulate. If they approve, all of New York will approve as well."

Ian stood a bit taller. "I have no doubt that the lady, with her quick mind and ready wit, can manage quite nicely."

At Lana's gasp, the young man turned to her and closed a hand over hers. "You're a smart woman, Lana. Smarter than most women I know. And you have rare courage. Those two virtues will take you wherever you choose to go in this world. You'll do just fine. You'll see."

Jesse studied their two hands before lifting his gaze to the young man's face and fixing him with a look guaranteed to freeze his blood. "Thank you. You may go now and collect your pay from Maria on the way out."

At the finality of his tone, Ian gave a nod and turned away. As he stepped through the open doorway, he turned. "It has been a pleasure working with you, Lana."

"Thank you for all your kindness, Ian."

Lana clasped her hands together and waited for Jesse to say something. The way he was studying her, she wondered if she had a smudge on her cheek.

Now that they were alone, Jesse couldn't seem to find his voice. Seeing her in that elegant ivory gown, her dark hair held back with mother-of-pearl combs, and the toes of brand-new shoes peeking out from beneath the ruffled hem had his throat going dry.

The change in her was astounding. These few weeks of good food and restful sleep had erased the circles from under her eyes and had given her skin a radiant glow. Her hands, clasping and unclasping at her waist with obvious nerves, no longer bore the effects of years of hard work, but were gradually growing soft and smooth. Anyone looking at her would think she'd been born to a life of wealth and privilege.

When he realized that the silence had stretched awkwardly, and that he'd been caught staring, he covered his lapse by looking her up and down and speaking in measured tones. "Maria said the rest of your wardrobe should be here before the weekend. Are you pleased with what you've seen so far?"

Lana wondered at his tone. She had the sense that something was wrong, but she was so happy to finally see him again, she couldn't dwell on anything else. In the past few weeks, he'd been gone before she came below stairs in the morning, and no matter how late she'd stayed awake at night, listening for the sound of his footsteps in the hall, she'd never managed to hear him return.

And why should he come back to this house that was not a home but merely belonged to a friend, when he could indulge himself with fine dinner parties, escorting wealthy women back to their homes, and possibly spending the night with them? There was no need for him to bother about his new houseguest. He knew she was in good hands with Maria and the staff of servants. Why should she matter at all to him? Especially when he was busy plying his trade on all those silly, empty-headed women?

Oh, the thought was too painful.

"Does your silence mean you're disappointed in the clothes Nadia has made for you?"

"Disappointed? Is that what you think?" She took in a breath. "For all my life, the only thing that mattered was that I had enough to eat and something dry and warm to wear. Now, I find myself dressed in silks and satins, with cloaks of fur and velvet, and fancy shoes so soft, my feet hardly know they're there. And you ask if I'm disappointed?"

He couldn't help but smile at her honesty. No wonder young Hyde-Smythe had been dazzled by her. She was as refreshing as the sunshine after days of gloom and rain. Just looking at her had his spirits lifting. Especially now that Ian was gone and they were alone.

"Well then." He put a hand under her elbow and steered her toward the door. "If you'd like, we'll take our meal in the formal dining room tonight, and you can wear your best new gown and impress me with all you've learned since I've been gone."

"You're staying home tonight?" She couldn't keep the excitement from her tone.

"I am. And happy to be."

And he was, he realized as they stepped inside. In fact, he was feeling so pleased with himself, he decided to send Hyde-Smythe a handsome bonus.

There. He hadn't been jealous at all, only weary after so many weeks of dancing to the tune of society hostesses.

Tonight there would be no pressure. Tonight he would eat what he pleased and watch and listen as critically as he could to determine if his money had been well spent.

And he would, he admitted with some reluctance, indulge his fantasies by spending an entire evening in the company of this fascinating creature.

FIFTEEN

———◆◆◆———

"SIT STILL, MISS." Rosa put the finishing touches on Lana's hair, adding pretty silver combs to the dark curls, before stepping back to survey her handiwork. "Oh, don't you look grand. Maria said this is to be a rehearsal for the Vanderbilt dinner party."

"Rehearsal?"

The little maid laughed. "I suppose you wouldn't know about such things. Actors must run through the complete play on the night before it opens to learn their lines and to make certain they have all the proper moves onstage."

"I see." This confirmed what Lana had suspected. Even Rosa was one of them. Actors, cons, loose women. The house was filled with them. Even Ian had been reluctant to say what his relationship was to them. Ah well, hadn't she asked for this? Besides, whatever their choices in life, they were helping her, and for that she would be grateful.

Lana barely took time to glance at herself in the looking glass before turning toward the door. "Thank you, Rosa. Now don't wait up. You've been working far too hard these past weeks. I want you to promise me you'll get your rest."

The little maid giggled behind her hand. "I have never served anyone like you before. Besides, I can't promise to rest, because Ernst, who tends the horses in the stable, has asked me to walk with him in the moonlight."

"Does Maria know?"

Rosa merely smiled. "There are some things I'd rather not mention to my aunt. When it comes to me, she's like a mother hen. She thinks I'm too good to be wasting my time on a man who cleans the stables."

Lana looked horrified. "But if he's a good person, what does it matter how he earns his money?"

"It is simply the way of things. My aunt thinks no man is good enough for her niece. Go now, miss. And good luck on your rehearsal."

Lana flew from the room and down the stairs, wondering at the way her heart began racing. Outside the dining room she stopped and ran a damp hand down her skirts, hoping to catch her breath. It was imperative that she make a good impression on Jesse, and make him proud of the things she'd learned. If this was the rehearsal, she must reflect all the things her tutors had taken such pains to teach her.

When she stepped into the dining room, Jesse was standing by the fireplace, staring into the flames. In his hand was a glass of ale. When he turned to her she thought he seemed distracted. But as she drew near, he blinked and the look was gone, replaced by that rogue smile that always did such strange things to her heart.

"You look lovely, Lana. That color is perfect on you."

Lana glanced down at the ruby satin. "Thank you. It was Nadia's choice, not mine."

"You can always trust Nadia's taste." He reached for a glass on a silver tray. "I asked Maria to pour you some champagne." As he handed it to her, their fingers brushed and she felt the rush of heat all the way to her toes. She could feel them actually curling in her new kid slippers.

"Thank you." Knowing he was watching and judging, she took no more than a sip.

"I like what Rosa has done with your hair."

She gave a slight nod of her head and wondered at the way her heart soared at the simple compliment.

One of the servants entered with a silver tray on which rested several triangles of toast with something spread on them.

"Cavier." Jesse watched as she took one and lifted it to her mouth. "From Russia."

Lana took a tiny taste and turned to him with a look of surprise. "It's very good. Did you know that Nadia told me she was seamstress to the Tsarina of Russia?"

"What do you think of that?"

Knowing how intensely Jesse was watching, she merely shrugged. "I think it makes a fine story, and one she's told so many times it comes easily to her now."

He smiled. "Your tone tells me you don't believe her. I suppose dear Colette has shared her tale of heartbreak, as well?"

"Many times. Each day when we get together she embellishes the story more, until I swear I can almost see her in the arms of the Prince of Wales." Lana polished off the toast point and had to force herself not to reach for another. "You surround yourself with very believable storytellers. I'd say they're your equal as actors, Jesse."

He gave a slight bow. "Thank you." He looked over when Maria entered, followed by several servants.

The housekeeper greeted them with a smile. "Clara has taken great pains to see that your dinner is just as you'd requested."

"I hope you'll give Clara my thanks."

Jesse extended his arm, and Lana placed her hand on his before moving beside him to the table. When he held her chair she sat and forced herself not to react when his fingers brushed her neck.

They began with a light consommé slivered with tiny strips of carrot and leek. As she had been instructed by both Maria and Clara, Lana ate only a few spoonfuls before touching the linen napkin to her lips. At once a servant removed the bowl.

A second servant paused beside her and lifted the lid from a serving platter, placing a small amount of potatoes on her plate. This was followed by another young woman who served vegetables and a third who served the fowl.

Maria poured wine into their glasses before stepping back. "Do you wish to be alone while you eat?"

Jesse nodded. "Yes, thank you, Maria."

When the servants were gone, Lana took a tiny bite of the fowl. "I've never tasted anything like this. What is it?"

"Duck roasted in wine and glazed with liqueur."

"And to think that Clara can make such a fine dish. Did you know that she told me she once cooked for the Duke of Argyll? After he wed the princess, poor Clara was sent packing, saying his wife preferred her own cook to his. Can you imagine such a cruel thing? Not that I believe her," she added softly.

"And why not?"

"You don't expect me to believe all the lovely fairy tales spun by the women in this house." At his look she felt her cheeks grow flushed. "Not that they aren't fascinating stories meant to imply amazing lives. But I realize that in reality they're probably just like you, Jesse. Actors who've perfected their craft until they're so good at it, they almost believe their own lies." She bent to her meal, obviously relishing each new food.

When at last she sat back, she couldn't resist a little sigh of pleasure. "That was . . ." She reached for the word Ian had suggested she use whenever she was in the company of wealthy women. "That was simply divine."

Jesse bit back his smile. "I'm glad you like the duck. It seems to be one of society's favorites this season."

"Do their favorites change?"

Now he did smile. "As often as the seasons change. And not only in foods, but in clothes, charities, even people."

"I don't understand."

He grew serious. "This year, because the VanEndels toured Europe, they have decided that English royalty is to be emulated. Which is why I've become so popular. By this time next year, New York society may decide that's all passé and move on to actors or jugglers or East Indian mystics. Whatever happens to catch their fancy."

"But of course, that should make no difference to you."

He arched a brow in question.

"Whether they want English royalty, actors or jugglers, or even East Indian mystics, I'm sure you'll manage to become whatever you must to gain entry to their world."

Jesse sipped his wine and studied her in silence. After a moment his smile returned. "I believe I detect a note of censure in your tone. Do you disapprove of how I choose to live?"

"Certainly not. Who am I to judge you, when I'm guilty of doing the same thing?"

"But you're not proud of what you're doing, are you, Lana?"

"I'll not be made to feel ashamed, either." The brogue was back, thick as ever. She tossed her head and lifted her chin in defiance, even while her fingers restlessly played with a silver spoon. "I'll do what I must to gain custody of Colin, and let no one judge me for it."

He closed his hand over hers, stilling her movements. His tone softened. "I'm not judging you, Lana. Nor will anyone else. You're not alone, especially here in this place. We're all forced to do things we aren't proud of to survive."

"But you could be so much more, Jesse." She pulled her hand away and looked up at him with eyes that had gone wide at his touch. "Look at you, in those fine clothes, looking better and talking better than even the Prince of Wales.

Why, if you were to turn your talents to more noble deeds, you could be as rich as the VanEndels or the Vanderbilts, I'd wager."

He couldn't keep the warmth of laughter from his tone. "Such trust, Lana. Be warned. If you're not careful, you'll start believing in me."

"But you should believe in yourself, Jesse. You're so much better than you think."

"And what's that supposed to mean?"

"Why do you always try to hide your goodness? Nadia thinks the world of you. So does Colette. Even Maria and Rosa and Clara have nothing but good things to say about you. Every day I must listen to their stories of praise. How you helped them come to America and found them jobs when they were desperate. How many times you've given them money when they were down and out. I've seen you speaking with each of them in their own language, lifting their spirits, leaving them always with a smile. And look how you let them live here in this fine big mansion with you until you're forced to move on. You may be nothing but an actor and con, but deep inside I believe you have a good heart. You just need to find an honest job, and there's no telling how far you could go."

He was looking at her with the strangest expression. Somewhere between wry humor and annoyance.

Now that she'd opened up, there was no backing down. Taking a deep breath, she said, "People are drawn to you, Jesse. Look at the way Stump and Toomy and Ned took to you. It would be the same with society people. I think if you were to tell Mr. VanEndel the truth, he might be willing to forgive you your little deceit and even give you a job in his company."

"You mean, if he didn't have me jailed for my, as you call it, little deceit?"

She was clearly shocked at the idea. "Jail? Could he do such a thing?"

"What do you think VanEndel and his wife would do if they were to learn that their guest of honor was not what he claimed to be? Especially if their friends were to learn of the deception and mock them for it?"

Lana thought about his words and slowly nodded. "I can see now that you have no choice but to continue as you began, or face the consequences."

"That happens to be true for both of us." He touched his napkin to his lips. "After your debut in society, there will be no turning back, Lana. I hope you have the fortitude to see this through."

They both looked up sharply as Maria knocked and entered the dining room.

"Clara has made one of your favorite desserts." The housekeeper nodded to a servant, who stepped toward the table while lifting the lid from a silver tray. "Bread pudding."

Jesse gave a sigh. "I'm sorry. Please give Clara my regrets, but I couldn't manage another bite."

"Miss Dunleavy?" The housekeeper turned to Lana, who shook her head.

"I couldn't possibly."

"Clara will be disappointed."

Jesse relented and accepted the dessert. Before taking a bite, he offered the first taste to Lana.

It was the strangest sensation, allowing him to feed her. Though he didn't touch her, she could feel his eyes on hers as she closed her mouth around his spoon.

She sighed with pleasure. "Oh, that's grand."

"Indeed." Jesse took several bites before setting it aside. "Give Clara my regards on this fine meal, Maria, and most especially on the bread pudding." He drained his glass before glancing across the table at Lana. "Would you mind if I smoked?"

"Not at all."

Jesse pushed away from the table before holding Lana's

chair. The two of them crossed the room and settled on a sofa in front of the fire.

Jesse touched a match to the tip of his cigar and drew deeply before emitting a stream of smoke.

Lana breathed in the fragrance of tobacco and was reminded of that first night she'd spoken with him on the wharf. "Have you seen Stump and Toomy and Ned lately?"

"There's been no time. I'm sorry for that. I genuinely enjoy their company." He glanced at her. "Do you miss them?"

"Sometimes. Like you, I've been so busy, there's been little time to think about them. I suppose that's good. If I had time to think, I'd probably go mad thinking about what Colin must be enduring in that place."

"I know this isn't easy for you, Lana." Without thinking, he took her hand and allowed his thumb to play with her fingers. "But if you can convince society of your regal lineage, it could all be settled within a matter of a few weeks."

"Oh, Jesse." She gave a sigh that seemed to come from deep within. "If only it can be."

"Trust me." He squeezed her hand, and then, because he desperately wanted to offer some comfort, closed his arm around her shoulders and drew her close. "I know these people. How they think. How easily swayed they are by the power of suggestion. Leave it all to me."

She wanted to. Oh, how she wanted to. But hovering on the edges of her mind was the realization that this man was nothing more than a slick con, who could just as easily manipulate her as those others he claimed to know so well. If she were to disgrace herself and him, it would be an easy matter for Jesse to toss her to the wolves and wash his hands of her entirely.

"I suppose I have no choice."

At her words he withdrew his arm and stood, tossing the rest of his cigar into the fire. When he turned to her he was still smiling, but she noted that the smile didn't quite reach his eyes.

"It's been a long day, Lana. I'll see you up to your room now."

She moved along beside him, cursing herself for spoiling the moment. Still, if she didn't look out for herself, who would? Certainly not this man, who'd made it all too clear that he enjoyed playing the part of a dandy.

It was one thing to playact to save Colin from the cruelties of life. It was another to allow herself to believe, for even one minute, the lies that had been so cleverly crafted. The closer she got to Jesse, the clearer became the truth. He and his "associates" were far more skillful than she could ever hope to be. They were so persuasive, and had repeated their lies so often, they seemed unable to discern fiction from fact. But if she couldn't trust them, at least she could learn from them. And she could achieve her goal, as long as she never allowed herself to get caught up in the lies.

As for Jesse, she couldn't lay any blame on him. He simply couldn't help being charming. It was as much a part of him as the phony English accent that slipped from his lips as though he'd spoken this way all his life.

They stopped at the door to her suite of rooms. Jesse opened the door and then stood aside to permit Lana to enter.

As she brushed past him she felt the tingle of awareness and stepped back, keeping as much space between them as she could manage.

Jesse gave her a long, lingering look. "When you see Nadia and Colette tomorrow, tell them that I approve of the work they've done. I believe you're more than ready to make your debut into New York's society."

"Thank you." She looked up and realized he was staring at her mouth. For just a moment she felt a quick little thrill, wondering if he might kiss her.

Just as quickly the moment passed and he stepped back, putting the open door between them. "Good night, Lana."

"Good night, Jesse." She firmly closed the door and stood listening as he moved down the hall until she heard him open the door to his own suite of rooms.

She wasn't disappointed, she told herself. Not at all. In fact, she was relieved. She walked to the window and stared at the night sky.

It wouldn't do to invite anything personal. She was here for one reason only. When Colin was returned to her, she must be free to walk away without regrets. She need only look at what happened to Siobhan to know that sweet words and honeyed kisses were no promise of happiness.

But if that be true, why was it, she wondered sadly, that she was feeling so cold and empty inside?

JESSE PROWLED HIS suite of rooms like a caged tiger, back and forth, back and forth, pausing at the balcony to stare at the garden below. Often, all he'd needed to soothe his weary soul was to drink in the carefully manicured trees and rose gardens, the stepping-stones that led along a grassy path from fountain to stone bench, and all of them gilded in moonlight. This night, the perfect symmetry of it, the restful beauty of it, failed to touch him. In fact, he stared into the darkness without really seeing any of it.

All he could see was Lana, and the way she'd looked tonight. As regal as any queen. For those few hours at dinner, he'd actually enjoyed himself. Instead of having to make tedious conversation with empty-headed debutantes, the conversation had been witty and charming. Sparkling, in fact. And though her brogue slipped through whenever she got careless, it only added to her charm. He'd never once thought about escaping her sweet company to the privacy of his own room.

The fact that she disapproved of him hurt more than he'd expected. It had been like an arrow to his heart. He'd never before cared what others thought. In fact, he'd taken particular delight in shocking people. It had always been part of his charm. But tonight, feeling her censure, he'd found himself wanting desperately to take her into his arms and promise her that she'd never be disappointed in him again.

What was happening to him? If he didn't know better, he'd think he was turning into some sort of empty-headed fool.

Why should Lana's opinion of him matter?

It didn't, of course. Not a whit.

He tore off his jacket and shirt and tossed them into a ball in the corner of the room, then kicked off one boot, then the other, taking pleasure in hearing them slam against the wall.

And then, because he knew sleep was impossible in his present mood, he dressed in casual clothes and ordered up a carriage. If he couldn't spend any more time with Lana, perhaps a game of poker with her old friends at the Blue Goose would be the perfect distraction.

SIXTEEN

—◆◈◆—

"MARIA." JESSE'S VOICE was rough with frustration. "What's keeping her?"

"She'll be along soon enough." The housekeeper merely smiled as she rushed past him and opened the door to Lana's suite of rooms. Before he could peer inside, she slammed the door in his face.

He swore and turned to Withers. "They've been all day getting her ready. What could there possibly be left to do?"

The elderly butler shrugged and did his best to look bored.

From inside came Nadia's voice raised in excitement. "*Dah.* It is perfect."

"It shows too much skin." That was Lana's tone, sounding a bit frazzled.

"*Nyet.* Not nearly enough, but it will be fine for your first time. You must stop tugging at the sleeves. They were meant to be worn like this, off the shoulders."

Colette's voice interrupted. "Now you will turn and walk for me one last time."

There was the angry tap tap of footsteps from inside the room, a curt order before the sound softened, and then all went silent.

Jesse turned to the butler, who merely lifted his brows in a question. At that moment the door opened and Maria waved both men away.

Jesse's eyes narrowed. "If you don't mind, I'd like to see what I'm paying for."

"And you shall. But first you will go below stairs, if you please."

Without a word Jesse walked away, trailed by Withers. Minutes later, as the two men stood in the foyer, they were allowed their first glimpse of Lana, standing at the top of the stairs.

Jesse's breath caught in his throat. She was a vision in silver lace, a long sleek column of it, with a low neckline framed by sleeves that fell off her shoulders and trailed her arms, falling in little points over her wrists. The exquisite lace was so fine, so intricately woven, it could have been spun by angels. The gown hugged her body like a second skin before flaring out at the hem into an elegant swirl.

As she descended the stairs, Lana's dark hair flowed down her back and over one breast in soft waves, held away from her face with silver combs.

Maria and the women remained on the landing, watching in silence. When Lana reached the bottom step, they hurried down and gathered around like a flock of birds, awaiting Jesse's verdict.

He smiled at the dressmaker. "You've outdone yourself, Nadia."

"*Dah.* Easy, when I am sewing for one as beautiful as this."

He turned to the beaming French woman. "If I didn't know better, Colette, I'd swear she walks like one trained for the ballet."

Colette touched a hand to Jesse's cheek. "She is my finest student."

He still hadn't spoken to Lana, and she stood as quiet as a statue, except for her hands, which were gripped tightly together at her waist.

Jesse reached into his breast pocket and removed a satin roll. He opened it to reveal a delicate filigree of platinum and diamonds necklace and matching ear bobs. Without a word, he handed Lana the ear bobs, waited until she'd fastened them, and then drew the necklace around her throat.

As he fastened it, he pointed to a gilt looking glass hanging above a marble table in the foyer. "I think this adds the perfect touch, don't you?"

Lana stared at her reflection, wondering at the way her poor heart was pounding. It wasn't the touch of his hands at her nape, she told herself. It was the sudden realization of what she was about to do.

Her eyes narrowed. Without turning she studied Jesse, reflected behind her in the mirror. "That must have been a very successful card game to afford something this fine."

He gave her one of those rogue smiles. "Indeed." He turned to Withers. "Do you have the lady's wrap?"

The butler held out a silver cape in the same fine lace, lined with shimmery velvet. Jesse took it from him and draped it around Lana's shoulders.

He saluted the others. "We'll say good night now."

"Good luck, miss," Rosa called.

"Remember to glide, child," Colette said.

"They will all be blinded by you," Nadia said in her broken English.

"You mean dazzled," Maria corrected.

"*Dah.* Dazzled."

Withers surprised Lana by giving a slight bow. "For tonight at least, you truly are royalty."

Lana gave him a halting smile before accepting Jesse's arm. And then she was moving out the door and down the steps, into the waiting carriage.

As they sped off into the night, she wondered that her poor heart didn't burst clear through her chest, it was beating so furiously.

"LISTEN WELL, NOW." Jesse's voice was low, and Lana had to strain to hear him over the clip-clop of the horse's hooves. "At an event of this importance, I can't always be at your side. I have . . . certain obligations."

"To charm the women. I understand."

He hissed out a breath. "I'll try to stay close, but if you look around and find me gone, stay calm."

"Will we be seated next to one another during dinner?"

"Probably not. I suspect our hostess will want me on one side of her, and our host will probably claim you for his dinner partner."

Lana could feel the beginning of a headache.

"Whenever possible, slip your champagne glass onto a tray. That will permit a gentleman to fetch you another."

"I don't understand."

He looked over at her. Even in the fading light of evening, she seemed to shimmer and glow. "The guests are about to be charmed by my mysterious, glamorous cousin who is visiting me from abroad. At least permit the men to pay you some small attention."

"I see." And she did. She must never lose sight of the fact that this was all a game. A silly game that would have been great good fun if it weren't for the seriousness of the prize for which she was playing.

The carriage slowed as they turned up the long, curving drive of the most magnificent mansion Lana had ever seen. How was it possible for every structure on Millionaire's Row to be finer than the last? The three-story building seemed to take up an entire block. Light poured from every window, and the driveway was lit with lanterns mounted on tall pillars. There must have been a hundred of them.

Their carriage paused behind a long line of carriages, each one pulling up to the wide porch steps where a uniformed man assisted the passengers down and handed them over to another liveried servant before turning to the next in line.

"There's one more thing I must tell you, Lana." Jesse moved closer, keeping his tone low enough that he wouldn't be overheard by the coachman. As he did, he breathed in the light floral fragrance that she had chosen as her own. It suited her perfectly, and he found himself wondering if the scent would be stronger at her throat and between her breasts. The thought had him sweating.

"There is a reporter for the *New York News and Dispatch*. His name is Farley Fairchild."

"The one who wrote about Mrs. VanEndel and Colin?"

Jesse nodded. "I've taken the time to . . . cultivate his friendship."

"Why?"

Jesse merely smiled. "He writes a column that is read by everyone in New York who can read, and even a few who cannot. If he writes something flattering about you, all of New York will have read it by tomorrow."

"And why would he say anything nice about me?"

"I may have mentioned a thing or two about my lovely cousin, distantly related to England's queen, who was visiting during the season in the hope of meeting some of New York's most eligible bachelors."

"You didn't." Lana drew away, her eyes widened with horror.

"Because he always travels with a photographer, I want you to be prepared to smile as you are assisted from the carriage, even if you feel you're being assaulted by the flash of gunpowder."

"Gun . . ."

"There's no time. I see him just over there." Jesse's voice turned commanding. "Smile, my dear. And look regal."

It was the last thing Lana heard before the door to the carriage was opened and the liveried servant was handing her down. Even as Jesse's hand closed over hers, there was the sound of an explosion, a flash of brilliant light, making Lana feel that she was under siege. She was led, nearly blinded, up the steps of the Vanderbilt mansion.

Jesse leaned close to whisper, "Welcome to society, Lana."

"JESLIN JEREMY JORDAN Hanover, Duke of Umberland."

The Vanderbilts' butler intoned the name that had an entire roomful of guests turning eagerly toward the man framed in the doorway.

"His cousin, Lady Alana Dunning Griffin Windsor, of Shrepshire, England."

There was a collective gasp from both the men and women who watched as Jesse led the stunning young woman into the room to greet their host and hostess.

The Vanderbilts were beaming at this coup. They had snagged not one, but two royals for their first dinner party of the season. That would surely set them above all the rest and make them the most talked-about couple in New York.

While they presented Jesse and Lana to their esteemed guests, Lana wondered how she would ever keep all the names straight in her mind. She recognized most from the society pages of the newspaper, but it was quite another thing to call the publisher of the paper by his first name, or to see his wife actually bow before greeting her. It was hard not to giggle when a Supreme Court Justice asked if she would save him a dance, and to have Gustav VanEndel squeeze her hand just a little too long before turning to include his wife and son in the introduction.

It was the first time Lana had actually seen Wilton Van-Endel, except for that brief moment when she'd come upon him with Swede. The thought of what he'd done to that poor, unfortunate girl was seared into her memory. And now, seeing this tall, smiling young man, his pale hair curling around a boyishly handsome face, she was grateful for that insight into his true nature. She found herself wondering how many innocent young women had been tricked into believing that such a good-looking man, wearing such fine clothes and enjoying the company of such important people, must be the epitome of all that was fine and good and noble.

"Lady Alana." He bowed over her hand. "I look forward to sharing a dance."

"As do I." Lana turned from him to accept yet another introduction, and another.

Through it all, she kept her smile in place and sipped her champagne. She refused any food from the passing trays, afraid the nerves gnawing holes through her stomach would only be made worse if she were to attempt to eat a single thing.

She found herself distracted by the maids in their spotless uniforms as they moved among the guests, offering food and drink while appearing invisible. How long had they been on their feet this day? And how much longer must they labor before they could take to their beds?

And what of this lavish lifestyle? What had it cost to furnish this room, with its gold leaf adding sheen to the carved mahogany ceilings? How much marble had been mined to provide that dazzling mantel and surround at the fireplace? How many hungry people in the tenements of the lower east side could be fed, clothed, and comforted by the cost of this single dinner party?

When the guests had all been presented, their host offered his arm to Lana, while Mrs. Vanderbilt linked her arm with Jesse's, and they led the entire assembly to the dining room, which was even bigger and more opulent than the one in the VanEndel mansion. The table glinted with ornate china and crystal and silver. Above it shone a chandelier alight with hundreds of flickering candles. The dining hall was adorned with masses of white roses and magnolias, lending their perfume to the festive air.

Lana found herself at one end of the table, to the right of their host, while Jesse was at the other end, to the right of their hostess. While the servants circled the table, offering rare beef, quail, and poached salmon, the room was abuzz with conversation, much of it centered on the royal guests.

". . . where she bought that gown?"

"Certainly not here in New York. Probably Paris or London or Rome. Did you see the fluid way it moves with each step?"

". . . the diamonds at her throat. A king's ransom, at least."

"Most likely a gift from Victoria. I've heard she is a favorite of the queen's."

"Are she and the duke distantly related enough that there could be a love match between them?"

"I'm not certain, but I believe Jesse said she was his third cousin once removed."

A rumble of laughter from one of the men. "Definitely distant enough for marriage, though I'd be tempted even if she were my sister."

"Enough, Gustav." Evelyn VanEndel shot her husband a withering look.

"It doesn't matter," one of the women whispered behind her hand. "I have it on good authority that Jesse intends to never marry."

"And why should he, when he can have any woman who pleases him without the bother of exchanging vows?"

Lana stared hard at her plate, hoping to shut out the buzz of gossip around her, and wondered if her stomach would ever settle. The thought of taking even one bite of the food from her plate left her physically weak. But as she glanced across the table she saw Jesse watching her. At that moment he smiled and winked, and her lips curved in a shy smile. How was it that he was able, with the slightest look, to touch her?

She would remember that this elaborate charade was all for Colin. Dear, wee Colin.

"Have you ever been to Alaska, Lady Alana?"

Lana turned to her host with a bemused expression. "Not yet, but I do hope to. I've heard so much about that fascinating, primitive part of the country."

"As have I." Delighted to have a guest who shared his latest interest, Richard Vanderbilt launched into a serious discussion about the animals he hoped to hunt on his first trip to Alaska, planned for the following year.

"Perhaps you and the duke might join us."

Lana touched a napkin to her lips. "As for me, my schedule appears quite full for the coming year, but I'd be happy to ask Jesse if he would care to join you."

Her host closed a hand over hers. Squeezed. "I'd be ever so grateful for anything you might say to him on my behalf."

When Lana glanced at Jesse, she caught the hint of a frown line between his eyes before he turned to his hostess and said something that had her laughing and blushing in delight.

After what seemed hours in the dining room, their host pushed away from the table and offered his arm to Lana. With Marguerite Vanderbilt and Jesse following close behind, they led their guests to a large parlor, where the maids had prepared tea and lovely little frosted cakes. While the ladies reclined around the fireplace enjoying their desserts, the men excused themselves and made their way to the library to indulge in brandy and cigars.

As Lana took a seat by the fire, she was approached by none other than Enid Morgenthall. At once Lana glanced down, terrified that, up close, the young woman would recognize the maid who had once mended a rip in her fine gown.

"Have you known Jesse, I mean the duke, all your life?" Without asking permission, Enid settled herself on the settee beside Lana.

"I have, yes." Cursing herself for the slip of her brogue, Lana added, "Though we were apart for many years as children."

"And why was that?" Enid accepted tea from a servant.

"Jesse attended a boarding school, while I was educated by tutors at home."

"Where is your home?"

Lana relaxed. She had been carefully rehearsed to respond to just such questions. "Though I call London home, we have a lovely country place in Shropshire, and another in the Midlands, as well a hunting lodge in Scotland."

The other women had gathered around, eager to learn all they could about this visitor.

Anya Davis finished her champagne and snapped her fingers in summons to a servant. At once the little maid held out a tray, accepting the empty glass and offering a full one in exchange.

Anya dismissed her with a frown before turning to Lana. "How long do you plan on staying in America?"

"I'm not certain." Lana had to force a smile as she answered this vain woman. In truth, she would have rather spent endless hours washing the pots and pans in the Vanderbilt kitchens than spend another minute here with someone so rude. "I suppose it will depend on whether I find something that amuses me."

"Something or someone," Enid's high-pitched screech had the others laughing and nodding.

"If you're looking for the most eligible, you need look no further than Wilton VanEndel." Anya Davis glanced toward the others for confirmation.

"If he is the most eligible, I would imagine you want to keep him for yourself."

Anya gave a smug smile. "Oh, Wilton and I have . . . had our moments. But I find your cousin, the duke, much more interesting. Perhaps you can thank me for that bit of information about Wilton by putting in a good word with your cousin that I'm eligible as well."

Lana managed a thin smile. "I'm sure the duke is well aware of the eligibility of every woman in this company."

That had the others giggling behind their hands and glancing around with knowing smiles.

Lana was relieved when Mrs. Vanderbilt announced that the musicians were assembled and it was time to head to the ballroom for the evening's entertainment.

As Lana and her hostess led the procession to the library, where they were joined by the men, she had no opportunity to speak with Jesse, who was surrounded by a cluster of laughing gentlemen.

It would seem that he had mastered the art of being as delightful and charming with them as he always was with the ladies. Now if only, she thought fervently, she could prove to be the same.

SEVENTEEN

———◆———

THOUGH THE BALLROOM was larger than the solarium at the house she was currently sharing with Jesse, Lana thought it not nearly as enchanting. Without the lovely domed ceiling, it was just another room. What it lacked in charm, however, it gained in sheer size. On a raised bandstand, there were enough musicians to fill an entire orchestra. Dozens of round tables ringed the dance floor, and each table was covered in shimmering gold cloth anchored by centerpieces of gilded flowers surrounding flickering candles.

Spying their host and hostess leading their parade of guests, the leader lifted his baton and the musicians began to play. Richard Vanderbilt offered his hand to Lana, while his wife turned to Jesse, and the two couples took a turn around the dance floor before the rest of their guests were invited to joined them.

When the first dance ended, Lana found herself surrounded by half a dozen men, all of them smiling and all of them vying for the next dance.

"I believe my age should count for something." A be-whiskered old gentleman, whom Lana recalled as a highly respected bank president, bowed over her hand. "I claim this dance, and the rest of you will just have to wait your turn."

With that, he led Lana to the dance floor just as the musicians broke into a lovely waltz.

As they moved slowly around the floor, Lana's partner smiled. "Before going into finance, I was considered an excellent student of history at my alma mater, Harvard University."

"Is that so?" Lana reminded herself not to count, even as her mind ticked off the one-two-three beat Colette had taught her with each step of the dance.

"Indeed." He nodded and executed a graceful turn. "I'm familiar with Queen Victoria's lineage, as it's one of my passions. However, I don't seem to recall your name in the list of succession to the throne, my dear."

Lana swallowed back the quick little rush of fear and managed a smile, summoning the lessons she'd memorized. "Perhaps that is because I cannot claim succession."

"But as cousin to the duke, surely you must be in line to succeed as well."

"I'm afraid not. I'm told that my grandfather gave up that right when he chose to marry a divorced woman who was also a commoner."

"Ah." The old gentleman nodded in understanding. "It's reassuring to know that in this age of competition, the heart can rule even the nobility."

"It truly was a love match," she managed to whisper, though her heart was still pounding at the thought of being caught in this preposterous lie.

When the dance ended, Lana had no time to catch her breath before she was approached by Wilton VanEndel.

"Quick." He gave her one of his most charming smiles. "Before all those eager suitors storm the gates, I claim this dance for myself."

The others watched from the sidelines as he twirled her around and around the floor. He knew they made a pretty couple, with his fair hair and laughing blue eyes, and her dark head coming just to his shoulder.

"You are," he whispered, "by far the most beautiful woman in the room, and I've always prided himself on having the good taste to be seen with only the best."

Lana held her silence as he smiled and nodded to those watching. While he smoothly circled the dance floor, he gave a satisfied smile, knowing the men in attendance were jealous of his prize.

He looked down into her upturned face. "Very smooth, Lady Alana. I'd say you've done this a time or two."

If only he knew.

Lana merely returned his smile with one of her own. "Not nearly as much as you, I'd wager. Is this your favorite form of entertainment?"

At that he threw back his head and laughed. "Not dancing, but certainly holding a beautiful woman in my arms ranks right up there with holding a full house."

She recognized the gambling term from her days at the Blue Goose. "You enjoy gambling?"

"Don't you?"

Lana wisely held her tongue.

That only had his smile growing. "I thought as much. Perhaps you and I might try our luck at a game or two one day."

"Perhaps." Lana was relieved to hear the song ending. With a little sigh she stepped back, careful to keep her smile in place.

"Thank you for the dance." Wilton bowed over her hand before lifting it to his lips in a gesture he hoped would impress her.

"You are most welcome." She felt the touch of a hand on her arm and looked over to find Jesse standing behind her, holding a flute of champagne.

His eyes were hard when they met Wilton's. "VanEndel."

Wilton merely nodded his acknowledgment.

Lana glanced from one man to the other, wondering what there might be between them to make them both so formal.

Jesse ignored the young man and turned his attention to Lana. "I thought you might enjoy a rest between dances, cousin."

"I would, yes." She cursed herself for that nervous slip of the tongue, and added, "Thank you. I would be grateful for a little time to catch my breath."

Without a word to Wilton, Jesse placed a hand under her arm and led her toward an empty table, holding her chair, then pulling his own close beside hers.

"You and VanEndel looked cozy enough."

"Cozy?" She glanced across the room and watched as Wilton whispered something to Enid Morgenthall that had the young woman giggling behind her hand. "I wonder that you had time to watch me, when you were so busy charming Miss Morgenthall."

Jesse merely smiled. "All part of the game, Lana. About young VanEndel, I ought to warn you . . ."

"Oh, I understand perfectly." She picked up her glass and drained it before looking over at him. "As you said, it's all part of the game, and I intend to learn to play it well."

Before she could say more, the publisher of the *New York News and Dispatch* bowed before her and held out his hand. "I believe this is my dance, Lady Alana."

Her smile would have melted the polar ice cap. "I believe you're right."

She walked away with a swirl of skirts and was soon circling the room in his arms. To all who watched, her partner was clearly enchanted as he smiled and laughed his way through the dance.

When the song ended, Lana found herself in the arms of yet another man, and then another. There were so many, she soon lost count, and though she laughed and flirted her way through the rest of the evening, she gave up trying to recall their names. She'd realized after a while that all that mattered was that she keep her smile in place and accept their offer to dance, and these men were more than happy.

When Wilton VanEndel claimed another dance, she had to force herself not to shudder at the intimate way his arm encircled her waist, drawing her much too close. After several turns around the dance floor, he slowed his movements, and Lana was forced to do the same, until they were merely swaying to the music.

"I would like to call on you while you're here in New York."

"I don't . . ." Before Lana could frame a response, Wilton looked up with a frown to see Jesse standing behind him, tapping him on the shoulder.

Jesse's eyes were twin daggers. "In case you haven't noticed, the music has ended." He ignored Wilton and directed his words at Lana. "It's time we bid good night to our host and hostess."

"Of course." She stepped back and allowed him to take her hand and lead her to the doorway, where the Vanderbilts stood with a cluster of friends.

"Mr. and Mrs. Vanderbilt." Lana extended her hand to her host and hostess.

"You're being much too formal." Their host closed a hand around hers. "You must call us Richard and Marguerite."

"Of course." Lana's smile was dazzling. "Richard. Marguerite. This has been a lovely evening."

"It was our pleasure. I do hope we will see you again while you're here in our country, Lady Alana."

As she started toward the front door, where the butler was holding her wrap, Richard Vanderbilt touched a hand to her shoulder and whispered, "And I do hope you'll speak with your cousin about my hunting trip to Alaska."

"Of course. I'll be happy to."

Lana slipped into her cape and accepted Jesse's hand as they stepped out the door and climbed into a waiting carriage. Behind them, the other couples had begun taking their leave as well.

As the carriage started along the gaily lit driveway, Lana leaned back and closed her eyes for a moment, wondering at the sudden lightness around her heart. She'd actually made it through the evening without stumbling, without making a fool of herself. Not a single person at that dinner party had suspected that she was anything other than Jesse's cousin.

The relief was so great, she could hardly keep from shouting. But when she glanced over at Jesse, the look in his eyes had her sitting up straighter.

"Is something wrong?"

"What could possibly be wrong?" His voice was as hard, as tight, as his eyes. "You did everything exactly as you'd been taught, and as a result, every man in New York's society is dazzled by you, especially young VanEndel."

"Really? Then I must have played my part well."

Jesse crossed his arms over his chest. "From where I was sitting it didn't look like you were playacting."

"You sound . . . annoyed."

"Annoyed? Why should I be annoyed?"

"But you are. I can tell by your tone." Wide-eyed, Lana turned to him. "I don't understand you. First you caution me to conquer my fear and make you proud. And now you're angry because I did as you ordered."

"Maybe it's because I didn't expect you to enjoy it quite so much."

"But I . . ."

"Don't lie, Lana, and try to tell me that your sweet smile and those fluttering eyelashes were just an act. You even had Vanderbilt whispering in your ear. And right in front of his wife."

Lana's smile was gone, replaced by a look of absolute fury. "How dare you! Do you have any idea what our host said to me?"

"Probably what any man with even half a brain would say. I think it best not to repeat it now, in my present mood."

"You aren't the only one in a mood. Oh! You're no better than those louts in the Blue Goose, whose minds were always below their waists. No wonder Verna Lee made so much money on men like you. You pig-headed, empty-brained, son of a barnyard sow . . ."

Before she could continue her litany of insults, Jesse's temper snapped. Though it was the last thing he'd planned, he hauled her roughly into his arms and silenced her in the only way he could.

The kiss was hot with temper. At least that's what he'd thought as his mouth covered hers. But as she struggled in his arms, he felt something else. Something stronger than anger. Something deeper than fury.

He wasn't even aware that his hands at her shoulders had gentled, slowly gathering her close against him until he could feel every part of her body imprinting itself on his. His mouth, too, softened, moving over hers until her lips parted in a sigh.

He wanted this. Only this. All night he'd been forced to watch the most beautiful woman in the room dancing with other men, when he'd wanted desperately to claim her for himself. And now, for these few moments, he would take what he wanted and to hell with convention.

Lana had every intention of fighting him. Her mouth was a grim, tight line of anger. Her hands were balled into fists at his chest. But the moment his touch grew gentle, instead of pushing him away, she found her fingers curling into the front of his shirt, unconsciously holding him close. At the first touch of his mouth on hers, she found herself forgetting everything except the quick sizzle of heat through her veins and the tiny curl of ice along her spine.

And then they were both lost in the wonder of the kiss they were sharing. Lost and helpless to do more than cling as the heat flowed between them, leaving them at once hot and cold and trembling with need.

Jesse knew he'd taken a wrong turn, but now that he was holding her, kissing her, there was no going back. All he could do was ride the tidal wave of pleasure that was carrying him along. The thought of releasing her was too painful to imagine.

One more second, he thought as he allowed his hands to move slowly along her back, drawing her close enough to feel the wild thundering of her heartbeat inside his own chest. One more moment to savor the sweet taste of her. But he knew that a single moment would never be enough. Nor would a single kiss stolen in the darkened carriage satisfy the hunger that was driving him. The feelings he was experiencing were about to consume them both unless he found the will to do what was right.

Calling on all his willpower, he lifted his head, breaking contact. Taking deep draughts of air he sat back, his eyes still fixed on her with a look that was almost searing in its intensity.

Lana, too, fought to fill her lungs as she drew away and struggled for control.

They were both startled and grateful when the carriage came to a halt and the driver climbed down to pull open the door.

Lana accepted his hand and stepped out, followed by Jesse. Offering his arm, they climbed the steps together. Before they could knock, the door was opened by Withers, who stepped aside to allow them to enter.

Inside, they found the women spilling out of the parlor, where they'd been eagerly awaiting their return.

"Well?" This from Maria.

"It went well." Jesse's tone was abrupt.

"Well?" Nadia frowned and brought her hands to her hips. "What does that mean?"

"It means that Lana played her part to perfection."

"Perfection? You hear that?" Colette eyed the others before turning back to Lana. "Did you dance?"

"I did, yes." Lana wondered if these women could tell, by looking at her flushed face, that she'd just been kissed breathless.

"And did she move as I taught her?" the ballerina demanded of Jesse.

"She did you proud." He handed his coat to Withers and then turned toward the stairs. "If you don't mind, I'll say good night now. Lana can fill you in on all the details."

The women looked at each other in consternation as Jesse climbed the stairs without another word. Withers accepted Lana's cloak before following Jesse up the stairs.

Lana pretended to yawn behind her hand. "I'm so tired. Would you mind if I waited until tomorrow to tell you about our evening?"

"Don't even think about such a thing." Maria answered for all of them. "Come into the parlor right this minute and tell us everything, or we'll follow you up the stairs and sit on your bed, denying you sleep until we've heard all the details."

Lana knew she had no choice. But as Jesse disappeared along the upper hallway, she wondered at the way her heart was behaving. He could provoke her anger more than any man she'd ever met. But all he had to do was kiss her and she couldn't even remember what she'd been angry about in the first place.

"All right." She led the way to the parlor, vowing to tell them only about the dinner and dance while conveniently leaving out what happened afterward. "You've all worked so hard to prepare me for this first . . . performance. You deserve to hear all the details."

As she settled herself on a chaise drawn up before the fire, the women gathered around her, eager for every detail.

"First you must tell us about the Vanderbilt mansion." Maria motioned for a servant to fetch a tray of glasses and a bottle of champagne.

For the first time in the entire evening, Lana was free to actually enjoy the burst of bubbles inside her mouth and the silken slide of the liquid down her throat. She sat back, smiling at the eager faces around her. "It's bigger than this, but not nearly as welcoming. The ballroom is as large as the gardens here, but very cold. The only thing that kept me warm was the dancing."

"Tell us who you danced with." Colette drained her glass and filled it, before reaching over to refill Lana's as well.

"I think I danced with every man there. And with Wilton VanEndel twice."

"That one." Nadia frowned. "He is a vile young man. You must keep your distance from him."

Intrigued, Lana studied the Russian woman more closely. "What do you know about him?"

"Only what I have heard, but it is enough to know that he is not an honorable man." Her tone softened. "Was Ansel Beecham there?"

Lana had to strain to remember the distinguished, gray-haired man who had claimed a dance shortly before the evening had ended.

"I don't believe we exchanged two words while we danced, but he struck me as a gentleman."

Nadia smiled and glanced at the others. "You see? It is as I told you."

Lana looked puzzled. "Do you know him?"

Nadia sipped her champagne. "In a manner of speaking."

Maria's tone was dry. "His wife died more than a year ago, and he told Jesse that he wanted to meet a woman who would soothe his broken heart."

"You?" Lana's eyes widened.

Nadia merely shrugged. "He is a kind man. And a lonely one."

"Not to mention generous," Colette said with a laugh.

As the voices swirled around her, laughing, joking, gently teasing, Lana sipped her champagne and sat back, feeling oddly comforted. For the first time in her life she felt as though she belonged. These women may be actresses and street women, but they were also kind and good and funny and irreverent. And they had, without knowing anything about her, accepted her as one of them without question.

They were more family than any she had ever known, and at this moment, she was so grateful for all of them in her life.

"Listen to us going on and on." Maria took the half-empty glass from Lana's hands. "You've been on your feet for hours, and now you must sleep. Tomorrow will be time enough to tell us the rest of your story."

"Oui." Colette kissed her cheek. "Sleep now, little one. And tomorrow you will tell us everything, down to the smallest detail."

Lana allowed herself to be led up the stairs by Maria and Rosa. While the housekeeper turned down the bed linens, the maid helped Lana out of her dress and into a nightshift.

In the darkness of the room she closed her eyes, expecting to fall asleep quickly. Instead, she felt again the quick rush of heat, the steady pulse of need, as she replayed Jesse's kiss over and over in her mind.

It didn't matter to her that he'd kissed her in anger. There was no denying that the feelings he'd wakened in her had nothing whatever to do with temper. But she'd had so little experience with men, she didn't know if what she was feeling was love or mere lust. She knew only that, to her shame, she'd give almost anything to feel his mouth on hers again.

EIGHTEEN

———◆◆◆———

Lᴀɴᴀ ᴡᴀs ᴘᴀssɪɴɢ Jesse's study when she caught sight of him seated at his desk, with Withers and Maria standing to either side of him. All were busy reading something lying atop his desk.

Jesse looked up as Lana paused in the doorway. "You might want to see this."

As she started across the room, she realized that both Withers and Maria were smiling brightly. "What is it? What's happened?"

"See for yourself." Jesse handed her the newspaper, and she gasped at the photograph taken of her the previous evening as she stepped down from the carriage. Underneath was the caption, "Duchess of Fifth Avenue."

She glanced over. "I don't understand. Why would Farley Fairchild call me such a silly name as that?"

"Don't you see?" Maria was practically gushing. "It means you were a success. According to the accompanying article, all of New York society has fallen under the spell of the mysterious and beautiful Duchess of Fifth Avenue. He calls you a cool English rose that puts all the other flowers to shame." Maria clapped her hands together. "Remember this, Lana. Farley Fairchild only gives special names to those people he considers extremely important."

While Lana read the accompanying article, Jesse studied the way she looked, wearing a day dress of lemon yellow, her hair tied back with yellow ribbons. This morning, without any of the trappings of wealth, looking as fresh as a daisy in a meadow of wildflowers, he realized that New Yorkers weren't the only ones under her spell. He'd spent a miserable night thinking about the way she'd looked in the arms of all those lecherous men at the Vanderbilt party and replaying in his mind that angry, shocking kiss in the carriage. He'd have to watch his temper and see that it didn't get the better of him again.

He nodded toward a silver tray atop his desk littered with small, white envelopes. "Since your debut into society, the invitations have already begun arriving."

"Invitations?" She glanced at Maria for confirmation.

"More than I've ever seen." The housekeeper sighed. "To the theater, the opera, and so many dinner parties, I've lost count. Everyone wanted to be the first to include you in their plans. I was just suggesting that we cut back your lessons to one hour a day so you can rest each afternoon. Otherwise, you'll never be able to keep up with such a demanding schedule."

Lana put a hand to her throat to stem the sudden rush of panic. "You mean I'm expected to playact every night?"

"You are, duchess." Jesse circled his desk. "That is, if you want to move to the next logical step."

"Colin." She spoke his name on a sigh and experienced a wave of shame for complaining about something as trivial as playacting, when that poor, sweet boy was surviving what must be a hellish existence in that horrible place.

Her voice lowered. "I've not forgotten." This would be her last complaint, she vowed. From now on, all her energy must be focused on Colin and how to save him. If that meant making conversation with silly, empty-headed women and dancing with lewd men, she would do it without question. "Do you think I might be allowed to visit the orphanage now? It's been so long, and I'm hungry for the sight of him."

Jesse nodded. "Now that you've gained the proper notoriety, I think the time is exactly right. But a woman of your stature wouldn't simply drop by. I'll arrange an appointment for you to visit."

"AN INVITATION FROM Mrs. VanEndel." Maria paused beside Lana's chair at the breakfast table and handed her a small, white envelope.

With a quick glance at Jesse, Lana broke the seal and withdrew a small card. After reading it, her eyes widened in surprise. "Evelyn VanEndel has invited me to join her Ladies' Aid Society. They will be visiting the East Side Orphan Asylum tomorrow."

Jesse's smile was quick. "Excellent timing. This is even better than going alone. With Evelyn VanEndel as your sponsor, what better way to see for yourself just how Colin is doing?"

"But what if he should recognize me? How will I explain his reaction? Oh, Jesse, what will I do if he falls into my arms weeping?"

Once again Jesse showed how quickly his mind could grasp any situation and make it work to the best possible benefit. "You'll need to be prepared for just such a thing. In fact, nothing would be better. If that should happen, you'll do what any kind woman of royal blood would do. You will explain to the others that his mother was once in your employ, that you have always loved him like a son, and that you owe it to the lad to make a home for him. If Evelyn

VanEndel still feels that she'd rather not be burdened with this orphan, you may find her eager to be done with this obligation."

"Oh, I pray it's so." Lana pushed away from the table, suddenly too nervous to think about finishing her meal. "If you'll excuse me, I need to go up to my room."

When she was gone, Maria paused beside Jesse's chair. "Do you believe that Mrs. VanEndel will give her the boy without a fight?"

Jesse shrugged. "I wish I knew. With a woman like Evelyn VanEndel, there's no telling how she'll react. She may not truly want the boy, but I'm betting she'll be reluctant to let him go for fear of how it might look to others."

Restless, he pushed his chair back and tossed down his napkin. "I'm going to inquire about a lawyer who's been causing quite a stir in court these days." At Maria's arched look he added, "A wise gambler always covers his bets."

LANA STUDIED HER reflection in the looking glass and wondered what Colin would think when he saw her. Would he recognize her in all this finery? Or would she appear to him to be just another society woman more concerned about her public image than the plight of those poor orphans?

She lifted a hand to the pins in her hair.

Rosa looked alarmed. "What are you doing?"

"I believe I'll do without the hat."

"It wouldn't be proper." Rosa anchored the hat with another pin for good measure. "All the society ladies wear hats to their afternoon functions. And gloves."

Lana sighed and relented, too nervous to argue. She'd been too tense to eat a thing at breakfast, and the thought of finally seeing Colin had her hands trembling.

She jumped at the knock on her door.

From outside the room came Maria's voice. "Your carriage is here."

She was grateful to turn away from the image in her mirror. As she started out of the room, she saw Jesse waiting for her at the bottom of the stairs.

Once Withers had helped her on with her cloak, Jesse escorted her outside and tucked her up into the carriage. As always, whenever he touched her, he felt the quick rush of heat tangled with need and had to struggle to ignore it. "Nervous?"

"Terrified."

"You'll be fine. Just remember that however the boy acts, you must similarly react. If he's surprised to see you, act the same about him. If he's tearful, it will be all right for you to show the same emotion."

"I'll not cry in front of those women." Her brogue was thick with emotion.

"Of course not." Jesse fought back his smile and then, without thinking, leaned into the carriage and drew her close while brushing a kiss over her cheek, wishing he could hold her. "You'll do fine, Lana. Just remember who you are."

Just remember who you are.

Even the warmth of Jesse's arms and the quick skitter of heat along her spine at his simple kiss, failed to lift her spirits. All she could hear were those words playing through her mind as the carriage moved along the curving drive and into the street, taking Lana past houses that were as far removed from the tenements where she and Colin had once lived as heaven was to hell.

When the carriage stopped in front of the tall, bleak building, Lana swallowed back the knot of fear threatening to choke her. She started up the steps and could already smell the familiar, fetid odors, so much a part of this building, that were taking her back to her own childhood, her own private hell.

* * *

"Here you are." Evelyn VanEndel was waiting with the others in the director's office, looking, in their finery, like a bright flock of birds. "We've brought the children cotton stockings."

"How . . . thoughtful."

"It's what the director of the orphanage told us was most needed. Now come and meet her."

Lana instinctively ducked her head, afraid that Mrs. Linden would recognize her from their earlier encounter.

"Mrs. Linden, may I present Lady Alana Dunning Griffin Windsor. Lady Alana, this is Mrs. Linden, the director of the East Side Orphan Asylum."

"Your ladyship. I mean, Lady Alana." The woman ducked her head and gave a clumsy bow.

"Mrs. Linden." Lana offered her hand, and the woman was so flustered, she merely held on to it a moment before stepping back.

When the director found her voice she managed to say, "I've told the women in my employ to gather the children in the dining hall. If you'll follow me."

Eager to show off, she led the way along a dingy hallway, with the society ladies trailing behind.

With each step she took, Lana could feel her breath coming harder and faster. Despite the fact that she'd already passed her first test, meeting the director without being recognized, this next step was infinitely more frightening. She was actually feeling light-headed and feared that at any moment she might faint.

Pressing a hand to the wall, she paused a moment and struggled to breathe.

When the others stepped into the dining room, she followed just as Mrs. Linden was heard to call, "Children, stand up and greet these lovely ladies who are your benefactors."

With some prodding by the uniformed aides, the children got to their feet and called in unison, "Welcome, dear ladies."

"Aren't they sweet?" Evelyn VanEndel turned to Lana and then caught her hand. "Are you unwell, my lady?"

"I'm fine." Lana stared around the room until she spotted the one she'd been hungrily seeking. Her hand went to her throat and his whispered name was wrenched from her lips. "Colin."

The boy hadn't yet spotted her, and she drank in the sight of him, wondering if her legs would continue to hold her or if she might embarrass herself by falling to the floor in a heap.

"The children have been learning a song to entertain you." Mrs. Linden was clearly in her element with these visitors as she turned to one of the aides. "Have the children begin."

Lana recognized the pink-cheeked woman who had greeted her on her first visit to the orphanage and watched as the boys and girls, under her leadership, began a halting, off-key rendition of a nursery rhyme.

She couldn't tear her gaze from Colin, standing with the others, eyes vacant, lips unmoving. Dear heaven, he was so sad. So . . . damaged. And why would he be otherwise? He'd lost his mother, father, and beloved aunt in the blink of an eye. All that had been familiar had been wrenched away, replaced with cold, unfeeling people whose only job was to enforce the rules. Lana knew from experience that there would be barely enough to eat, and his only refuge would be sleep, wrapped in a blanket on the hard, cold floor.

She stood there, feeling her heart breaking, while all she could do was stare hungrily and twist her hands together to keep from running to him and gathering him close.

Just as their little song ended the door was opened and Jesse was striding inside, followed by two muscular youths carrying bushel baskets.

"Jesse." Evelyn VanEndel couldn't hide her pleasure or her surprise. "Come and meet Mrs. Linden, the director of the orphanage. Mrs. Linden, this is the Duke of Umberland."

The director was so impressed, she curtsied before realizing that he had offered his handshake. She accepted it and then looked beyond him to the two young men. "What have you brought us, your lordship?"

Jesse merely smiled and turned to Lana. "My cousin wanted to do something special for the children and asked me to seek out fresh fruit, as that is something not always allowed within the overburdened budget of a place such as this."

Lana absorbed a tingle of pride that Jesse had paid such attention to the details of her time spent with Colin. She hadn't expected him to remember such a simple detail as the apples.

Jesse nodded toward Mrs. Linden. "Would you mind if we pass out these apples to the children?"

When the director agreed, the two young men passed among them, holding out the baskets so each child could reach inside. Lana felt tears spring to her eyes as the children laughed and clapped their hands in delight before biting into the fruit. But as she watched, her joy turned to horror at Colin's reaction. The lad stared at the apples for long, silent moments, before taking one and tucking it into the pocket of his shabby pants.

Sensing Lana's pain, Jesse moved to her side and said in a barely audible whisper, "Steady, Lana. Hold on."

"Look at him, Jesse. He's so sad. I can't bear it."

"You must. You will." Dear God, how he wanted to take her into his arms and comfort her. "You'll see . . ."

Evelyn VanEndel's voice could be heard above the children's laughter. "Isn't that sad little boy the one who will soon be coming to live with me?"

The director nodded. "His name is Colin."

"Why isn't he eating?" Evelyn demanded.

Mrs. Linden couldn't mask the anger in her tone. "We've detected a spoiled and willful streak in him. But don't worry, Mrs. VanEndel. The aides have been working with him, and by the time he joins your lovely household, he'll have put aside such behavior and will be a perfect child who will make you proud."

"I should hope so. I wouldn't want him hoarding food. I wonder what other vile habits he may have picked up." Evelyn shuddered, and the women around her nodded in silent agreement.

From the looks on their faces, it was clear that they thought their friend a saint or martyr for taking on the task of raising such an unpleasant child.

Evelyn turned to Lana. "Have you heard that I'll be adopting one of these poor, unfortunate orphans?" At a clap of her hands, one of the aides shoved Colin toward her.

"His name is Colin O'Malley," the director said with a trace of disapproval. "His parents were Irish immigrants."

"Colin!"

Jesse could feel the way Lana stiffened and knew she was barely able to contain her emotions. If she couldn't pull herself together, he would carry on without her.

He gave a cheery smile that encompassed all the women. "I'm sure all of you can see that my cousin is in a bit of a shock."

"And why is that?" Evelyn backed away when Colin got too close and shook down her skirts to shake off any dirt that might have contaminated her gown.

Knowing he had an attentive audience, Jesse used his most persuasive tone. "A sad tale, actually. That very lad's mother, Siobhan O'Malley, was a dear, devoted maid to my cousin. They'd planned a happy reunion here in this country. Alas, by the time my cousin arrived the boy's mother was dead, and no one knew what had happened to her son. My cousin and I have been doing all we could to locate him. You can imagine our shock at seeing the boy here in this very place."

"How can you know this boy"—Evelyn glanced down at Colin's blank stare—"when he doesn't seem to recognize you?"

"He was just an infant when his mother came to this country." Jesse dropped an arm around Lana's shoulders, as much to hold her up as to comfort her. If she swooned now, he would just have to claim that the shock was too great. To her credit, and Jesse's great relief, she remained standing. Barely.

"But my cousin gave her word that if anything happened to his mother, she would take him to live with her and love the boy as her own."

Lana took a halting step toward Colin and dropped to her knees before him. "Colin, don't you know me?"

The boy stared at her with that same bland expression.

Hearing the stunned silence in the room, knowing that all her friends were waiting for her response, Evelyn Van-Endel stood a little straighter. "Such a sad story. But we must all put the boy's needs ahead of our own. I doubt that any unmarried woman, even one as fine as you, Lady Alana, could make a real home for an orphan."

Jesse was aware of Lana's quick intake of breath. "My cousin's promise to the boy's mother means nothing to you?"

Evelyn VanEndel gave Jesse her sweetest smile. "It may be as you said. Still, I know nothing about such a promise. What I do know is this. I publicly offered to give this orphan a home. I would be less than honorable if I didn't keep my word."

Hoping to ease the tension in the room, Mrs. Linden called out, "What do you children have to say to these lovely ladies for their generosity?"

In sing-song fashion as they'd been taught, the children called out, "Thank you, lovely ladies."

Mrs. Linden turned to Jesse. "The children weren't pre-pared to thank you, but I'm sure they're grateful for the ap-ples, too, your lordship."

Jesse's smile was guaranteed to melt every heart in the room. "They can thank my dear cousin for that." He helped her to her feet and gave her a long, lingering look, hoping to lend her the courage to get through this interminable event. "She is the kindest, most generous and loving woman I know."

"How is she?" Jesse looked up when Maria paused in the doorway of the library.

"She has taken to her bed."

He rubbed at his temple, where the beginning of a headache throbbed. "Can't say I blame her. The lad looked at her and didn't even recognize her. He was like a whipped puppy."

Maria thought about the woman asleep upstairs. Until the potion had worked its magic, Lana had looked much the same. "Will you now take the fight for the lad to court?"

He nodded, his eyes hot and fierce. "Count on it. We've gone too far to back down now.

NINETEEN

———❖———

Lana looked up when Jesse returned home in the early evening. "I thought, because we were free of any obligations tonight, you'd spend your time at the Blue Goose."

"I'd planned on it." He handed his topcoat to Withers. "But I've changed my mind. I'd like you to accompany me to The Encore tonight."

"Just the two of us?"

He nodded.

"Are you doing this to cheer me up?"

He gave her that rogue smile. "I don't know about you, but it will cheer me considerably."

Despite the fatigue she'd been suffering since her visit to the orphanage, Lana was surprised and pleased. It was the first time Jesse had ever suggested dinner alone. They had been to The Encore several times with others, as it was one of the finest restaurants in the city and the one most frequented by the wealthy and the famous.

"I'll change my gown." She touched a hand to the soft waves spilling down her back. "And I'll ask Rosa to pin up my hair."

His smile faded. "Leave it." Then, because he'd spoken sharply, he softened his tone. "I think it would be a shame to pin it up, just to mirror society's matrons. Why not set your own style, as it's much more attractive than anything they can come up with."

Puzzled at his strange mood, Lana relented. "All right. I'll just be a few minutes."

Jesse started toward the library, where he poured himself a glass of whiskey from a crystal decanter. He'd learned from experience that once Rosa and Maria set about preparing Lana for an evening out, their minutes usually turned into hours. Not that he minded. That first glimpse of Lana after their pampering was always a thrill.

Did she have any idea how she looked? Rosa had privately told him that she'd never served a mistress with so little conceit. Lana had to be reminded to glance at her reflection in the mirror, just to approve all their hard work. Once she'd been properly dressed and coifed for an evening out, she never once paused to tuck up a curl or repair her toilette.

She was such a contrast to the women Jesse had known all his life. His own mother had been obsessed with beauty. And his sister seemed determined to pursue pleasure, regardless of the cost to those who loved her.

Love. What a foolish, overused word. Those he'd loved had been unwilling or unable to actually give love. Not their fault, he thought, draining his tumbler and filling it a second time. There are people in this life who, through example or circumstance, are simply incapable of putting others' needs ahead of their own. As a lonely, neglected boy, he'd discovered that his greatest happiness lay in choosing his own path. Whatever lifestyle was expected of him, he could manage well enough, as long as he could slip away now and then and live the life he chose.

For now, he chose to be here, involving himself in Lana's cause. Not that it was love, he thought with a quick shake of his head. But there was no denying that Lana had become . . . important to him, her well-being and happiness his main concern. When her spirits were up, so were his. When she was down, he could feel his own spirits plummet.

How had one little female made such a difference in his life?

"I'm ready."

Jesse turned and felt the familiar jolt at the sight of Lana framed in the doorway. Light from the foyer seemed to surround her like a halo. As he'd requested, her hair was long and loose, pinned away from her face with jeweled combs. Her gown was pale green, the color of foam that frosted the ocean's waves after a rain. It skimmed her lithe body, flaring below her hips, falling in a column of silk to her ankles. The neckline was rounded, spilling just off each shoulder and anchored with a jeweled bow.

"I told you I wouldn't be long."

He set aside his glass and hurried to offer his arm. "A woman of her word. Rare indeed. I like that. But then, there are so many things about you I like, Lana. Not the least of which is," he added with that rogue grin, "the fact that you can dress like a lady, walk like a lady, and still hide that damnable dagger in your sash."

"Guilty." With a laugh she closed a hand around the pale green sash, knowing no one but Jesse was aware of her hidden weapon.

THE ENCORE WAS crowded, with several couples waiting, but as soon as the owner caught sight of Jesse, a booth in the middle of the room was made ready.

As they threaded their way between the tables, they were aware of a sudden hush, followed by a buzz of conversation. As soon as they were seated, a waiter arrived with a bottle of wine and two glasses.

"Andre says this is the finest bottle in his wine cellar. Only the best for you and the Duchess of Fifth Avenue."

Jesse smiled at the owner, hovering across the room. "Give Andre our thanks."

While Lana sipped, she realized that Jesse was distracted. Though he appeared to be merely asking the waiter about the night's menu, she'd come to know him well enough to realize that he was actually studying the faces around the room.

When they were alone she whispered, "Are you searching for someone special?"

Jesse smiled and took her hand as though she'd just said something amusing. "Don't look just yet, but in a minute, if you glance over my left shoulder, you'll see a bewhiskered man seated with two other, younger men. His name is Zachariah Frederick. He's the lawyer I'm hoping to engage on your behalf in your custody battle for Colin."

Lana waited a discreet time before observing the man. She fought a wave of disappointment. The man was badly in need of a haircut, his beard needed trimming, and his clothes looked as though he'd slept in them for a week. This was hardly the sort she wanted taking up her cause in court. What could Jesse be thinking?

While he ordered dinner for both of them, Lana sat back, deep in thought. Could it be that Jesse was merely pretending to care about her goal? Had he lured her into this game for some reason unknown to her? Or had her obsession with Colin dragged on too long, causing Jesse to lose interest?

Perhaps that was it. He was tiring of this game.

What did she really know about Jesse? He was such a private man that, even though they were sharing a house, she'd been able to glean little by observing him. She knew only what the others had told her. Nadia and Colette, and even Maria and Rosa and the cook, Clara, were constantly singing his praises. According to them, their lives would have been bleak indeed without his intercession. And yet, what did they do with their lives except cater to his whims? Couldn't Colette have continued to be a famous ballerina if she had remained in France? Didn't Nadia tell her often that she had once been a dressmaker to the Tsarina of Russia until she'd been rudely dismissed? Couldn't she have impressed other wealthy Russian nobility with her talents? And what of Maria and Rosa? Both had all the mannerisms, all the proper bearing of high-born women, yet they acted as maid and housekeeper. Clara could cook for any of the society matrons here in New York, and yet she hid her talents cooking in the house Jesse was borrowing from a friend.

Was she correct in believing that all of them were nothing more than actors, playing the parts given them by Jesse? Why else were they all here, seeing to the needs of a man who was obviously a charlatan and a rogue?

And right now that charlatan, that rogue, was about to sabotage her chances of winning Colin.

Unless she managed to outsmart him.

"You're quiet." Jesse topped off her glass and sat back as a waiter presented them with a plate of oysters.

"I was wondering what I might do to earn some money."

"Money?" His eyes narrowed. "What need have you of money? I thought you didn't care about clothes and jewels."

"I care not about such things. But it isn't right that my friend Siobhan is buried in an unmarked grave."

"Forgive me, Lana." Jesse closed a hand over hers. "I've been thoughtless. You've never even had a chance to grieve over the loss of your best friend. Tell me where Siobhan is buried, and I'll see that her body is moved and given a proper grave marker."

Lana swallowed back the rush of guilt that stained her cheeks. Would she ever learn to lie with the ease of Jesse and his friends? "I'd rather see to it myself."

"As you wish." He released her hand and bent to his meal. "First thing tomorrow I'll see that you're given enough money to buy a plot in St. Patrick's and a marker. There's a marvelous Italian stonecutter in the West End who can carve an angel or a saint from granite, or engrave whatever you would like on a slab of marble. The choice will be yours."

Lana ducked her head to hide the tears that threatened.

Oh, Siobhan, how I wish I could give you what you deserve, but I know you'll understand. For now, I must use the money to secure a fine, expensive lawyer to assure me custody of Colin. Though I'm ashamed of the lie, I do it to keep my promise to you. Please forgive me.

Her whispered prayer was little comfort to Lana. The deceit that she'd set in motion lay like a stone around her heart. But what else could she do? With no one to confide in, she had to do as she'd always done. She would keep her own counsel, hoping the choices she made were for the best.

"THE DUCHESS OF Fifth Avenue. This is a rare treat. How did you find me, duchess?" The handsome, immaculately groomed man was up and around his desk the minute Lana stepped into his office.

"I read your name in the *New York News and Dispatch*. You represented Enid Morgenthall in that . . . misunderstanding with a shopkeeper."

"That." With a single word, spoken like a curse, he dismissed the lurid trial that had made headlines for weeks.

He held a chair and waited until Lana was seated before settling himself behind his desk. "Greedy businessmen are always threatening to sully the good name of someone of wealth and privilege, in the hope of getting a settlement to go away."

Lana had heard the rumors that a shopkeeper had caught Enid with several expensive pieces of jewelry hidden in her clothing, and that it had taken a great deal of money to get him to drop his charges.

Hunter Schuyler steepled his fingers atop the desk and studied her. "Is that why you're here? Is someone threatening your good name?"

She took a deep breath and thought about all she'd been rehearsing on the way here. "Mr. Schuyler, I want you to represent me in court."

"For what purpose?"

"There is a lad."

His brows shot up. "Yours? An illegitimate child?"

If she was offended by his misjudgment, she brushed it aside. After all, a lawyer of his reputation was often forced to look at the seamy side of life. "He's an orphan. The son of a dear friend. I gave her my word that if anything happened, I would raise him and love him as my own. Though I would dearly love to keep my promise, I'm being thwarted in my efforts."

"Extortion?"

She held up a hand. "Nothing like that. It's just that Evelyn VanEndel has agreed to adopt the boy, and it is my belief that, though she may regret that decision, it was made publicly, and she is reluctant to publicly renege on her promise, for fear of how it might look."

"Evelyn VanEndel?" Suddenly alert, Hunter Schuyler studied Lana more closely. "You realize that it will require a great deal of money to go up against such a formidable foe?"

Lana swallowed. "Money is no object, Mr. Schuyler. I am determined to win custody of the lad."

For the first time his smile reached his eyes.

He opened a drawer and pulled out a pad of paper. Dipping a pen into an ink pot, he glanced up. "I'll want as much information as you can give me, beginning with the boy's full name and date of birth."

While Lana dictated, he scribbled furiously before setting down the pen. "How much money are you prepared to give me today?"

Lana carefully unfolded the bills and watched as he counted them out. His hands were soft and smooth. His hair was perfectly trimmed, and his wardrobe was that of a man of means. She felt a measure of relief. She had made a wise choice. This man would be comfortable in the world of Evelyn VanEndel.

He looked over. "You'll need a great deal more than this before we go to court."

She sucked in a breath and realized that she'd been afraid, not because of the money, but because a man of his stature might not be willing to take on such a minor case. "You'll represent me?"

His smile was as smooth as his velvet voice. "I'll accept this modest sum as my retainer, duchess, and begin work at once."

JESSE PULLED A cigar from his pocket before stepping into the waiting carriage. As he rode along the darkened streets, his mind wasn't on the successful game of cards, but rather on Lana.

He was worried about her. The bloom was gone from her cheeks. Though she continued valiantly playing her part in the social whirl, it was plain to him that her heart was no longer in the game. Seeing the lad had wounded her so deeply, he wondered how she would recover if she were to lose the looming custody battle.

She wouldn't lose, he vowed. He'd done all in his power to see that she was successful.

He leaned back and closed his eyes. He'd always loved these nights when he was free of social obligations. The sailors at places like the Blue Goose were so much more entertaining than the social climbers he met at those stuffy dinner parties. Still, he would have preferred to stay at home tonight, enjoying a book, a cozy fire, and a brandy. But now that Lana was there, he couldn't afford the temptation. Knowing she was just a room away caused him too many sleepless nights.

There were times he actually paused outside her door and thought about inviting himself inside.

That path would lead to disaster.

He thanked his driver and made his way up the steps. Inside he greeted Withers and handed over his topcoat before climbing the stairs.

Outside Lana's suite of rooms he paused and tempted himself with the thought of knocking. It would be pleasant to chat with her, and tell her about Verna Lee's latest conquest, and fat Toomy's four aces that had everyone in the saloon gathered around to congratulate him.

He stood a moment, smiling at the thought of how she would look, barefoot, wearing something long and loose over her nightshift, dark hair tumbling. The need to see her, to share his evening with her, was like a hunger.

He shook his head and, thinking better of it, let the moment pass as he moved on and stepped into his own room.

The last thing they needed, when they were so close to their goal, was to give in to any weakness now.

TWENTY

━━━━◆◆◆◆━━━━

JESSE OPENED THE envelope, read the enclosed letter, and then stared at the bank draught. Puzzled, he went in search of Lana. He found her in the ballroom, surrounded by Nadia, Colette, Maria, and Rosa. As was usually the case when these five got together, their laughter was a joyous sound as they giggled over something Colette had just said.

Seeing him in the doorway, Nadia hurried over to catch his hand and lead him farther into the room. "Colette was just telling us about the time the Prince of Wales managed to sneak her into his quarters at the castle, right under the nostrils of his mother, Queen Victoria."

"Nose," Jesse corrected. "And I'm sure there were many such instances." His smile was strained. "If you'll excuse us, I need to speak with Lana."

She looked up. "Yes? What is it?"

"Alone." He turned and started away, leaving Lana to shrug and roll her eyes at the others before running after him.

She caught up with him at the doorway to the library. "What is it, Jesse? Why couldn't you just say whatever you had to say in front of the others? By now they know as much about me as I know about myself."

"That gives them the advantage over me." He stormed to his desk.

"I don't understand." Lana remained where she was. "What's wrong?"

"That's what I'd like to know." He picked up the sheaf of papers and held them out.

Lana crossed the room, read the letter, and then glanced at the bank draught on his desktop.

"Why has Zachariah Frederick returned my retainer? You're required to appear in court tomorrow, and according to this, you've never even once been to see him."

When she remained silent, he stepped closer. "Where have you been going every week, if not to Zachariah's office?"

"I . . . didn't want to meet with him."

"Why not?"

"I . . . didn't like the way he looked."

"The way he looked?" Jesse stepped back, studying her as if she'd gone mad. "Since when does a man's looks determine his ability?"

"He looked . . . shabby."

"I'll remind you that you did, too, the first time I saw you."

Lana ducked her head and felt the sting of humiliation. Then just as quickly, she lifted her chin, determined to make him understand. "I read about a lawyer in the *New York News and Dispatch* and thought he would be the perfect man to fight someone as important as Evelyn Van-Endel."

"You read about some stranger? And without asking advice, you sought him out?"

"He assured me that I'd be more than satisfied with the outcome. Thanks to him, there is to be no trial."

"What do you mean, no trial?"

"He told me that this will be an informal hearing in the judge's chambers. The judge will listen to the facts and decide which of us can offer Colin a better home."

"And if the judge should decide against you? What recourse will you have then, Lana?"

She caught his hand. "Please don't be angry. I didn't mean to deceive you, but this was something I had to do. And this will be so much better, don't you see? I'll not have to take an oath, I'll not have to lie or cover up anything. I'll just tell the truth about Siobhan and Colin. Once this judge hears the facts, how could he possibly decide to grant custody to anyone but me?"

Jesse stared down at her hand covering his and wondered at the jolt of pure pleasure that shot through him. How could he stay angry when she was touching him like this? When those big eyes were looking into his with such hope and trust?

He cleared his throat. "Would you prefer to go alone to this . . . hearing? Or would you like company?"

"You'll go with me?"

"If you'd like."

She stood on tiptoe and kissed his cheek. "Thank you, Jesse. You don't know what this means. I was dreading the thought of facing this alone. Ten o'clock tomorrow."

He watched her dance away and wondered at the conflicting feelings churning inside. A touch, a kiss, and he'd been reduced to a fool, never once asking the name of her lawyer or how she'd come by the money to pay for him.

As he sat down at his desk, it occurred to him that he might not have the lawyer's name, but he had the answer to the source of money in a flash of sudden insight. Siobhan's grave marker.

That little con.

He'd taught her well.

Much too well.

* * *

LANA RUBBED HER sweating palms down her skirts as she stepped into the judge's chambers, with Jesse trailing behind. She'd dressed carefully for this day, in a navy skirt and jacket and prim little matching hat. She wanted the judge to see a proper, sensible young woman.

Mr. and Mrs. VanEndel were already there, with not one, but three men in plain black suits.

Jesse put on his best smile and extended his hand. "Evelyn. Gustav."

Following his lead, Lana did the same.

Evelyn glanced around the room. "Where is your legal counsel, my dear?"

"I'm sure he'll be here soon." There were only three empty chairs left, so Lana took a seat while Jesse remained standing.

Minutes later the door opened and Hunter Schuyler entered, carrying a stack of papers. He greeted the VanEndels and their lawyers and then bowed over Lana's hand.

She said softly, "Hunter Schuyler, my cousin, the Duke of Umberland."

Jesse's smile disappeared. "We've met." He looked from Schuyler to Lana, but before he could say more, the door to the judge's inner chamber opened, and a white-haired man in judicial robes stepped to his desk.

Jesse sat beside Lana, and the judge settled himself behind his desk. A sudden silence settled over the room while he opened a folder and read a document before looking up.

"As you know, this is an informal hearing to determine temporary custody of the orphan, Colin O'Malley. In most cases, temporary custody becomes permanent only after a thorough inspection of the home in which the child is to be raised."

He glanced at Hunter Schuyler with a frown. "I have read the case you presented for your client, Lady Alana Dunning Griffin Windsor."

He focused his gaze on Lana. "These documents emphasize the fact that you are an unmarried lady. Is that correct?"

Lana could barely speak above a throat clogged with absolute terror. "It is. Yes."

"I understand that you claim to have made a promise to the orphan's mother, to raise her child as your own."

Lana's brogue thickened. "I did."

He pinned Hunter with a look. "Your documents state that you were not present when this promise was given."

Schuyler shook his head. "That is correct, your honor. I was not present, and therefore must accept the word of my client as fact."

The judge turned to the VanEndel's lawyers. "You have made an excellent point about the fact that these good people are willing to use their wealth and social position to help a less-fortunate boy reach his full potential."

Three solemn heads nodded in unison.

The judge returned his attention to the paper on his desk and began to read aloud from his prepared notes. "Though both petitioners claim the right to custody of the orphan, Colin O'Malley, it is the judgment of this court that it would be in the best interest of said orphan to be raised in a home with two parents, rather than by an unmarried woman. Therefore, I grant temporary custody of the orphan, Colin O'Malley, to Mr. and Mrs. Gustav VanEndel. Pending any extenuating circumstances, permanent custody will be granted within six months."

The judge closed the file, pushed back his chair, and walked through the door to his inner chambers.

When the door closed behind him, Evelyn and Gustav shook hands with each of their lawyers and then paused beside Lana.

Evelyn lay a hand on her shoulder and said softly, "I'm

sorry, my dear. If it's any consolation, I believe your claim of a promise made to the boy's mother, and that is a noble thing indeed. We considered letting you have the boy. But our lawyers convinced us that, after all the publicity, it would not be in our best interest to give up custody without a fight. Some people might think we didn't want to take an immigrant into our home. Bad for business, you understand. I'm sure our friends will agree with Judge Lawrence's decision that two parents are better than one. Why, the very thought of an unmarried woman trying to raise a boy alone in these trying times is simply too horrible to contemplate."

Without waiting for her response, Evelyn and Gustav left the room, trailed by their lawyers.

Lana continued sitting perfectly straight-backed in her chair, her hands folded primly in her lap.

Beside her Hunter Schuyler gathered his papers before turning to her with a grave look. "I'm truly sorry, but it's hard to argue with the judge's logic. I will be happy, however, to continue to represent you until the judge makes a determination about permanent custody. For a fee, of course."

Jesse's tone was pure ice. "My cousin won't be needing your services any longer, Schuyler."

The lawyer shrugged. "As you wish."

When they were alone, Jesse helped Lana to her feet and kept his arm around her shoulders. She moved along beside him like one in a trance.

As the carriage bore them home, Lana thought about all the hopes and dreams she'd carried in her heart for so long. She'd had such grand plans for the future. And now they'd all been dashed.

"Say something, Lana."

She turned to him. "What is there to say? There is no future without Colin. Only endless days of work and worry and a fear that will never leave me."

"The VanEndels won't harm him, Lana. They're not monsters."

"I know that. But I also know what I heard. Though they will not abuse him, they'll never allow themselves to feel anything for him. My sweet, innocent Colin will once again be thrust into a life of neglect." Seeing that Jesse was about to argue, she added quickly, "Oh, he will have all the trappings of wealth now. A big house. Servants to see to his every need. Fine food and an excellent education. But will they love him? Are they capable of loving him? Or will that sweet lad grow up to be as vain and self-centered as Wilton?"

With a cry of pain, she covered her face with her hands and began to sob.

Beside her, Jesse felt a sense of relief at her tears. He'd been watching and waiting as she'd held herself together, looking as brittle, as fragile, as glass. He'd been afraid she might withdraw into her sorrow to a place he wouldn't be able to go. But now, with the tears begun, so also could the healing begin.

He drew her close and pressed his mouth to a tangle of hair at her temple, waiting while she wept bitter tears. When at last they subsided, he handed her his handkerchief.

"I failed him." She blew her nose and dabbed at her eyes. "All those fine hopes and promises, and in the end, I failed Colin."

"You didn't fail, Lana. You were sabotaged."

"No." She shook her head. "You don't understand. I lied to you. I used the money you gave me for Siobhan's grave marker, just so I could hire some fine, fancy lawyer. And even that couldn't get me what I wanted. It's my punishment, don't you see? I had no right to pretend to be anything other than what I am."

"And what is that?"

"A poor, dirty immigrant who works in a saloon and tried to pass herself off as a titled lady to keep a promise to a dead friend and raise her child as my own."

"You love that boy."

"I do. Yes." She sniffed and blew her nose again. "More than anything. More than my own life. But I don't deserve him because of the lies I've told and the horrible things I've done. And this is my punishment."

Jesse found himself marveling at her words, which had touched him more deeply than he cared to admit. She loved the lad more than her own life. He'd never known anyone capable of such love.

They pulled up the curving driveway and rolled to a stop. As they climbed the steps, the door was thrown open, and Withers and the women fluttered around, eager to hear the outcome and to celebrate Lana's success.

Jesse shook his head in silent warning, and they stepped back, allowing him to lead Lana toward the library.

Once there he closed the door, shutting them out, and led her toward the chaise in front of the fireplace. Filling two tumblers with whiskey, he handed her one and downed the other in one long swallow. After refilling his tumbler, he turned to see her staring at the amber liquid without tasting it.

Her voice was little more than a whisper. "I'm sorry about the money. If Wilbur Hasting will take me back, I'll start paying you a little each week until it's all paid."

"I'm not worried about the money, Lana." He sat next to her and stretched out his legs. "I don't think you were listening earlier, or maybe you just weren't ready to hear what I had to say. Are you ready to listen now?"

She looked over at him and then away.

He took her hand in his. Such a small, delicate hand. "You didn't lose custody, Lana. It was stolen."

"You're not making any sense."

"If you'd told me the name of your lawyer, I could have warned you that he's one of this city's biggest gamblers. I've been in enough poker games with him to know that he's in debt to practically everyone in town."

"But what has that to do with me?"

"Not you, Lana. Gustav VanEndel. Schuyler owes him a fortune. I have no doubt that Schuyler went to Gustav and offered to throw this case in his lap if Gustav would forgive his debt."

"But the judge . . ."

"Someone had to plant that seed in Judge Lawrence's mind. I'd bet all my money that someone was Schuyler. It was his emphasis of you as an unmarried lady. Once the judge read that, he wasn't able to get beyond it."

Lana sighed. "Still, the choice of lawyer was mine. And the fact that I lost Colin is my fault. Now, there's nothing to be done about it."

"What you lost was round one." Jesse drained his glass and set it aside. "Now let's talk about round two."

"I don't understand."

"Permanent custody, Lana. That's what we have to think about now. I know that Zachariah Frederick doesn't present an attractive appearance."

She glanced over, but before she could say a word he held up a hand. "All right. He probably frightens small children and even grown women. But that disheveled appearance masks a brilliant mind. He has the reputation of having never lost a case in court."

"I see." She took a tiny sip of the whiskey and felt it burn a path of fire down her throat. "Are you saying that you want me to stay and try again?"

"It's your battle, Lana. Are you willing to keep on fighting it?"

She took another sip and felt as though she were coming out of a fog. Maybe it was just a first step, but at least the fog was lifting. "What about the money?"

"I've made bad investments before. All part of the game." He waited a beat before asking, "Are you in?"

She drained her glass and closed her eyes a moment, welcoming the heat. "I am. Yes. As long as you think there's a chance."

"I've always loved a game of chance." He took her hand and helped her to her feet. "But this time we do it all my way, no questions asked. Deal?"

She nodded. "Deal."

He brushed a kiss over her cheek.

Lana wondered at the way the room seemed to tilt for a moment before settling.

He closed his hands over her upper arms to steady her. "And to cover my bet, I'll find out more about Judge Lawrence. Maybe he has a weakness for cards, or maybe exotic women."

Her eyes widened. "You would try to influence a judge?"

"Not influence, duchess. Let's just say I'd be happy to . . . cultivate his friendship."

Lana felt her eyes fill with tears. Not the tears of despair, that she'd shed earlier, but tears of hope. "I'll never forget this, Jesse."

He gave her his best rogue smile and saw the way her eyes found some of their old sparkle.

"It's too soon to thank me. We still have our work cut out for us."

"But you think there's hope?"

He winked, and she felt the quick flutter around her heart. "There's always hope, Lana. It's there in every turn of the card. That's what keeps a gambler in the game."

"I'm not much of a gambler."

"You? You're the best I've met." He chuckled. "I'd say you've been gambling, and beating the odds, since the day you were born."

TWENTY-ONE

———◆———

"Do you think I have a chance of gaining custody of Colin, Mr. Frederick?" Lana perched nervously on the edge of a chair in the lawyer's office, an office that reflected the man. Shabby chairs scattered about the room in a haphazard manner. A desktop cluttered with files and documents. More boxes filled with files that littered every corner of the room.

"If I didn't think so, I wouldn't have taken your case." Instead of sitting behind his desk, the lawyer leaned a hip against an overflowing file cabinet and regarded her with interest. "Jesse has given me the details."

She turned wide eyes to Jesse, who gave a slight nod of his head. "Zachariah said he would only help us if we were completely honest with him. So I've told him everything. The truth, Lana."

Lana found herself relaxing. It was a relief to be able to speak freely, without the lies that had become so much a part of this new life.

The lawyer's bushy brows drew together as he frowned,

and Lana found his dark, probing eyes almost hypnotizing. "I know the facts, Miss Dunleavy, but I wanted to meet you before moving ahead with this."

Despite the fact that he looked more like a grizzled old vendor than a man of letters, Lana found herself trusting him. Perhaps it was the honesty she could read in his eyes. Or the fact that he hadn't tried to sweet-talk her when they'd first met, but rather had insisted on asking probing questions. "I'll do whatever you ask."

He folded his arms over his chest. "Tell me, in your own words, why you think you should be granted custody of the orphan."

"That orphan has a name. It's Colin. When he was born, his mother named her wee babe for her father."

"Did you know the boy's grandfather?"

Lana shook her head. "I met Colin's mother, Siobhan, in a foundling home in Ireland. I never knew her family."

"What was Siobhan like?"

Lana thought back to their first meeting. "Terrified. When she first arrived there, she cried for hours and then hid in the corner. I understood, because I'd often wanted to do the same."

"But you didn't?"

Lana's head lifted fractionally. "I'd never let the others see me cry."

Across the room, Jesse grinned.

"How did Siobhan overcome her fear?"

"I told her that I'd be her friend and promised to take care of her. And I did everything I could to keep my promise. When it was time to flee the foundling home, we ran away together. And when it was time to leave Ireland, we came to America together."

"How did you know it was time to leave the country of your birth?"

"We were starving. We knew life had to be better somewhere else. It couldn't get worse."

"What about the father of her child?"

"Billy O'Malley." Lana dismissed him with a wave of her hand. "He was handsome and charming, and after we arrived in America, just another mouth to feed."

"He didn't contribute?"

"Only to his own comfort."

"You believe he killed your friend?"

"I do. Yes. But I can't prove it, and because Billy is dead, I think it best for Colin if that part of his family history is never mentioned again."

"You say Colin's mother named her baby for her father. How do you know this? Were you there when he was born?"

"I was. Yes. I was the first to hold him." She smiled at the memory. "I saw him take his first steps. Taught him his first words. And saw him every day of his life until Siobhan told me about another baby on the way. That was the day I gave up my job at the Blue Goose and took a job as a maid so I could afford a place for Siobhan and Colin when Billy left them."

"You were that certain Billy would abandon them?"

She nodded.

"And this is why you believe you should have custody of Colin O'Malley?"

"I didn't carry Colin in my body, but I carried him in my heart, even before he was born. From the day of his birth I've loved him more than my own life. That makes him mine, as surely as he was Siobhan's."

The lawyer glanced at Jesse, who was staring at Lana with fierce concentration.

"It looks as though I have my work cut out for me, if I'm to help you gain custody of your boy." Zachariah smiled then, and Lana thought his eyes reminded her of a hound's eyes. A sweet, gentle hound.

She decided that, unless he gave her some reason to

doubt him, she would follow Jesse's example and put her trust in this funny-looking, odd little man.

THE NEXT SEVERAL weeks were a constant round of dinner parties, the opera, the theater. Whenever Lana's picture appeared in the *New York News and Dispatch* under the title "Duchess of Fifth Avenue," twice the copies were sold than on other days. The ordinary people of New York had begun to enjoy reading about this lovely, fascinating creature. Her face had become more familiar than that of the mayor or city officials.

It occurred to Lana that she saw the same people at every social event. Despite the size of New York City, the circle of acquaintances in which she now traveled was as small as the crowd she'd once served at the Blue Goose. And just as predictable.

Except for Jesse. He'd become her fierce protector, staying close to her whenever they were out in public. It was Jesse who now claimed the first and last dance and who watched with concern while she danced with other men. It was Jesse who fetched her champagne, who sat close beside her whenever possible at dinner.

She wondered how much more of this she could bear. Sometimes when they were dancing, she had to close her eyes and take deep breaths to keep from simply throwing her arms around his neck and begging him to take her home. To his bed.

The very thought had her cheeks going bright with color. He was so good to her. So thoughtful. If he knew what she was thinking, he would no doubt laugh at her. She couldn't bear it if he should laugh at these strange new feelings, and so she kept them carefully hidden.

This art of playacting, she'd learned, was very serious business.

*   *   *

"LOOK AT YOU." Nadia pointed to a grainy photograph of
Lana in the arms of Benson Blair, taken at a dinner party to
celebrate the opening night of the opera.

As was their custom, the women of the household were
gathered in the ballroom to continue their tutoring of their
prize pupil, though they'd begun to realize that there was
little left to teach her. Now they gathered as friends, to
tease, to laugh, to share stories of their lives before they had
come to this country, and to pry from Lana every bit of gossip they could about a society that was as closed to them as
the former lives of wealth and privilege they constantly
boasted of.

Nadia smiled. "Benson Blair is considered one of New
York's most eligible bachelors."

"An eligible bachelor?" Lana was shocked. "Why, he
must be seventy years old."

Colette gave a throaty laugh. "The older the better, my
darling. That way a woman doesn't have to wait so many
years to inherit his estate."

The women chuckled at the horrified look on Lana's
face.

Nadia patted her arm. "Hasn't anyone told you, darling?
If you marry the first time for money, you can afford to
marry the second time for love."

"That's disgusting."

Nadia cast a knowing look at her French friend. "You
and I know better, don't we, Colette?"

"*Oui.*" The French woman nodded. "Only one who has
never been desperate would be disgusted by survival in any
manner possible. Nadia and I know what it is to wander the
streets, never certain where our next meal will be or where
we will lay our heads in sleep."

"I know that fear." Lana thought about those first few
frantic days and nights after she and Siobhan had slipped

away from the foundling home and had been forced to live on the streets, until Lana found employment with a kind soul willing to take a chance on a girl with no family. She and Siobhan had been so desperately hungry and terrified of what might happen to them.

Their first weeks in America hadn't been any better, despite the presence of Billy O'Malley in their lives. In fact, Billy had become one more problem, one more mouth to feed.

Colette broke into her thoughts. "I think you are not as desperate to gain custody of this lad, *cherie,* or you would see that marriage to a millionaire could be the solution you seek."

Lana paused. "Do you think a judge would give more consideration to the wife of a millionaire than he might to a high-born Englishwoman?"

"He might. Especially if the millionaire happened to travel in the same social circles as the judge. What do you care if your husband is seventy, or seven times seventy, so long as he serves his purpose?"

"The older the better," Colette said with a wink. "That way you need not warm his bed, but simply adorn his arm whenever he is out in the public eye."

Jesse stood in the doorway, eyes narrowed in anger. "I believe Lana has had enough of your silly chatter." From the gruff tone of his voice, it was clear he'd been standing there listening for some time.

"Silly?" Colette grinned at Nadia, and the two women shared a knowing look. "Do you expect her to remain an innocent forever, Jesse? It is up to us to impart our vast store of knowledge about such things to our pupil."

"Be careful." Jesse's tone lowered. "Or she will be your pupil no more."

All except Lana seemed amused by his display of temper.

She got to her feet, shaking down her skirts. "Jesse's right. I have better things to do."

As she stepped past him, she could almost feel the sting of his fury.

He wasn't the only one annoyed. She'd long ago learned that when Nadia and Colette got together, they seemed to enjoy shocking their innocent young friend.

But there was no escaping the seed that had been planted in Lana's mind. Would she be better off considering marriage before taking on Evelyn VanEndel in court?

"LADY ALANA. I thought I recognized you across the room."

Lana looked up in surprise at the sound of Evelyn Van-Endel's voice beside her in the parlor of the Carter mansion. Helena and Bertram Carter were hosting a dinner party after a night at the opera.

Lana glanced around for some sign of Jesse, but he was busy entertaining a cluster of guests in front of the fireplace. When he caught her eye and made an attempt to go to her, one of the men stopped him with a hand to his arm, and Jesse was forced to remain.

"Mrs. VanEndel. How nice to see you."

"Please, don't be so formal. I'd hoped we could be friends. Please call me Evelyn."

"Evelyn," Lana said through clenched teeth.

The woman waved away a maid who had started over with a tray of drinks. "I was hoping I might speak with you." She glanced around. "Alone."

"I don't think . . ."

Evelyn stopped her with a hand to her arm and leaned close to whisper, "It occurred to me that there might be a simple solution to . . . our little problem with the boy."

Lana thought about reminding this woman that the boy had a name, but she was too intrigued. "A solution?"

Seeing that she now had Lana's full attention, Evelyn

smiled. "You are a lovely young woman with impeccable taste, as befits a member of English royalty."

Startled, Lana could only murmur, "Thank you."

Encouraged, Evelyn continued. "My son, Wilton, has confided in me that he finds you devastatingly attractive, Lady Alana. I believe you are not immune to his charms, as well. What woman could resist him?" Evelyn's smile was pure honey. "If you were to marry Wilton, you would be part of the family, and therefore would have access to our newly acquired orphan whenever you wanted."

Again Lana's first thought was to correct the woman and insist that Colin was neither a piece of newly acquired property, nor an orphan without a name, but those things faded at the enormity of what had just been offered her.

For the first time in her life, Lana couldn't think of a single word to say. She stood there, jaw dropped, staring at this woman with a look of complete astonishment.

Evelyn patted her hand. "I see I've caught you by surprise. My son, Wilton, seems to have that effect on women. I'll just leave you alone now, to think over what I've said."

She soon joined a group of women, laughing and chatting easily, as though she hadn't just offered Lana the most exquisite gift of a lifetime.

Lana remained where she was, lost in thought, until Jesse came to find her and escort her to the dining room.

Later that night, as rain battered their carriage, Jesse was forced to endure the entire ride in silence while Lana sat beside him, ignoring all his attempts to engage her in conversation.

When they were finally standing outside Lana's suite, Jesse paused before saying good night. "You and Evelyn VanEndel looked cozy in the parlor. What were the two of you chatting about?"

"She offered me a way to share Colin."

"Share him?"

Lana nodded. "She thinks I'd be a perfect match for Wilton. She said that if I were to marry her son, I could be with Colin whenever I chose."

"So that's her game." Jesse gave a shake of his head. "I'm not surprised."

"You aren't?" Lana gave a short laugh. "I'm afraid her offer left me quite speechless."

"And well it should. Of course, this would be the solution for several of her problems. Word on the street is that Wilton attacked a helpless young maid in their employ, and a doctor brought in to treat her made a police report. Naturally, it will all be hushed. Nothing will come of it. The girl will be given some money and will conveniently leave town. But his parents have to know that sooner or later he'll become more violent."

"Oh, dear heaven." Lana closed her eyes and was instantly thrust back to that horrible scene with Swede. She found herself wondering again what had happened to the little maid. Had Wilton returned and exacted revenge, as he'd vowed?

"On top of that, Wilton's gambling debts are piling up, and his father is tired of bailing him out of his troubles. I can see where they might believe that marriage to a wealthy woman would be the perfect solution." His eyes narrowed on Lana. "As a titled English lady, you could pay Wilton's debts and maybe settle him down. If not, at least you could take him off to England for a while, to give his family some peace. And if you were to agree to take Colin along, all the better. With the wayward son and the orphan both out of the country, Evelyn and Gustav would be done with all their troubles in one clean sweep."

Jesse fell silent for a moment before muttering almost to himself, "All of this reinforces my opinion that Evelyn is feeling a bit desperate. I say now is the time to have Zachariah petition the judge for a change of custody."

"No." Lana put a hand on his sleeve. "Please, Jesse. Not yet."

He struggled to ignore the sizzle caused by her touch. "Don't you see, Lana? The woman is looking for a way out."

"But she will never admit defeat. At least not in public. If I were to lose again, I'd have no more chances." She closed her eyes, her mind racing. "Think about this instead. Not that I'd ever consider marriage to Wilton. But if I were to appear interested, at least I could get the opportunity to see Colin. To spend some time with him."

Lana was shocked at the change in Jesse. His eyes darkened like the sky before a storm. His hands closed around her upper arms, dragging her roughly to him until her feet no longer touched the floor.

"Do you have any idea what Wilton is capable of?"

"Of course I do. Now unhand me, Jesse."

Her whispered command only served to further inflame him. "You think you know, but someone as sweet, as innocent as you wouldn't have a clue."

"Jesse." Her tone sharpened. "You're hurting me."

"Am I?" His eyes had gone from stormy to nearly blind with rage in a matter of moments. "This is nothing to what a monster like Wilton would do, given the chance to be alone with you. I forbid you to entertain such a notion for even one second. Do you hear me?"

"You forbid? You forbid?" With her temper full-blown, her voice carried through the hall.

"You'll wake the entire household." When Jesse put a hand to her mouth to stifle her words, she bit him.

With a yelp of pain he hissed, "Little fool. You can fight and bite and kick and scream, but I forbid you to even consider feigning interest in that monster just to win the lad."

Her eyes flashed fire while her brogue thickened. "I'll remind you that I don't belong to you. I'll do what I think best, and you'll not stop me."

She lifted a hand to shove him aside, and he clamped his arms around her, pinning her arms at her sides. He knew he'd gone beyond reason, but he no longer cared. He backed her up until he felt the door to her suite give way. Shoving her roughly inside, he kicked the door shut and ducked when she swung at him.

She reached for the knife she carried concealed at her waist, and he closed his fingers around her wrist, squeezing until she was forced to drop her weapon or feel her bones snap like twigs.

"You disgusting, dim-witted, overbearing son of a sow." Despite the tears in her eyes, she stood facing him, toe to toe, spewing the familiar litany of insults that sprang instantly to her lips from all those years at the Blue Goose.

"You're right. I'm all of those things and more. But I'm not without a soul, Lana. I won't have you bargaining your body for the boy. That would make you no better than Verna Lee."

Both of them were breathing hard, chests heaving, bodies taut with fury.

"You've no say in what I do. Not now. Not ever."

"You're right, of course." His words were clipped. "All right. Give yourself time alone with Wilton VanEndel. And when he discovers the truth, that you have no money and no ties to English royalty, what do you think he'll do? Oh, not right away, of course. First he'll have to punish you for having lied to him. So when he slaps you around the bedroom and forces you to do things you'd have killed a drunk for doing at the Blue Goose, you'll have no one but yourself to blame. And when you've been publicly beaten down and humiliated, don't expect little Colin to thank you for your sacrifice. Not that you'll ever see the lad again. I'm sure Evelyn VanEndel will make certain of that."

His words had the desired effect. Lana blanched and stepped back, all the fight gone out of her.

"I'm sorry, Lana." Seeing her like this, Jesse felt lower than a slug. All he really wanted to do was gather her close and offer her some comfort, but this was no time for tenderness. "I've come to care too much about you to allow you to do something so destructive. I'd never forgive myself if any harm came to you. Though I hadn't meant it to happen, you've become . . . very precious to me. For now, we both need to stay the course we've set, and very soon now, I'm confident you'll have your heart's desire." He turned away and yanked open the door, eager to escape. "I'll say good night now."

As he made his way along the hallway, Jesse absorbed a wave of self-hatred. The look of pain in her eyes had nearly stopped his heart. Why hadn't he just slapped her? It would have been kinder than what he'd just done. But he was desperate to make her see the truth before it was too late.

He stormed into his suite of rooms and crossed to a decanter of whiskey on a side table. Picking it up, he snagged a tumbler as well and carried both into the bedroom. After tearing off his jacket and shirt and viciously kicking his boots against the wall, he slumped into a chair in front of the fireplace and filled the tumbler to the brim, drinking down the fiery liquid in one long swallow.

The rain battering his windows added to his gloom.

It was his intention to get as drunk as humanly possible in the shortest amount of time.

TWENTY-TWO

———◆◆◆———

ON TREMBLING LEGS Lana made her way to her bed and sat on the edge, feeling too numb to weep. She untied the laces of her shoes and set them aside.

Jesse was right, of course. Leading on Wilton VanEndel was out of the question. She'd known that in her heart of hearts. But she'd been so startled by Evelyn's proposal, she'd actually allowed herself to contemplate the impossible, if just for a few moments.

It was just that she wanted so desperately to see Colin. To save him.

Still, Jesse had taken particular delight in scorning her suggestion. She hadn't known him to have such a cruel streak. After such a vicious attack, he had a nerve calling Wilton a monster. How could Colette and Nadia and the others practically swoon over all Jesse's virtues? Obviously they had never seen this side of the man.

He'd been like a madman when she'd told him about Evelyn's offer. In fact, he'd changed before her very eyes, going from kind and considerate to mocking and taunting in the blink of an eye. And then he'd excused his boorish behavior by suggesting that he'd said those cutting things for her own good.

Her own good. Ha! The man was a liar and a cheat and had shown himself to be a bully, as well.

She struggled to recall his exact words.

"I've come to care too much about you to allow you to do something so destructive. I'd never forgive myself if any harm came to you. Though I hadn't meant it to happen, you've become . . . very precious to me."

Very precious to me?

He had an odd way of showing it.

Now that she was replaying his words, she remembered something else. He'd been reluctant to make such an admission, as if, by merely saying the words, he was somehow showing a sign of weakness.

Weakness? Disgust would be more like it. He actually seemed disgusted with himself for admitting such a thing.

With a little glimmer of understanding, she lunged to her feet and began to pace. Had he unwittingly revealed a depth of feeling for her? Or was she foolishly making this into something more, only because she so desperately wanted it to be so?

Oh, if only she had someone in whom she could confide. She dared not go to Maria or Colette or Nadia. They were so worldly wise, so jaded. They would find her ignorance amusing. She knew so little about men and women.

She stopped her pacing. This much she knew. Jesse's temper had grown in direct proportion to her determination to consider Wilton VanEndel as a husband.

He'd been quietly confident, almost cheerful, while discussing the VanEndels' problems. Had been glib and condescending toward Evelyn VanEndel. It was only when he realized that Lana was considering cozying up to Wilton that he had become enraged.

He'd admitted to caring about her. Was that the same as an admission of love?

She had to know. Had to. All her life she'd had to be sensible. But just this one time, she decided to go with her impulse. Without giving herself time to change her mind, she dashed from her room and raced down the hall.

JESSE LOOKED UP at the insistent knock on his door and called out irritably, "I don't need you tonight, Withers."

The knock came a second time, only louder.

Jesse swore and crossed the room, yanking open the door with a scowl. "I said . . ."

The words died in his throat when he saw Lana standing there, looking flushed and breathless.

Without a word, she pushed past him and stepped into the room, crossing to the fireplace.

Jesse leaned against the door, struggling in vain for a careless pose. "Haven't had enough? Did I forget an insult or two? Or have you come for vengeance?" He tipped up his glass and drank, hoping to ease his suddenly parched throat. "Go ahead then. Plunge your dagger through my heart. I suppose I deserve it."

"That's what I thought when you first walked away." She hugged her arms across her chest and prayed that the fire would warm her suddenly chilled body. Her legs were actually trembling. She'd forgotten her shoes. Not that it mattered, in his present state of undress. She hadn't expected him to be barefoot and shirtless. The sight of that hair-roughened chest and all that expanse of naked flesh had her heart leaping to her throat. Still, she'd been the one to start this. Now she was committed to seeing it to its conclusion. "And then I thought about all you'd revealed."

"That Wilton is a monster?" His hand involuntarily tightened around the tumbler. "Doesn't take any brains to figure that out."

"This isn't about Wilton." She took a step toward him. "I suppose it never was."

"What's that supposed to mean?" He was suddenly wary. There was a look in her eye that troubled him. A cat-like gleam. As if she had just discovered some new feminine power inside herself.

"You care about me, Jesse."

"Of course I care." He saw the knowing smile that curved her lips and amended quickly, "The way a brother might care about a sister. A sister who was about to make a foolish, fatal mistake."

"You feel brotherly?" She took another step toward him and noted that he took a step back. That had her smile growing, along with her confidence.

He glowered at her. "Whatever game you're playing, Lana, I'm not interested. It's late. I have"—he lifted his glass—"this whiskey to drink before turning in for the night."

"Go ahead and drink your whiskey." She took the glass from his hand and lifted it to her lips. "In fact, perhaps I'll join you."

"Stop that." He snatched the glass from her hands and watched the liquid slosh over the rim before he set it aside. "Whatever you've come to say, Lana, have at it and leave me."

"All right." She drew herself up as tall as possible and spoke the words in a rush, before she could lose her courage. "That display in my room wasn't mere anger. It was jealousy."

"Don't be silly. I was . . ."

"Don't deny it, Jesse. You flew into a rage when you thought I might seriously consider getting close to Wilton

VanEndel, because you were jealous. And whether you're willing to admit it or not, you were jealous because you . . . want me for yourself." When he opened his mouth to protest, she lifted a hand to his lips. "There's more. Let me say it all now, so we're perfectly clear about our feelings. I . . . want you, too."

He could think of so many reasons why he needed to get her out of his room as quickly as possible. Especially now. But the press of her fingers against his lips was the sweetest of torments, and he could feel his body already betraying him and his mind going blank along with his good intentions.

She saw his eyes narrow before he closed his hand over hers. Instead of releasing it, he continued holding it while he chose his words carefully. "I'm honored that you share my feelings, Lana. But we can't possibly act on them."

Her eyes widened. "And why can't we?"

"Because, as anyone will tell you, I'm a black-hearted rogue, and you, Lana Dunleavy, are an innocent."

Her smile was back. "Only because I'd never met anyone who tempted me enough to want it otherwise. But now, with you, my black-hearted rogue"—she stood on tiptoe and brushed her mouth over his—"I'd be happy to give up my innocence."

He couldn't seem to get a breath. All the air had been sucked out of his lungs. Everything he'd ever known was wiped from his mind. All he could see was Lana. All he could taste was Lana.

"You don't want to do this." Feeling a sense of panic, he framed her face with his hands, hoping to push her away. Instead, he combed his fingers through her hair. With a muttered oath, he fisted a hand in the tangles and watched as the silken strands sifted through his fingers. Soft. So soft.

In that instant, he knew he was lost.

Still, he had to try. For her sake.

"Think about this, Lana. And think about tomorrow. If

we give in to these feelings tonight, there will be no going back to the woman you are now."

"I won't want to go back, Jesse." She wrapped her arms around his waist and felt a quick skitter of fire and ice at the touch of his naked flesh against her palms. Growing bolder, she pressed her mouth to his throat. At his quick intake of breath she felt a moment of triumph that overcame whatever fear lingered. He wasn't nearly as immune to her charms as he pretended to be. "Don't send me away. I want to stay here with you."

He drew her so close she could feel the wild thundering of his heartbeat inside her own chest. "God help me, I wish I were stronger. If I were good and decent and noble, I'd send you packing without so much as a glance. But I'm only a man, Lana. And a weak one at that."

"One more thing, in case you need persuasion." Lana reached beneath her sash, pulled out her dagger, and tossed it aside.

It fell to the floor with a clatter.

In the silence that followed, Jesse lowered his mouth to hers and kissed her long and slow and deep, pouring all the hunger, all the longing into that one kiss, until they were both trembling.

Against her mouth he muttered, "I could no more send you away now than I could stop the rain. But I warn you, Lana, I can't promise to be gentle. In fact, I can't make you any promises at all."

His mouth crushed hers with a fierceness that had her gasping. His fingers dug into the tender flesh of her upper arms as he dragged her firmly against him.

If he'd hoped to frighten her, it had the opposite effect. She returned his kiss with a sense of urgency, giving herself up to the purely sensual pleasure.

How could one man's mouth be so clever? How was it that, with one simple touch of his fingers, her body could feel so alive?

His lips left her mouth to nuzzle her throat. With a purr of pleasure, she arched her neck to give him easier access. When his mouth closed around the bodice of her gown, she gave a sudden gasp and instinctively pushed away. Despite the layers of clothing that acted as a barrier, she had felt the jolt of that simple touch to her breast all through her body to her very core.

His smile was quick and dangerous. "Does that mean you'd like me to stop?"

In reply, she cupped his head and drew him down for another drugging kiss.

"That's a relief." He gave a ragged laugh. "We've gone beyond stopping."

This time, when he began exploring her neck, her shoulder, and the sensitive hollow of her throat, she clung to him and rode the pleasure, trusting he wouldn't take her where she didn't want to go.

"I need to see you, Lana. All of you." Impatient for more, he slid the bodice of her gown from her shoulders. In his haste, several buttons gave way, freeing the garment to pool at her feet. With his eyes steady on hers, he untied the ribbons of her delicate chemise, parting the fabric until it, too, drifted to the floor.

Lana had always wondered if she would be embarrassed to have a man look at her like this. Now, seeing the dark desire in Jesse's eyes, there was no discomfort, only the awareness that he wanted her as much as she wanted him. That knowledge was more erotic than any touch.

When he bent his head to take her breast, all thought fled. Her blood heated, even while her bones began to melt like candle wax. Pleasure built upon pleasure until she feared that she would surely explode with all the strange, new feelings building inside her. Her body was alive with need—a need that only Jesse could satisfy.

Growing bolder, she reached for the fasteners at his

waist. When her fingers fumbled, he helped her until his clothes joined hers at their feet.

At last they were both free to touch, to taste, to feast.

Jesse nibbled his way from her jaw to her throat to her breast, all the while moving his fingers along her back, causing the most amazing heat to dance through her veins.

When he felt her trembling response, he gathered her into his arms, intent upon carrying her to the bedroom. Halfway there he made the mistake of taking her mouth for another kiss. That was his undoing.

The need that sizzled between them had him moaning and lowering her to the chaise in front of the fire.

The world seemed to slip away. The rain beating against the windowpane was nothing compared to the thundering of their two heartbeats. The hiss and snap of the log on the grate was muted next to the sound of their shallow breathing. Each seductive touch, each heady taste, sank them deeper into a murky pool of passion. The heat of it slicked their bodies, clouded their vision, and clogged their throats until their breathing was ragged.

"I've wanted you for so long, Lana. So long."

His admission, whispered fiercely inside her mouth, had her wrapping herself around him, offering him whatever he wanted. All he wanted. She was desperate to give and take and give even more, until this strange new hunger was sated.

With a moan of pleasure he took her on a wild, dizzying ride, until she gripped his shoulders and pleaded for release. Needs so long denied took over her will. The need to have his hands on her, all of her, until she quivered and trembled. The need to have his mouth on hers, devouring. The need to forget all the rules she'd set for herself.

"Jesse, please . . ."

In his arms she experienced such pleasure, pleasure so intense, it bordered on pain. She wanted, more than anything, to give him the same pleasure, and so she returned kiss for kiss, touch for touch, and found his reaction deeply arousing.

She looked up into those eyes, always before filled with secrets. Now they were staring deeply into her eyes with a look that told her in every way that he found her beautiful, desirable.

The knowledge that she was the reason for that look of love gave her a sense of power unlike any other. He wanted her. He could no longer hide behind a rogue's mask.

Jesse knew he was teetering on the edge of reason. Need, deep and compelling, was like a beast inside him, struggling to be free. If he didn't take her soon and end this terrible battle, he would go mad.

And still he hesitated, needing to hear the words. "Tell me you won't regret this, Lana. Tell me this is what you want."

"No regrets, Jesse. Never." Needs unlike anything she'd ever known had taken over her will. Raw, primitive, gnawing hunger. A need that ached, rocking her world, sending it tilting out of control.

And then, though she hadn't meant to make such an admission, the words spilled out of a heart overflowing with feelings. "I want you. Only you . . ."

It was too late. The words were lost in the frenzy that caught them both by surprise.

Jesse heard her cry and knew he was hurting her. Dear heaven, she was an innocent, and he was taking her like some sort of barbarian. For the space of a heartbeat he paused, filled with remorse, and struggled to rein in the passion that was already out of control.

"I'm sorry, Lana. I didn't mean to hurt . . ."

"Shhh." She lifted a hand to his cheek. Just a touch, but he felt his heart contract. And then she looked up into his eyes, and what he saw there shook him to his very soul.

In her eyes was the same hot, fierce flame he was trying

so desperately to bank. The same hard, driving need. The same out-of-control passion.

"Please don't stop, Jesse."

Their mouths mated as they began to move together, bodies slick, hearts thundering, flesh to flesh. They climbed higher, then higher still, until they broke free of earth and soared to the heavens.

"DID I HURT you?" Jesse's face lay in the curve of her neck, his breath tickling her ear.

"Ummm." She gave the slightest shake of her head. Anything more would require too much effort, and right now, she just wanted to lie here and wait for her heart and her world to settle.

"Am I heavy?" His fingers played with a tangle of hair at her temple.

"Ummm." She closed her eyes to stem the moisture she could feel building behind her lids.

"That's what I've always liked best about you." He lifted his head enough to brush his mouth over hers. "The talkative type." His grin faded when he caught sight of one big wet tear squeezing from the corner of her eye. "God in heaven, I did hurt you."

"No." Horrified to have him see her weeping, she brushed the tear with her fist, but a second one spilled over, and then a third.

Jesse felt his heart stop as he wiped the tears with his thumbs. "I'm sorry, Lana. I never meant . . ."

"This isn't what you think." She smiled through her tears. "It's just that I never dreamed it would be this wonderful."

Wonderful? He wheezed out a breath. "I didn't hurt you?"

"Of course not. I was . . . overcome for a moment."

"Ah." Jesse felt his heart start to beat once more.

She looked away. "You must think me silly."

"I think you're delightful, and beautiful, and full of surprises, Duchess. But never silly."

She latched on to the only thing that had snagged her attention. "You think I'm beautiful?" The very thought had her glowing.

"You know I do. And have since the first time I saw you in the Blue Goose."

"I didn't think you saw anything except the cards."

"You'd be surprised at all I managed to see." He rolled over on the narrow chaise and managed to settle her on top of him. As she snuggled close, he was struck by the thought that they fit together perfectly, like two pieces in a puzzle.

"About that display of temper." He cleared his throat. "You were right, Lana. I was jealous. Jealous of every other man who made you smile. I was jealous of every old lecher who danced with you. I was jealous of your dinner partners, and the men who fetched your champagne. But the very thought of you being alone with Wilton sent me over the edge. That was more than a twinge of jealously. That was some sort of black rage, the likes of which I don't believe I've ever experienced before in my life."

His admission had her brushing her lips over his. Against his mouth she whispered, "Then you need never experience it again, for I know without a doubt that I'll never consider Evelyn's proposal."

"We'll find another way to win custody of Colin. I promise you."

"Thank you." She was touched by his concern. She sighed and wrapped her arms around his neck. "Do I have to go back to my room now?"

He couldn't hide his surprise or his pleasure. "Would you like to stay the night? I'm sure I can find a way to . . . make you comfortable while we pass the time."

That had her bursting into laughter. "You really are a rogue, aren't you?"

She was still laughing when he drew her head down and kissed her, long and slow and deep, pouring into it every bit of tenderness he was feeling.

Gradually the laughter turned to a sigh, and the sigh to a moan of pleasure as they lost themselves in the wonder of their mutual passion.

TWENTY-THREE

———◆◆◆———

LANA STIRRED IN her sleep. Sometime during the night Jesse had carried her to his bed, where they had alternately loved and dozed.

Aware that Jesse wasn't in bed beside her, she sat up, shoving a tangle of hair from her eyes. "Jesse?" She watched as his shadowy figure moved restlessly around the room. "What's wrong?"

He paused. Turned. "Sorry. I didn't mean to wake you."

"Why are you pacing, Jesse? Tell me what's bothering you."

When he remained silent, she swung her legs from bed and got to her feet. "I'm sorry. I shouldn't have stayed. I'll go now."

"Wait." He was across the room in quick strides, catching her by the arms. "It isn't you, Lana."

"Then what . . . ?"

"You're so sweet. So generous. Here you are, giving me all I could have hoped for, and I have nothing to give in return."

"I've asked for nothing."

"Which only makes it worse, don't you see? I watch you, fighting so hard to win a boy, not because of what he can give to you, but only because of what you can do for him. And you're the same with me. Asking nothing and giving everything."

She smiled in the darkness. "I'd say you've given me a great deal."

"Things. I've given you things. A place to stay. Tutors. Clothes. But I can't give you any promises. I can't give my name, or my vow to be here for you in the future."

"I don't need your name or your vows, Jesse." She shivered at the intensity of his words. In her heart a tiny seed of doubt began to sprout. Was there a lover in his life? A wife?

"You're cold." He tore a blanket from the bed and wrapped it around her and then crossed to the fireplace and stirred the embers before placing a fresh log on the grate. Within minute flames licked across the bark.

Jesse stood staring into the fire. "You're the most amazing woman, Lana. You give your love so generously. But there are some people who are incapable of love."

She said nothing, only walked closer to stand beside him. Whatever was on his mind, it was tormenting him, and she sensed his need to talk openly. If he told her he had a wife, she wasn't certain she could bear the pain. But she had to know what had him walking the floor.

After a long silence he said softly, "My mother was never faithful to her vows. She took so many lovers, I lost count. No doubt she did, too. She claimed it was because her family forced her into a loveless marriage, but whatever the reason, the choices she made afterward were hers."

"Have you told your mother how you feel?"

"I've told her nothing. We rarely see one another. It's better that way."

"How can you be so forgiving of Colette and so unforgiving of your own mother?"

"Colette did what she had to to survive. Perhaps in her case, she truly was in love. As for my mother, she was incapable of thinking about anyone but herself. The world revolved around her needs. She never gave a thought to what her children might need."

"Children?" Lana's eyes widened. "You have brothers and sisters?"

"A sister. Who is as vain, and as unfaithful, as our mother. Which is why I will never marry." He turned to her with a look of such sadness, it twisted a knife in Lana's heart. "I would rather live my life alone than risk hurting someone that way. Especially someone who mattered to me."

Though his admission was heartbreaking, it wasn't what she had feared. There was no wife. No other lover.

Lana touched a hand to his cheek. Just a touch, but she saw his eyes narrow on her with a fierce hunger. "In that case, I'll ask nothing more of you, Jesse, than what you've already given so generously."

Keeping his gaze steady on her, he caught her hand and brought it to his lips. "I wish I could give you more."

"This is enough." Even as she said the words, she wondered if she spoke the truth or if she was fooling herself.

Pushing aside the twinge of regret, she offered her mouth, and he took it with a hunger that startled them both.

"WELL, DUCHESS. ABOUT time you surfaced." Jesse watched as her lids fluttered and then lifted. He'd been lying here watching her sleep and waiting for the moment when she would wake and he could see himself in those jeweled eyes.

"Is it morning yet?" She yawned and stretched before wrapping her arms around his neck.

"Not even close. Thank you for agreeing to stay the night." He nibbled the corner of her mouth. "I'm sorry I haven't given you more time to sleep."

"I'm not complaining." She arched her neck when he began nuzzling her throat, her shoulder. "You're a man of your word. So far you've managed to keep me . . . entertained."

"My pleasure, Duchess." His mouth moved lower, nibbling, teasing.

Lana couldn't hide her gasp as he began moving down her body. All through the night they'd been learning each other's secrets. And with each hour that passed, they'd uncovered new and wonderful surprises. Like two children turned loose in a garden of delights, they couldn't seem to get enough.

"Jesse." She clutched the bed linens and felt her toes curl.

His words were muffled. "I thought you liked this."

"I do, but . . ." Whatever she'd been about to say died in her throat as she gave herself up to the intense pleasure.

Before she could catch her breath he took her up and over again. Almost blind with passion, she drew him close as he entered her.

Would she ever have enough of him? Would he one day tire of her?

Those questions fled, replaced by the most amazing sensations as he showed her how, together, they could make the earth tremble.

"WHAT ARE YOU doing?" Jesse watched as Lana's shadowy figure returned from his sitting room carrying her gown.

"I thought I'd dress and get to my room before I'm missed."

"You're already missed. By me." Jesse held open a corner of the bed linens. "Don't leave me yet, Duchess."

"You know what will happen if I get back into bed with you."

His grin was quick and dangerous. "I'm counting on it."

"I should go."

He stopped her with a hand on her arm. "Stay. Please."

Lana looked at his hand and then gave a laugh as she dropped her gown and crawled into his arms. "You know I can't resist you when you beg."

"I'll have to keep that in mind."

"I THINK I see sunlight peeking through that window." Lana lay in Jesse's arms, floating on a cloud of pure contentment.

He nibbled her ear. "Would you like me to draw the draperies and see if it's daylight?"

"Too much trouble."

He kissed the tip of her nose. "I don't mind. I'll just . . ."

At the sound of footsteps in the sitting room, Lana turned wide eyes to Jesse. "Who would that be?"

He merely smiled. "If you saw sunlight, that would be Withers, with my morning tea."

"Withers?" Lana began rummaging around the bed for a coverlet. Finding none, she did the only thing she could think of, and slithered out of bed, rolling underneath just as the bedroom door was opened.

She watched as two perfectly polished boots appeared just inches away. "Good morning, sir. Your tea."

Jesse's voice sounded from above. "Thank you, Withers. You can set it on the night table."

"As you wish." Lana watched the boots disappear, then reappear a moment later. "There's a good bit of excitement this morning."

"Is there? And what's it about?"

"It seems Miss Dunleavy wasn't in her suite when Rosa brought up her morning chocolate. Her shoes were beside her bed, but the bed hadn't been slept in."

"You don't say?" Lana could hear the hint of a smile in Jesse's voice and felt her face flame. She was grateful no one was here to witness her humiliation.

Just then, to her horror, she spied her gown, lying in a heap where she'd dropped it.

She inched her fingers from under the bed, determined to hide the evidence.

"I say. What's this?" As Lana watched, a hand and the cuff of a starched white shirt came into view. To her horror, the hand closed around her gown and snatched it away before she could retrieve it.

"Looks like one of Lana's gowns to me." Jesse's tone was matter-of-fact.

"So it does." Withers's voice faded as the boots moved away. From across the room he said, "It appears a few of the buttons have come off. I'll see that Maria gives it to Nadia to repair."

"Thank you, Withers. I'm sure Miss Dunleavy will be grateful."

When the door closed, Lana crawled out from under the bed only to find Jesse convulsed with laughter.

She put her hands on her hips, too upset about Withers's discovery to give a thought to her nakedness. "How will I ever go back to my room now?"

"You can wear one of my shirts. Or if you'd like, I'll wrap you in a sheet like a mummy before you leave. Or better yet, I could just order Rosa to fetch your robe."

"This isn't funny, Jesse. You realize that very soon now the entire household will know that I've spent the night in your bed."

"Soon? Duchess, I'm sure it's public knowledge already."

"Oh, how can you laugh at a time like this?"

He slid out of bed and caught her hand. "You should have seen Withers's face when he realized what he'd stumbled upon. Oh, Lana, it was priceless. That poor man."

"That poor man? What about me, forced to lie under the bed, knowing that he knew I was there?"

Suddenly the ridiculousness of the situation had her laughing, too. "I almost had the gown. A minute more and I'd have been able to hide the evidence."

"It wouldn't have done you a bit of good." Jesse buried his face in her hair and shook with laughter. "Withers nearly tripped over your chemise when he came through the doorway. It was actually caught on the sole of his boot for a step or two. And then, while he tried to pretend not to know what was going on, he was forced to stand here and behave like a gentleman's gentleman, grim as a statue."

The two of them fell into each other's arms, choking with laughter.

"HAVE YOU SEEN them?" Rosa stepped into the kitchen, where the staff was gathered around the big wooden table, sipping tea and sampling Clara's honey-glazed biscuits.

"I did." Maria glanced at the others. "I must admit, I doubted you at first, Withers. But the way they were looking at each other over breakfast confirmed everything you said."

"I told you." Colette gave a smug smile.

"So you did." Nadia bit into a biscuit. "I confess that I'm surprised at Jesse."

"And why is that?" Clara poured boiling water into the teapot. "After all, the lass is every bit as lovely as any of those society ladies."

"Oh, indeed. I quite agree." Nadia glanced around. "It's just that I never expected Jesse to trifle with an innocent like our Lana."

"What makes you think it's mere trifling?" Withers accepted a cup of tea from the cook. "Who's to say he doesn't have feelings for the lass? After all, we've all come to love her."

"Indeed we have. But Jesse?" Colette giggled behind her hand. "We know better. Not that he's a philanderer. Jesse has always been . . . discreet when it comes to affairs of the heart. But we can certainly all agree that Jesse will never commit his heart."

"Perhaps not willingly." Withers sipped. "But love, real love, has a way of sneaking up on a man."

"Some men. But Jesse isn't like other men. I can't see him letting his heart rule his head." Colette winked at Nadia, who nodded in agreement.

"No matter." Maria set down her cup with a clatter and turned toward the door. "For now, the two of them are happier than they've been since coming here. I say we leave them alone to enjoy this new intimacy."

"*Dah.*" Nadia sniffed. "Even if, in the end, they will surely break one another's hearts."

"GOOD DAY, MISS Dunleavy."

"Mr. Frederick." Lana took a seat in the lawyer's office. These weekly visits had given her insight into the man's sharp mind. Though his office was still untidy, his brain was far from cluttered.

"I have some news."

Lana glanced at Jesse before asking, "Good news, I hope?"

"I suppose that would depend upon your point of view." He cleared his throat. "One of my . . . employees has befriended a maid in the VanEndel house, who confided that the boy was found sleeping on the floor under his lovely new bed."

"I see." Lana thought back to her own painful adjustment to life outside the confinement of the foundling home.

"You don't seem surprised. Does this make sense to you?" The lawyer was watching her eyes.

"It does. Yes. When Siobhan and I escaped the foundling home and finally managed to find a place to stay, we huddled together in a corner of the room for weeks, even though it had a bed, for fear of having someone discover us in the night and snatch away our freedom."

Zachariah leaned back in his rickety chair. "I don't believe you've ever told me how you managed to escape the foundling home."

"A farmer had delivered potatoes and was busy accepting his pay from Mother Superior. Siobhan and I hid in his wagon, under the empty potato sacks. When he stopped at a tavern, we were able to sneak off into the night."

"You make it sound simple enough." He glanced at Jesse, who was staring at her with a thoughtful expression. "My . . . spy, reported other things. When Evelyn VanEndel ordered the boy to clean his plate before leaving the dinner table, he did as he was told and then promptly gagged and threw up. Since then, she hasn't allowed him to eat with the family. Instead, he has a tray in his room. The boy is a virtual recluse, except for a maid assigned to see that he bathes, eats, and sleeps."

Lana put a hand to her mouth to cover her gasp of dismay. This was even worse than she'd expected.

Zachariah nodded in grim agreement. "You were right in your assumption that Mrs. VanEndel was more concerned with how she would look to society than how she might best care for the orphan. Not that she is cruel, mind you. I have it on good authority that she has been taking her instructions on how best to handle the boy from the director of the orphanage."

Lana gave a snort of disgust. "Mrs. Linden, who believes Colin has a willful streak that must be curbed."

Ignoring Lana's outburst, Zachariah continued. "I believe that now, more than ever, Mrs. VanEndel is beginning to wonder how to extricate herself from this dilemma." For the first time he smiled, and Lana realized that it wasn't a sweet lapdog he resembled, but rather a ferocious hound on the scent of prey. "It will be my job to help her find a way out of this while allowing her to save face."

JESSE ROLLED TO his side and reached out in his sleep for Lana. It was amazing how quickly he'd become accustomed to having her here with him. It was her scent that filled his lungs. Her taste that lingered on his lips long after their lovemaking.

He'd begun to look forward to their nights together. The anticipation had him watching the door until that moment when she would step inside, wearing some soft, drifting garment, her hair long and loose, her smile full of secrets.

When had the girl become a woman? A woman who had him completely bewitched. He'd never known such contentment.

Finding her side of the bed empty, he was fully awake and sitting up to peer into the darkness. "Lana?"

His room echoed only silence.

Puzzled, he dressed in haste and hurried down the hall to her suite of rooms. Without knocking, he entered the sitting room and could see, by the embers on the hearth, a shadowy figure just slipping out the window.

Dashing across the room, he peered into the darkness and watched as the figure dropped to the ground and started running.

With a muttered oath, he raced to his room to find his shoes and coat. Minutes later he was running across the lawn. Far ahead he could see Lana turning into the curving driveway of the VanEndel house.

Little fool!

With a string of curses, he ran like a madman to catch up to her.

* * *

LANA MADE HER way to the back door of the VanEndel mansion. Cook always left this door unlatched at night so the farmer who delivered fresh eggs and milk each morning could set his wares on the big kitchen table.

Pausing on the porch, she peered in the window. Seeing no lights and no sign of life, she reached for the door. Though she was intimately familiar with the kitchen area, she knew the living areas of the mansion were another matter.

How would she figure out which bedroom was Colin's?

No matter. She would simply tiptoe from room to room until she found the lad.

As she started to shove the door inward, a hand closed over her mouth, stilling the cry that sprang to her lips.

Her heart was pounding as she was pressed against the door. A mouth touched her ear, causing the hair at the back of her neck to prickle.

"Not a word."

"Jesse." As she breathed out his name, he covered her mouth with his hand.

"I said not a word."

"But I . . ."

Just then light spilled into the kitchen and footsteps headed toward them.

Quick as a flash Jesse flew down the steps, dragging Lana with him. Beside the porch he drew himself firmly against Lana, keeping them both in the dark as a maid stepped out, holding a glass of milk.

With a sigh she settled herself on the top step of the porch and slowly sipped her drink. Though it seemed an eternity before she finally stood and walked inside, it was actually only a few minutes.

As soon as the door was shut, Jesse closed a hand around Lana's arm and began dragging her away.

"No." She dug in her heels. "I have to . . ."

Without a word Jesse picked her up and carried her like a sack of flour over his shoulder. After checking to see that the driveway was empty, he strode along the path and cut across the lawn. It wasn't until they had left the VanEndel mansion behind that he finally set Lana on her feet.

She looked like some sort of wild creature caught in a bow-hunter's site. She was dressed in a pair of his pants, the long cuffs rolled to her ankles, an ascot tied at the waist to hold them up. Into this she'd tucked one of his shirts, the sleeves hanging over her hands.

Despite his fury, he couldn't help grinning. "The Beekman's masked ball isn't until next week. Too bad I've already ordered up our costumes from a shop on Lexington. I think New York society would enjoy seeing the Duchess of Fifth Avenue looking like this."

"How dare you carry me away before I could save Colin. You miserable, cowardly, son of a sow . . ."

He caught her by the arm and began dragging her toward their house. "Call me whatever you please, Lana. But if you'd have been caught inside the VanEndel mansion, you'd have lost your last chance to ever win custody of Colin."

"I can't wait any longer, Jesse. You heard Zachariah. Colin is suffering. I can't bear the thought of it."

"Zachariah said he'd get another . . ."

She shook her head. "Even if Zachariah should get the judge to allow another hearing, there's no way of knowing if I'll ever get custody of Colin. I can't afford to lose him again. I don't believe either of us would survive it."

"And so you thought you'd just climb up to the second story of the VanEndel mansion and kidnap the boy? God in heaven, Lana. How could you ever hope to get away with such an outrageous scheme?"

"You saw how easy it was. I know the layout of the first floor of the VanEndel house. Though I've only once been on the second floor, I figured I could find my way to Colin's room. From there we could just slip away before they discover him gone. Once we leave New York, we won't be recognized in Boston or Chicago."

He gave a hiss of disgust. "Kidnapping may be a solution in the short term, but think about what it will do to you and the boy for the rest of your lives. You'll spend a lifetime running, hiding, always looking over your shoulder. Is that what you want for Colin?"

"It's better than being locked in a room, with no one to love him, or hold him, or give him comfort." She turned away to hide her tears. "I can't bear thinking about my wee Colin being forced to live like that."

Jesse drew her back against him and wrapped his arms around her waist, pressing his face to her hair. "I know how much you love the boy, Lana. And I can't blame you for wanting to do anything, no matter how dangerous or foolish, to save him. Come home with me now. We'll come up with a better way."

"How?" She sniffed and wiped at her tears.

He turned her to him and tipped up her chin, staring into her eyes. "Maybe we could use your notoriety to our advantage once more."

"I don't understand."

"I believe it's time to share our news with Farley Fairchild, so he can announce it in the *New York News and Dispatch*."

"Our news?"

Jesse gave her one of his best rogue smiles. "The news that the Duke of Umberland and his cousin, Lady Alana Dunning Griffin Windsor, are engaged."

"But you've made it plain that you will do anything to avoid the trap of marriage. Why would you . . . ?"

"You're right, of course. I didn't say we'd actually marry. But I have no problem staging a mock engagement. After all, it's for a very good cause."

She hesitated as another thought intruded. "What if the judge should learn about our deceit?"

He merely smiled. "Let me worry about that."

Lana's eyes were as big as saucers in the moment before she threw her arms around his neck and hugged him fiercely. Her words were muffled against his neck. "You would do that for me, Jesse?"

He gathered her close and decided he rather liked playing the part of a hero, especially when the rewards were so satisfying. "It would be my pleasure, Duchess. And now, after all those nights of getting you out of your clothes, let's see how quickly we can get home and get you out of mine."

TWENTY-FOUR

———◆◆◆◆———

"YOUR LORDSHIP." FARLEY Fairchild arrived at Central Park, breathless and rumpled. "I can't tell you how honored I am to be allowed to break this news."

"You've been most kind to my cousin since her arrival in your country, and we both thought this was the perfect way to thank you." Jesse lay a hand on Lana's. "My darling, this is the reporter from the *New York News and Dispatch.*"

"Mr. Fairchild." Lana extended her hand, and the reporter hesitated for a fraction, as though debating whether to shake hands or bow before kissing it.

In the end, the offered a limp handshake before indicating his ever-present photographer. "I hope you don't think me too bold? I'd like a picture for tomorrow's edition."

"Not at all." Jesse was all charm. "How about the two of us in front of the carousel?" He smiled down into Lana's upturned face before adding, "It's a particular favorite of ours."

The reporter was already scribbling in his notebook as

the handsome couple positioned themselves in front of the carousel. While the photographer snapped a picture, Farley fed them all the questions he dared.

"Did you get down on one knee to propose, your grace?"

"Indeed. It wouldn't be proper unless I followed protocol, now, would it?"

The two men shared a knowing smile. "And you, Duchess . . . I mean, Lady Alana?" Farley's cheeks colored, the only sign that he was aware of his little slip of the tongue. "Where you expecting this? Or were you caught by surprise?"

"A bit of both, I'm afraid." Lana glanced at Jesse from beneath her lashes and hoped she wasn't overdoing the acting. "The attraction was always there, but it was only after I arrived in America that we both admitted to our feelings."

"Will the wedding be here, or would you prefer the ceremony be held in your own country?"

Out of the corner of his eye Jesse saw that the photographer was ready for another shot.

"We haven't made a decision on that yet." Jesse caught Lana's hand and lifted it to his lips just as the flash momentarily blinded them.

Satisfied, Jesse signaled to his driver, and the carriage started toward them.

If Farley Fairchild was disappointed that the interview was ended, he was savvy enough to realize that he'd scooped every other newspaper in the city.

As Jesse helped Lana into the carriage, he called, "Thank you, your grace. Lady Alana. I'll never forget this kindness. I'm in your debt."

Jesse lifted a hand in a salute before the carriage carried them away. When they were safely out of sight he brushed a kiss over Lana's cheek. "Well done, Duchess. I do believe you're as good a con as I've ever met."

"Thank you. And since you've probably met them all, I'll count that as a high compliment indeed."

"I SUPPOSE IT'S only proper that I offer my congratulations." Withers extended his hand, and Jesse clasped it just as Lana stepped into the library. "Even an imaginary engagement calls for a celebratory handshake."

The entire household was gathered around Jesse's desk. They looked up as Lana walked toward them, and she knew, by the looks on their faces, that Jesse had told them everything.

"Look at this." Maria thrust the newspaper toward her. "You've made the front page."

"Of the society section," Lana corrected.

"Of the entire *New York News and Dispatch*." The housekeeper pointed to the headline.

"My word." Lana studied the photograph taken the previous day, showing Jesse and Lana, smiling broadly in front of the carousel in Central Park. Below was a caption that read:

Duchess of Fifth Avenue engaged to wed cousin, England's Duke of Umberland.

Colette was pouting. "Why a carousel, *cherie*? Couldn't you have picked something more glamorous?"

"It was Jesse's idea." Lana smiled, remembering. "I'd told him how much Colin enjoyed going to the park and riding the carousel, and it just seemed the perfect place to meet the reporter and photographer. After all, we didn't want them coming here."

The others accepted that without comment. They were, after all, a most curious household.

"But why the *News and Dispatch*?" Maria asked.

Jesse stepped around his desk. "We did it as a favor to Farley Fairchild."

Lana busied herself folding the newspaper.

"I still say we should have planned a proper engagement party." Maria was wringing her hands. "On such a momentous occasion, there should be music and dancing and champagne. We could still plan something . . ."

"That isn't necessary." At Lana's brisk dismissal, the others studied her with new interest.

It was Nadia who broke the silence. "I understand how much you chafe at these lies. But if you are to convince society that you two are serious, there should be an engagement party."

Jesse broke in smoothly, "Lana and I aren't feeling up to a party just now. We'd rather put all our energy into the looming custody battle."

Maria looked hopefully toward Lana. "Does this mean that you will soon be taking custody of the lad?"

Lana bit her lip. "We're hopeful that this might encourage the judge to reconsider his earlier decision, but as our lawyer has warned us, anything is possible."

"Exactly." Getting into the spirit of the charade, the housekeeper patted Lana's hand. "We will hold to that thought. Anything is possible."

"IT DOESN'T SEEM fair that, while we are denied a celebration, the rest of society seems to be doing nothing but celebrating your engagement." Maria pointed to yet another society report in the daily paper. "It would seem that every dinner party, every social event, has been an occasion of celebration."

Jesse sighed. "We've been toasted with champagne and forced to endure endless speeches about the joys and benefits of married life, especially from those who seem least joyful in their own marriage."

With Lana nowhere to be seen, he and the others were free to enjoy a good laugh at his statement.

* * *

AT THE BEEKMAN masked ball, Evelyn VanEndel was overheard in the ladies' parlor telling a cluster of women, "It will be the most spectacular wedding of the season. Of any season, according to Enid."

Spotting Lana, Evelyn gave a thin smile. "I understand congratulations are in order for you, as well."

"As well?" Lana wondered where this was leading.

Anya Davis put in quickly, "Enid's father is so delighted, he has promised her the most spectacular wedding of the season." She added with a laugh, "Or of any season." She turned to Evelyn. "We're all so happy to see Wilton and Enid together at last. They make a splendid couple."

Finally Lana understood. "Your son and Enid Morgenthall are getting married? Oh, that's such happy news." And of course, Enid's father was wealthy enough to wipe his soon-to-be-son-in-law's debts clean.

"Thank you." While the others refreshed their makeup and hair, Evelyn drew Lana toward a private corner of the room. "It wasn't very kind of you to permit me to bare my son's feelings for you when you were contemplating marriage to your cousin."

"I assure you, Evelyn, this sudden engagement was as much a surprise to us as it was to the world."

"You mean you didn't know about these plans when we last met?"

Lana shook her head. "Truly I didn't. Nor did Jesse, I'm certain. It's just . . . one of those delightful surprises that happens between people who have sometimes known each other for a lifetime. Just as . . ." she quickly added, "you've discovered with Enid and Wilton."

"Indeed." Evelyn looked relieved. "I can't tell you how foolish I felt when I read about your engagement in the paper, knowing how recently I'd approached you about marriage to my son. Of course, at that time, I had no idea he was losing his heart to another."

Lana was suffering such guilt, she actually took the woman's hand in hers before saying earnestly, "I am flattered that you would consider me worthy of such an honor. I do hope we can still be friends."

Evelyn's brows arched in surprise. Linking her arm with Lana's, she whispered, "Come. Let's join the men in the other room." As they made their way to the ballroom, the older woman leaned close to ask, "It's going to be such fun making plans for a lavish wedding, isn't it?" Without waiting for Lana's response she added, "I don't know about you, but I barely have time for all the details." And then, almost as an afterthought, she whispered, "Are you still interested in adopting your friend's child?"

"JUST DON'T GET your hopes up too high." Jesse kept his arm around Lana's shoulders as the carriage carried them to the courthouse.

"But Evelyn seemed genuinely agreeable to giving up the responsibility, now that she's to be involved in planning her son's wedding."

"Maybe. But we have to be prepared for any eventuality." He helped her down when the carriage came to a stop and tucked her hand in his as they made their way inside.

"Exactly." She leaned close. "There's still Judge Lawrence to contend with. I remember how coldly he sealed Colin's fate, and realize he won't be so easily swayed as the VanEndels."

Jesse merely nodded without bothering to enlighten Lana about the card game he'd attended with the judge and several well-placed officials from the city. It had taken considerable skill to lose to Judge Lawrence, who had turned out to be one of the most inept gamblers Jesse had ever had the misfortune to meet. He wondered how a man with such a fine mind couldn't figure out that three deuces would beat a pair of aces. One time, when the judge had dropped his cards on the floor, Jesse had gallantly picked them up, trading the king from his own hand and palming a four of clubs in its place. The difference between those two cards meant the judge won the largest jackpot of the evening. Of course, Judge Lawrence had no idea he was in Jesse's debt. Nor would he ever know it. Still, he might be disposed to look kindly on a poker-playing partner who was there to witness such a spectacular display of skill. At least Jesse hoped it was so.

"Here you are." Zachariah, standing outside the door, led the way into the judge's chambers.

Evelyn and Gustav VanEndel were there, along with their three lawyers. After handshakes, everyone settled down to wait for the judge.

When the door to his inner chambers opened, Lana pressed a hand to her stomach. She couldn't bear it if she lost custody again. And yet, she'd had no choice but to place her trust in these two men. She glanced at Zachariah, shaggy hair badly in need of a trim, jacket unbuttoned, tie askew. And then she shot a glance at Jesse, sitting solemnly beside her. He turned his head ever so slightly and winked. Her heart did a funny little dance in her chest, and she wondered again, as she had so often, what it was about this actor that caused her to trust him.

The judge took a seat behind his desk and opened a folder before steepling his fingers and peering at the assembled. "We are here to revisit a decision regarding custody of the orphan, Colin O'Malley."

He turned to the couple seated with their three lawyers. "Evelyn and Gustav VanEndel, I see by this document that you have spent weeks working with the child, whom you now deem mute and uneducable. The director of the orphan asylum concurs and recommends that the child should spend the rest of his life in a facility for the mentally insane. I understand that it is your reluctant decision to abide by her superior knowledge of such things and return the boy to the custody of the state of New York."

They answered in turn, "It is."

He turned to Lana, who appeared stunned. "Have you been fully apprised of the child's disabilities?"

Disabilities? They thought her wonderful, bright, sweet Colin impossible to educate?

She couldn't find her voice. Instead she nodded, while her lawyer answered for her. "We have, your honor."

"And still, knowing the difficulties that lie ahead, you petition for custody?"

Zachariah spoke firmly. "We do."

The judge began to read from the document opened on his desktop. "This Court wishes to state its gratitude to Evelyn and Gustav VanEndel for their patience and forbearance in what must have been a particularly painful situation. That they wished to use their finances and social standing to improve the lot of an immigrant to our shores is most praiseworthy."

Evelyn shot a triumphant smile at her husband, while Lana grasped Jesse's hand so tightly he almost winced.

The judge turned a page and read further. "It is the decision of this Court, in the case of the orphan Colin O'Malley, that, in compliance to the verbal request of the child's deceased mother, temporary custody will be granted to the petitioner, an unmarried lady, with the provision that permanent custody will be granted only after she weds, and the court's officers have thoroughly inspected the home in which the child will be raised."

Without a backward glance, the judge closed his file, pushed away from his desk, and walked from the room.

Evelyn and Gustav seemed absolutely delighted with the judge's words of praise, which had already been echoed by their friends. Their tale of woe about the orphan to whom they had opened their home had earned them near-sainthood in the eyes of society.

They hurried over to offer their congratulations to Lana and Jesse.

"My dear," Evelyn closed a hand over Lana's. "I think it very noble of you to take in this poor child, just to keep a promise to his mother. I'm sure, once you return him to England, you'll be able to find a suitable institution where he will be made comfortable for the rest of his life."

"Thank you, Evelyn." Lana was struggling to keep her expression bland, but the euphoria growing inside was threatening to unravel her best intentions.

"And now . . ." Evelyn tucked her arm in the crook of her husband's. "We have a grand wedding to plan, without the turmoil that has been in our midst these past weeks."

They strode from the chambers, followed by their lawyers, leaving Lana alone with Jesse and Zachariah.

She turned to her lawyer first. "I don't know how to thank you, Zachariah. I'm so very grateful for all you've done."

"You're more than welcome, Lana. I just hope you're as grateful a few weeks from now. According to the report I read of Colin's stay in the VanEndel household, the lad was a bit of a handful."

"I'm not worried. When will I see him?"

He picked up his shabby valise stuffed with documents. "A woman from the orphanage will bring him later today. I'm told the state of New York is more than happy to see a troublesome child placed in a home, even," he added with a wink, "that of an unmarried lady."

After shaking hands with Jesse, the lawyer walked away.

Lana turned to Jesse, eyes shining. "You did it."

He closed a hand over hers and brushed a kiss over her lips. "We did it."

She studied him from beneath her lashes. "You heard what the judge said about not granting permanent custody until after I'm wed."

He gave her his best smile. "We'll cross that bridge later." He linked her arm with his. "For now, let's go home and get ready for a very important houseguest."

"Do I hear a carriage?" Lana flew to the window to peer at the curving drive, which, to her dismay, was still empty.

"He will be here soon, *cherie*." Colette was wearing a festive gown of pale orchid that draped fluidly over her body, revealing every line and curve. When Lana had first seen her, she'd thought to ask the woman to change. It hardly seemed the sort of day dress appropriate for welcoming a child. What if the people from the orphanage should see her and change their minds about allowing the lad to remain? But Colette was as excited as the others, and for that Lana was too grateful to risk dampening her spirits.

"Have you thought what you will say to him?" Nadia sat by the window, her fingers busy sewing a piece of white cotton with fine, even stitches.

"I can't think." Lana twisted her hands together and walked over for yet another peek out the window.

She was wearing her best day dress of fine rose silk. At Lana's request, Rosa had piled her hair high on her head and secured it with jeweled combs. Lana was taking no chance on looking less than dignified, for fear the woman from the orphanage might be reporting back to the judge.

Clara entered carrying a fancy crystal plate. "I've baked sugar cookies. Children have always loved them."

"That was kind of you, Clara."

The cook merely smiled and joined the rest who were eagerly awaiting the arrival of the boy. They'd heard so much about this mysterious, troubled lad, and had watched Lana fight so desperately to have him with her. Her fight had become theirs, as well. And her victory had somehow become theirs.

"I believe I hear a carriage now," Maria announced.

At once everyone began peering out the window as a plain black rig and tired-looking horse rounded the drive and slowed at the steps.

Withers opened the door and Lana, too impatient to remain in the doorway, lifted her skirts and danced out the door and down the steps.

A woman from the orphanage stepped down, followed by Colin, who stared hard at his scuffed shoes.

"Lady Alana." The woman bowed slightly. "Here is the boy." She caught Colin's hand and drew him forward, all the while holding Lana's gaze. "These are the clothes he was wearing when he came to our orphanage. Our director, Mrs. Linden, hoped you wouldn't object to her decision to keep the fine wardrobe given him by the VanEndel's to be used by those less-fortunate orphans who must remain under our care."

"Of course not. I'll be more than happy to provide new clothes for Colin."

"Well then. Mrs. Linden wanted you to know that if there is anything she can do to help, any advice you might need in dealing with the boy's many problems, you have only to ask."

"Please thank Mrs. Linden for me."

The woman released Colin's hand. "This is to be your new mother, and this is your new home." With that she turned away and stepped into the rig, calling to the driver, "Let's be off."

As the horse leaned into the harness, the woman stared straight ahead, without a single backward glance.

Lana waited until they were out of sight before kneeling down in front of the lad. "Don't you remember me, Colin? Have I changed so much?"

He merely studied the ground.

"I'm your Auntie Lana."

There was no flicker of recognition in those haunted blue eyes.

With a sigh, Lana caught his hand in hers and led him up the steps. Inside, the others had gathered around the foyer to welcome him. Seeing all the strange faces peering down at him, hearing all those voices speaking in unfamiliar dialects, he shrank back against the door, only to find Withers standing there, looking down his nose at the pale, thin child.

Seeing the pain in Lana's eyes, Jesse dropped to his knees in front of the boy. "Hello, Colin. My name's Jesse."

Two red-rimmed eyes looked away, unwilling to meet his gaze.

"I'll bet you're hungry," Clara called.

The boy merely lowered his head further.

"Tell you what." Jesse picked him up and felt him stiffen in his arms. Quickly setting him on his feet, he motioned for Lana to take the boy's hand. "Why don't we take Colin upstairs and show him his room. And then we'll let him decide if he'd like to stay there or explore the rest of the house."

Grateful, Lana caught Colin's hand and followed Jesse up the stairs.

The others stood below, watching and speculating softly on the best way to ease the lad's fears.

"Food," said Clara firmly. "Good food can do wonders for a growing boy."

"Music," Colette said with a sigh. "Music can soothe the most wounded of hearts."

"Clothes that fit." Nadia held up the soft nightshirt she'd been sewing, small enough to fit the lad.

"Discipline," Withers said sternly. "The boy just needs a firm hand."

"A feeling of safety." Maria watched as Lana and Jesse, walking on either side of the boy, disappeared along the upper hall. "He's been given no chance to feel safe since his mother died."

"Love." Rosa clasped her hands together, eyes shining. "With enough love, he'll be fine. If anyone can love him, it's our Lana."

They fell silent and slowly began drifting back to their own rooms, hoping the little maid was right.

TWENTY-FIVE

———————

"IT'S BEEN FIVE days now." Maria moved about the dining room, overseeing the morning service. "Five days, and I've not heard the lad speak."

"I've been singing to him whenever I go to his room." Colette sighed. "I can still recall Mama singing to me when I was little. I was so hoping it would ease the lad's fears."

"I've made him fine little shirts and pants, and the softest underdrawers I could." Nadia held up her latest creation. "He wears whatever he is told to wear, but he seems not to notice."

"His eyes are so sad." Rosa turned to look out the window. "The saddest little eyes I've ever seen. It just breaks my heart."

Withers cleared his throat. "Hush now. Our Lana is coming."

As they did each time they saw her, the others put on a good face and did their best to talk about the fine weather, the latest society gossip, even the state of New York politics. Anything except the one thing that was on all their minds.

* * *

JESSE PACED HIS room, wondering what he could do to help Lana through this terrible situation.

Lana. He missed her. Missed having her here in his arms. In his bed. Since the boy had arrived, she'd spent every waking minute with him. At night she held the lad until he fell asleep and then dozed in a chair beside his bed, lest he should wake in the night afraid and alone. Each morning she hurried out at dawn to dress in her finest gown, her hair arranged just so, hoping this would be the day to celebrate with her long-lost Colin. But each day, the lad awoke looking lost and confused, without any sign of recognition of the woman who had devoted all her energy to his rescue.

What were they missing? What more could they do to pull this little boy out of his sorrow? Where had he gone in his mind that he couldn't even remember the woman who loved him so desperately?

In all the time here, they had yet to hear Colin say a single word. At Lana's coaxing, he ate what was put before him, but when he thought nobody was looking, he hid food in his pockets. Lana found food hidden around his bedroom, though it didn't appear that he'd actually eaten any of it.

The lad had resisted leaving the room and showed no interest in exploring his new home. Instead, he seemed content to sit at the little table Lana had installed in his room, listening to her as she chatted on about things she thought he might remember. His mother, his father, neighbors he'd once known in their crowded tenement—none of them seemed to spark any recognition in those lifeless little eyes.

Everyone in the household was concerned, and yet they were all feeling equally helpless.

Jesse stopped his pacing. He couldn't allow Lana to deal with this alone. Though he wasn't certain just what good he could possibly do for this strange little lad, he had to try.

He made his way along the hallway and paused outside the door to Colin's room. Hearing no sounds from within, he opened the door and peered inside. A fire burned on the hearth. He walked to the bed. Seeing no one there, he glanced around and saw the shadowy outline of something in the corner of the room. Walking closer he realized that Lana had made a nest of blankets and pillows on the floor and was lying beside a sleeping Colin.

Seeing Jesse, she touched a finger to her lips.

He knelt beside her. "Trying something new, are you?"

She nodded. "I remembered what Zachariah had said about Colin sleeping on the floor at the VanEndel house. I thought this might help, but I don't want him to wake and find himself alone in yet another strange new place. I need to be here for him, Jesse."

Without a word, Jesse reached for a pillow and stretched out beside her.

She touched a hand to his. "You don't need to do this."

"I want to." He pulled her close for a long, slow kiss. "This is probably the only way I'll get to sleep with you now. And besides . . ." He winked. "I'm not about to let you two have all the fun."

LANA SNUGGLED DEEPER into the blanket and was warmed by the now-familiar press of Jesse's arm flung around her waist. The feather bed seemed unusually hard and she rolled over, searching for a more comfortable spot.

Suddenly she became aware of where she was. Not Jesse's bed, but the floor of Colin's room.

Colin.

She was instantly awake. When her eyes opened, she saw, by the light of the embers on the grate, Colin, sitting up beside her, peering intently at her face.

Without a word he reached a hand to her hair, now spilling soft and loose around her shoulders. With a look of wonder he touched her face, tracing the curve of her brow, the softness of her cheek, the shape of her mouth.

The movements had Jesse waking. He lay beside Lana, watching in silence.

The boy appeared awestruck for the longest time as he studied the face he had carried in his memory for such a long, long time. Then came his breathless whisper. "Auntie Lana?"

For the space of a heartbeat Lana couldn't seem to find her voice. Had he actually spoken? Or had she simply dreamed it because she'd wanted it so desperately?

"Yes, my darling. I was hoping you'd remember me. I'm your Auntie Lana."

"Where have you been?"

She felt as if she'd just taken a sword to her heart. "I'm sorry it took so long. I've been doing my best to get you out of that place."

"They wouldn't let me look for you." His sad blue eyes filled with tears. "They took me away, and I couldn't find you. I couldn't find Mum. I couldn't find anybody."

"I know." Lana sat up and gathered him to her. "But we're together now, Colin, and I give you my word, nobody will ever separate us again."

"Promise?" His little voice was muffled against her shoulder.

"Promise." She knew her own tears were spilling down her face and wetting his hair, but she couldn't seem to stop. Nothing mattered now except that Colin was finally here with her, and remembering. At long last, remembering.

Jesse sat up and gathered them both into his arms, pressing a kiss to a tangle of hair at her temple.

They stayed that way for the longest time.

Safe, Lana thought as she absorbed each steady beat of Colin's heart inside her own chest. Finally, he was safe with her. As the minutes wore on, she realized that she could feel Jesse's heartbeat as well. Strong and measured and steady.

If she could, she would stay this way forever. Locked in Jesse's arms, and holding firmly to Colin. Because forever was too much to wish for, and because she'd already been granted her heart's desire, she would simply savor this moment and not risk the wrath of the fates by asking for more.

IN THE DAYS that followed, the boy Lana had once known began slowly emerging from the sad, sickly little boy who had been brought to her doorstep. And with each day, she watched the interaction between the lad and this strange band of actors who surrounded Jesse.

"Oh, look at you." Nadia was beaming when Colin came down the stairs, walking between Lana and Jesse and wearing the white shirt and dark blue short pants she'd made for him.

He clung nervously to Lana's hand, peering out from behind her skirts at these strangers who seemed to fill every room of the big house.

"Nadia was the kind lady who made your clothes, Colin." Lana paused and looked down at him. "What do you have to say to her?"

"Thank you, Nadia."

"You're most welcome. Next I think I make you a little coat, like the one Jesse wears."

She saw the boy's eyes widen at that and realized she'd snagged his interest. "*Dah.* A little coat and maybe boots to match." To Maria she added, "This will be such fun. I always wanted to have a little one of my very own to sew for."

The housekeeper pointed to a pile of books that had been stacked on one of the chairs at the table to accommodate the little boy's size. "Would you care to sit here, Colin?"

"You did this for me?" He stared at the books and then at Maria's smiling face.

"Indeed. I'm so pleased that you're ready to begin taking your meals with us now."

"Thank you." He allowed Jesse to lift him onto the books, where he perched as tall as the adults.

"Here you are." Clara entered the dining room and rounded the table to stand beside Colin's place. "I've made you something special."

"Gruel?" he asked politely.

That had everyone smiling.

"There is no gruel in this house. I made you crepes."

"What is that?"

The cook looked startled. "You've never tasted crepes?"

The little boy shook his head.

"Then you must try them and see if they're to your liking." She lifted the lid from a silver tray and placed one on his plate before adding warm cherry glaze.

Colin studied the round flat pancake with disinterest. But after his first bite, his smile widened and he managed to say, around a mouthful, "This is good."

Clara's face was wreathed with smiles. "Of course it is. And if you want more, you need only ask."

When she walked away the boy glanced at Lana. "Am I truly allowed as many as I want?"

"Truly." But despite her assurance, she saw him tuck the last of the sticky confection into his pocket for good measure. The sight of it caused a twinge of regret, knowing how often he must have gone to sleep hungry in the days after Siobhan's death.

Still, hadn't she done the same after leaving the foundling home? In time he would learn to trust again. Until then, she would make certain she was always nearby to ease whatever fears should arise.

When the breakfast ended Colette danced into the room and Colin's eyes followed every fluid movement. It was impossible not to watch someone so graceful, so flamboyant.

This morning there was a childish, playful look to the French woman that Lana had never seen before.

Colette smiled at Colin. "If you are finished with your morning meal, *ma petite,* I have a treat for you."

"A treat?"

"*Oui.*" She stepped out the door and retrieved something. "Look. A hoop and a stick. Do you know how to use them?"

He nodded. "I never had one, but Giovanni Genovese and I used to see some of the boys playing with them in the street."

Lana felt a wild rush of hope. This was the first time Colin had voluntarily mentioned someone from his former life.

Colette held out her hand. "Then come with me, little one, and we'll try our hand at it. If you'd like, we'll learn together."

As eager as he was to play, the little boy seemed unwilling to leave Lana. Seeing his distress, she pushed away from the table. "Would you mind if I watched?"

Relieved, he got to his feet and followed Colette outside, keeping Lana in his line of vision.

Jesse watched from the open doorway before strolling down the steps to join them.

At Lana's arched brow he shrugged. "Just thought I'd see how it's done."

As he joined Colin, Maria stepped up behind Lana to whisper, "Haven't you heard? Men are just boys at heart, only bigger."

The two women shared a laugh as they stood together, watching the man and boy and the French woman dashing about the curving driveway chasing after a hoop.

The sound of so much laughter had Lana touching a hand to her heart. How was it possible, she wondered, that something as simple as this should fill her heart with such joy?

* * *

LANA PAUSED OUTSIDE Colin's room. Hearing the sound of singing, she looked inside. In a chair by the window, Colette was rocking the little boy while singing a lullaby in French.

"What does it mean?" he asked.

"It is about a little boy who is lost. He wanders through a forest and suddenly he finds a kitten and the two of them play."

"Does he find his home?"

"He does. But first he must wander for many days. He sleeps in the cottage of a kind old woman and one night in a barn with a friendly horse."

"I lost my home." He yawned and snuggled his head against the French woman's shoulder.

"And now you've found a new one."

"With my Auntie Lana and all of you." His eyes closed.

"You are a very lucky little boy, *ma petite,* to have a loving aunt. To have, in fact, so many loving relatives."

Lana moved away, blinking back tears. Each day, thanks to the kindness of these good people, Colin moved closer to finding his way back.

"I BAKED YOUR favorite sugar cookies." Clara found Colin in the solarium with Colette and Nadia.

"Thank you, Clara." The little boy picked up a cookie and took a bite before setting it down.

Watching from across the room, Lana realized that he hadn't tucked the rest of it in his pocket.

"Listen to this, Clara." Colin's little face was animated. "Nadia was telling me about the time she and the Tsarina, that's a Russian queen, isn't that right, Nadia?"

"*Dah,* little one."

"Anyway, they were in a sled, wrapped in furs and pulled

by two big horses, when the horses bolted and took them on a wild ride down a mountainside." Colin's eyes were as big as the cookies on Clara's plate. "Weren't you afraid, Nadia?"

"Terrified. But there was nothing to do but hold on and pray the horses wouldn't lose their footing."

"Did they?"

The Russian woman laughed. "If they had, I wouldn't be here to tell the tale. In no time one of the Tsar's soldiers caught the harness and brought the sled to a halt. But though it lasted just a few minutes, it seemed like hours while it was happening."

Colin seemed to consider that a moment. "Does time always seem longer when you're afraid?"

"I believe so, little one." She ruffled his hair just as Jesse stepped into the room. She turned to include Jesse and Lana in the conversation. "He has such lovely golden curls, does he not?"

Lana nodded. "I've always loved Colin's curls."

"Curls?" Jesse stepped closer. "Curls are for girls." He caught hold of Colin's hand. "Come with me, little man."

Lana looked horrified. "Where are we going?"

Jesse winked at Colin. "We're going out to do man's work. You're staying here with the ladies."

Colin paused in the doorway to cast a quick, worried glance at Lana before disappearing.

By the time Lana reached the front door, she was told by Withers that Jesse and Colin had gone to the stable, but before she could follow them, she was forced to watch them departing along the driveway in the carriage.

As the women gathered around her, they could see her agitation.

Maria took hold of Lana's trembling hands. "You have to know that Jesse would never hurt the lad."

"Not knowingly, of course." Lana sighed. "But Colin's father was a tyrant. I'm certain the lad carries scars from such treatment. Oh, don't you see? Finding himself alone with Jesse might send him back into his shell." Inconsolable, she turned away from the others. "All our hard work could well be rendered useless by the time they return."

Even Withers seemed disheartened as he joined the others in watching Lana climb the stairs to her room.

"Auntie Lana! Auntie Lana!"

At Colin's shouts, Lana raced from her room and down the stairs. By the time she got there, the others, having heard the shouts, were coming from all parts of the mansion to join her in the foyer.

"What is it, love? What's happened?"

"Look." The little boy turned around, then back, with a smile as radiant as the sun. "Uncle Jesse took me for a haircut just like his."

"Uncle Jesse?" She glanced from the boy to the man. Both were wearing identical smiles.

"Boys should never be forced to wear curls." He turned to Colin with a wink. "Isn't that right?"

"It is, yes. And after our haircuts, Uncle Jesse took me for a ride through the park. He let me ride the carousel, and we stopped to buy an apple from a vendor. And then he took me shopping at a . . ." He turned to Jesse for help.

"A gentlemen's shop," Jesse prompted.

"And he bought me this." Colin held up a package wrapped in brown paper and handed it to Lana.

She opened it to find a jaunty little cap. "Oh, isn't that fine?"

Colin nodded. "Uncle Jesse said I must never wear it indoors. Only outside. And when we got to the driveway, he let me sit with the driver and hold the reins. In the stable he let me sit on a horse's back. And I petted one of the barn cats. Uncle Jesse said I can pet the cats whenever I want, as long as I ask permission of Withers first, because I can't go to the stables alone." He swiveled his head, peering up at the tall, white-haired butler. "Is that right, Withers? Will you go with me whenever I want to go to the stables?"

The butler stood a little taller, looking not only surprised, but immensely pleased. "I'd be honored to accompany you, Master Colin."

"Thank you, Withers." Colin looked beyond Lana to Colette, who was standing on the bottom stair. "You know that word you taught me? *Gato?* I met a *gato* in the stables."

"That's grand, *ma petite.* Soon you'll be talking to that *gato* in French. Now wouldn't that be grand?"

"*Oui.*"

At his unexpected reply, the entire company burst into laughter, while Colette merely beamed.

When she hoped the others weren't looking, Lana wiped a tear from her eyes. If she wasn't careful, she warned herself, she might very soon turn into a blithering crybaby.

TWENTY-SIX

———◆◆◆———

"HAVE YOU SEEN this?" Maria dropped a copy of the *New York News and Dispatch* on Jesse's desk.

He read the entire column, which was devoted to speculation about the coming nuptials of the Duchess of Fifth Avenue, including a list of the English royals who might be invited.

He tossed it aside with a careless shrug. "Nothing new. Farley Fairchild just wants to tease his readers a bit. He's been begging me to give him details."

Lana paused in the doorway, looking as fresh as a summer day in pale pink silk. It occurred to Jesse that he'd never seen her looking so relaxed. Now that Colin had warmed to all of them, she was sleeping better, even though she still left Jesse's bed each night to look in on the lad. Most nights he joined her, watching the way the boy slept, his dreams easy, his rest undisturbed. It felt so good, standing beside the lad's bed, knowing they'd made a difference in his life.

Having Colin in their lives had added a layer of tenderness to their relationship. Though he'd fretted that Lana would become distracted, it had the opposite effect. If anything, their lovemaking had taken on a new urgency, as though they were driven to make each night as special as possible.

Maria persisted. "You aren't concerned that people are beginning to wonder why you haven't set a firm date?"

Jesse smiled. "When have you ever known me to worry about what others think?"

"Think about what?" Lana strolled into the office and looked from Maria to Jesse.

"This." The housekeeper handed her the newspaper and started toward the door. "I'll see if breakfast is ready."

Lana read Farley's society column without expression. When she was finished she looked over at Jesse. "They're expecting a wedding."

"Then we'll give them what they want."

Her eyes widened. "I know how you feel about marriage."

"True enough, but now there's Colin to consider." Seeing that she was about to protest, he said quickly, "It doesn't have to be a real wedding, Lana, any more than the engagement was real."

He glanced over as Colin danced into the room, looking eager and breathless.

"Rosa said you're taking us someplace special, Uncle Jesse."

He nodded. "I am indeed, little man. I have a surprise for both you and your Auntie Lana."

Intrigued, Lana turned to him. "Where are you taking us?"

He merely winked. "First breakfast. Clara's gone to a lot of trouble, and we wouldn't want to disappoint her, would we?"

Colin was fidgeting. "Did she make me crepes?"

"She may have, though I believe I smelled cinnamon when I passed the kitchen earlier."

"Cinnamon biscuits." The little boy clapped his hands. "My favorites."

"Imagine that. Mine, too." Jesse caught Colin's hand, and the two started toward the door. Halfway across the room Jesse paused and turned to Lana. "Coming?"

"Of course." She put aside the nagging little thought that worried the edges of her mind and followed them to the dining room, where the others had already gathered.

"ST. PATRICK'S?" LANA turned to Jesse with an arched brow.

Without a word of explanation, he helped her down from the carriage and then lifted Colin down before taking both their hands in his.

They skirted the church and started toward the cemetery in back. That's when Lana realized what he'd done.

"Siobhan's grave. How did you find her?"

"I asked Zachariah to do a search. Once her grave was found in the pauper's cemetery, it was a simple matter to have her moved here."

Simple. Lana could only imagine the paperwork and money it had cost to arrange all this.

"It shames me to think of the way I squandered the money you'd given me."

"Not another word about that." Jesse dropped an arm around her shoulders. "She has a proper place to rest now."

"What about Billy?"

He gave a quick shake of his head, keeping his voice low enough that Colin wouldn't hear. "Zachariah is working on it, but so far, he hasn't been able to locate where he was buried. We'll find it. It's just a matter of time."

"Here we are." Jesse nodded and paused before a marble headstone depicting a mother holding a child in her arms.

The carving read simply: *Siobhan Riley O'Malley. 1870–1890. Beloved wife, mother, and friend.*

He knelt down beside Colin, who was mouthing the words he was struggling to make out on the headstone. "This is where your mother is buried. Do you remember her?"

The lad gave a quick nod of his head. "Mum had golden hair, and she looked like an angel." He turned to Lana. "Didn't she, Auntie Lana?"

"She did. And she loved you more than anything in this world."

They stayed a long time, kneeling beside the mound of earth, tracing the words on the headstone, and remembering all the little things about Siobhan that had them laughing and weeping.

When at last they turned to leave, Colin said gravely, "Mum shoved me out of the way of the horse and cart."

Lana stopped in her tracks. This was the first he'd spoken about that fateful day. "You remember?"

"I do." He nodded.

"Did you see anything else?" She hesitated, wondering if she had the right to prod. "The driver of the rig, perhaps?"

He stared hard at the ground. "When I looked up, the cart was moving away, and all I could see was my mum, lying in the street. I kept telling her to get up, but she wouldn't move. And then a crowd of people gathered around and someone said my da was dead in the next street, and a police officer said I had to go with him. And then . . ." His lips trembled and he swallowed back the rest of the words.

"You're safe now, Colin." Lana paused to kneel in front of him and gather him close. "And I'll do everything in my power to keep you safe always."

She stood, carrying him in her arms, following Jesse to their waiting carriage. "Whenever you feel like visiting your mum's grave, we'll bring you here. But remember, love, she isn't really there."

"Where is she then?"

"She's in heaven now, Colin."

"With the angels?"

Lana nodded. "You said she looked like one." Lana touched a hand to the lad's heart. "But she's also here, inside you. And inside my heart, too."

"Forever?"

"She is. Yes. For as long as we can remember her."

Jesse helped them both into the carriage.

On the ride home, Lana lifted her face to the sunlight and wondered at the lightness around her heart. Beside her, Colin was happily chirping the little song Colette had taught him, oblivious to the painful past he was already putting away.

She turned to Jesse with tear-bright eyes. "This was a kind and thoughtful thing you did, Jesse, and I'll not soon forget it."

He leaned close to brush a kiss over her lips and found himself marveling at the fact that his own happiness seemed to grow in direct proportion to hers.

When had this woman's happiness become so important to him? One moment he'd been living exactly as he chose, enjoying the luxury of answering to no one. Now here he was, taking pleasure in the simplest of things, so long as they brought a smile to Lana's eyes.

It defied logic. And yet, there it was. He was hopelessly, happily, wildly in love, and he didn't care if the whole world should know it.

JESSE SMILED AT Withers and handed him his coat before patting the little jeweler's box in his pocket. There was no answering smile from the butler.

Instead he leaned close to whisper, "There's a problem. Maria needs to talk to you."

"Tell her I'll be in the library."

Before he could take a seat behind his desk, Maria paused in the doorway with Rosa, Colette, and Nadia crowding around behind her. "Something has happened. I believe you should go up to Lana at once."

"Where is she?"

"In her room."

"Packing," Rosa added ominously.

"Packing?" Jesse's smile turned to a frown. "Why in the world would she be packing?"

The little maid was clasping and unclasping her hands.

"It is my fault," Colette said sadly. "Lana asked me about the wedding, and I told her I thought it was very brave of you to give up your freedom for the sake of her and the lad."

"You what?" Jesse's eyes narrowed on the French woman.

"Do not blame Colette." Nadia stepped forward. "I told Lana much the same thing when she asked."

Jesse swore. Before he could say another word Maria faced him. "Neither of these good women are to blame. You've made no secret of how you feel about marriage."

"That was before." He clenched his teeth. "Before Lana. Now tell me exactly what Lana said."

The housekeeper shrugged. "She told me nothing, except that she intended to pack her things and Colin's as well. None of their fine, fancy clothes. Only the things they'd come with."

While the others watched, Jesse stormed up the stairs. Without bothering to knock, he stepped into Lana's sitting room. A cozy fire burned on the hearth. There seemed to be nothing amiss. The door to the bedroom was ajar, and he could see Lana's shabby little satchel open on the bed. The sight of it had his jaw clenching.

He stepped inside and leaned against the door, struggling for a casual pose while his heart started pounding. "What's this?"

Lana's head came up sharply. Seeing him watching her, she turned away. "A letter came today from the court." She pointed to the paper on her night table.

Without a word Jesse picked it up and read. When he'd finished, he flung it aside. "They merely ask when they may inspect Colin's new home."

Her words were clipped. "In case you didn't notice, they asked the date of the wedding so the adoption can be completed."

"As I assured you earlier, that isn't a problem. We'll marry whenever you wish."

She kept her face averted. "I'll not enter into a sham marriage."

"Then we'll make it a real one."

"This isn't the time for playacting. I'll not do that to you, Jesse."

"Do what?"

She turned then and met his eyes. Her own were dry, though from the look of them it was obvious that she'd been through a bout of weeping earlier. "It was one thing to have a laugh at society while you helped me gain custody of Colin. I told myself I was doing this for an unselfish reason. And I was. But now, when you've been so good, so kind and thoughtful, I couldn't live with the guilt if I were to carry this any further."

"Guilt?" He was watching her carefully, trying to gauge how best to deal with her.

"I know how you hate the thought of marriage, Jesse. You've made it clear how repugnant the very thought of it is to you."

"It may have been, once upon a time . . ."

"I can't bear the thought of tying you down, even with a mock wife and son, and taking you away from the life you were happily leading before I . . . forced myself on you."

"And so you thought you'd just leave and take the lad with you while I was gone?"

"I'd never do that." A spark of temper came into her eyes. "I intended to wait until you'd returned before taking Colin."

Though he'd gambled a fortune on the turn of a card, this was the first time in Jesse's life that he found himself about to risk his very future in a game of chance. He hoped he was reading her correctly.

"I'm touched by your honesty, Lana. But this turn of events begs a question."

"A question?"

At least he finally had her complete attention. Her hands had paused in the act of packing the faded gown she'd once worn in the Blue Goose.

"A question. Just one." He paused a beat. "Do you love me?"

She looked away. "I'll not answer that."

"I believe you owe me that much. Just a simple yes or no. Do you love me, Lana?" While he waited for her answer, he wondered if it were possible for a heart to break with a simple word. Still, he'd been the one to risk it, and now he had to know.

Her chin came up in that way he'd come to recognize. Her brogue was as thick as the lump in her throat. "God help me, though I'd have agreed to anything to save Colin, I never planned for this to happen."

"Planned for what?"

"I'll not let you make this sacrifice for us. You have to let us go."

At her words Jesse felt his heart soar. He gave her one of those rogue smiles. "You see, Lana, that's precisely why I can't let you go. Though you refuse to say the words, I can see it in your eyes, the same way you once saw it in mine. You love me."

"I never said . . ."

He held up a hand. "Don't deny it. Though God knows I've tried. I never would have believed this could happen to my cold, cynical heart, but somehow you've managed to capture it, and now you'll just have to live with the consequences. You love me, Lana. At least admit that much. And

I love you. So much, in fact, that I'd planned on coercing you into marriage for the sake of the boy, knowing, even if you didn't love me, you would do anything for him."

Her eyes narrowed. "You were going to trick me into marriage?"

"If I had to. Or bribe you with this." He reached into his breast pocket and removed the small jeweler's box. When she refused to accept it, he opened the box to reveal a glittering ruby ring. "I know that diamonds are traditional, but I think rubies suit you far better. In fact, of all the stones I looked at, these were the only ones that seemed to call your name."

Lana had a sudden memory of her mother's ruby ear bobs, traded for a shawl aboard ship.

She wouldn't cry. Not now.

Too overcome to speak, she merely stared at the glittering bloodred stones in silence.

Seeing her reaction, he softened his tone. "There's something I need to tell you."

She shook her head. "No more. I don't think I can bear any more surprises. Is it a gambling debt I'll be responsible for?"

"No debts. In fact, quite the opposite."

She regarded him with suspicion. "I don't understand. What is the opposite of debt?"

"Too much money. So much so, I've had to spend my entire adult life avoiding women who wanted to marry me to get it."

"That's a likely story. An actor as gifted as you can do better than that."

"It's the truth. You see, Lana, as much as I enjoy occasionally pretending to be a gambler and actor, I really am the Duke of Umberland, and eighteenth in line of succession to the throne of England."

Lana sank down on the edge of the mattress and stared at him in total disbelief. "You see. You're like all the others here. You've repeated the lie so often, you've come to believe it."

"Everyone here told you the truth. It was you who didn't want to hear it. Each member of this household is related in some way to royalty. All of them, except Withers, who really is my manservant, had no place to go once they were turned out by the royals they once loved or served. I suppose that's another reason why I decided that love and marriage were not for me. I've seen too much heartache caused by the dictates of royal blood. And my blood is too bloody royal," he added with a wry smile.

"You're telling me their stories are true? That Nadia really was a seamstress to the Tsarina? That Colette was really lover to the Prince of Wales?"

He nodded.

Hadn't she known all along? And yet . . . "And Maria and Rosa?"

"Maria was royal housekeeper to the King of Spain. She was forced to flee or be taken to his bed against her will. She brought her niece with her, knowing Rosa would soon have to face the same fate. Like the others, they sought freedom here in this country. How could I not take them into my home, when I had so much I could share with them?"

Lana could only shake her head at all she was hearing. "No wonder they all praise you to the heavens."

"I don't deserve praise, Lana. I may not have been given love, but I was blessed with education and wealth. That is my good fortune. But because I doubt that the seventeen ahead of me in line for the Crown will die any time soon, I intend to continue living in this fascinating new country, enjoying the freedom I've come to love. I fled to America to escape a life of entitlement and to put an end to the hounding by females intent upon marrying me for my money and title, and to end, once and for all, my family's attempts to marry me off just to continue a title. What I found here in this strange new land, to my amazement, is that I enjoy the freedom to work and play with the wonderful, ordinary people who live here. I've also discovered an aptitude for making money."

"You mean as a gambler?"

He laughed. "As a businessman, buying land and selling to men with the vision to build great buildings. In truth, this mansion is really mine. It was my first investment when I came here."

He saw the way her mouth opened and closed, although no words came out.

"Think about sharing my life, Lana. If you should ever grow weary of life in New York, I'll happily take you and Colin to my estate outside London, or my home in Dublin, or the one in Spain, or the one just outside Paris."

That would explain how he could speak to each of these women in their own language. Still, she was too confused to take it all in. "If what you say is true, and I don't believe for a minute that it is, you can have your pick of women."

"Indeed. And so I have." He dropped to one knee before her and held out the sparkling ruby ring. "I've chosen you, Lana. Only you. Please say you'll be my wife and agree to allow me to adopt Colin, so that my life will be complete."

"But . . ." Dazed, she stood and brushed past him, struggling to make sense of all this. "Why didn't you tell me the truth a long time ago?"

He got to his feet to face her. "I almost did. That night you came to me at the tavern in tears, I wanted to tell you. But you were so insistent upon believing that I was some sort of dangerous, daring rogue, I didn't have the heart to spoil your illusions. And then it all got out of hand, and there was no way to tell you without losing you. And though I pride myself on being a gambler, that was one risk I wasn't willing to take."

"You?" She huffed out a breath. "Afraid of risk? I just don't know what to believe any more. One minute you have me believing you're nothing more than a rogue and an actor, and the next I'm to believe you're an English royal?"

"Believe this, Lana. Only this. When I saw how unselfishly you were able to love Colin, and how hard you were willing to fight for him, without a thought to the sacrifices you would have to make, I found myself believing in the power of love. Though it took me a long time to admit it, I finally realized the truth. I love you with all my heart. You're the finest woman I've ever known. Please say you love me, too, and that you'll spend the rest of your life with me."

"Oh, Jesse." In reply, she wrapped her arms around his neck and lifted her mouth to his in a kiss that showed him, as no words could, all the love that was in her heart.

At the sound of excited voices raised in a cheer, they looked up to see the entire staff clustered in the doorway. Nadia and Colette, Clara, Maria and Rosa, and behind them Withers, holding Colin in his arms so the lad could see over the women's heads. All of them were laughing and clapping their hands.

"We must publish the banns immediately," Maria called.

"I'll plan a lovely wedding supper," Clara shouted.

"I'll begin work immediately on the most beautiful wedding gown the world has ever seen," Nadia declared.

"How fortunate, *cherie*," Colette said with a smile, "that you are already accustomed to being called duchess."

Duchess. The word had Lana smiling and shaking her head in wonder. Who would have believed that Lana Dunleavy, orphan, immigrant, and an innocent in the game of love, would not only find herself wildly in love with a gambler and actor, and he with her, but also that she would actually become the Duchess of Umberland? It was, quite simply, too much to take in.

"For now"—she blew a kiss to Colin—"I'll settle for being called Auntie Lana."

"I have a better title." Jesse drew her close and kissed her, much to the delight of those watching. "How about wife?"

"Oh, yes." She wrapped her arms around his neck and returned his kiss, wondering at the way her heart had leapt to her throat and seemed permanently lodged there. "Of all the titles, I believe I like that one best of all."

While they kissed, the others continued smiling and making plans. But as the kiss deepened, Withers cleared his throat and pulled the door shut to give them the privacy they deserved.

Lost in the excitement of their newly discovered love, they never even noticed that the voices had faded away. The silence of the room was filled with soft sighs and the beating of two hearts in perfect rhythm.

"Welcome to my world, Duchess." The words were whispered against her mouth.

"Your world." Lana had been prepared to guard her heart against a life of luxury. But there had been no way to prepare her heart for the wonder of something as precious, as unexpected, as Jesse's love.

Love. The very thought of it filled her with quiet peace.

There was, she realized, nothing to do but savor it, now, and for the rest of her life, which she intended to spend with this black-hearted, mysterious, and oh-so-delightful rogue who had thoroughly captured her heart.

EPILOGUE

———•━━■◆■━━•———

New York—December 1897

"Mumi Mumi!"

Lana looked up just as Colin raced into the room and came to a skidding halt. His cheeks were bright pink, his fair hair tousled by the wind. "Da told Ernst that I could handle the team on the way home."

"That's quite a responsibility. How did you do?"

"Fine. Didn't I, Da?"

"You were exceptional." Jesse paused in the doorway with a dark-haired lass still perched on his shoulders. She was the image of Lana, with an angel face framed by a mass of coal-black curls that fell down her back.

When he lowered her to the floor she gave a shriek of delight and skipped across the room and into her mother's waiting arms.

"Well, Victoria." Lana snuggled the lass who had been named for her great-aunt, whose duties in England had kept her from attending the birth three years earlier, though she'd sent a lovely layette to New York bearing the royal crest. "Did you have fun with your da and big brother?"

"I did. Yes."

Jesse glanced around at Nadia and Colette, sitting amidst the clutter of boxes and bags and colorful paper. "I see you're getting a head start on the party."

As he strode across the room and brushed his mouth over hers, Lana felt the familiar flutter around her heart. "Once I started shopping for all the orphans, I couldn't seem to stop myself."

"I'm afraid I'm guilty of the same thing." He chuckled and nodded toward Withers, whose arms were laden with packages. "I'm willing to bet that this is the best Christmas party the Ladies' Aid Society will ever give for the children of the East Side Orphan Asylum."

"Oh, Jesse. The women are so excited, especially after seeing the lovely clothes Nadia made for the children. And thanks to your example, their husbands have been more than generous. Not only will the orphans receive warm coats and blankets, but books and puzzles, and even rocking horses and pull-toys."

"It's about time we involved the business men of this city in the lives of the less fortunate. I hope you don't mind that Farley Fairchild asked if he could attend and bring along a photographer."

"Not at all. Especially if it will encourage more people to reach out to the widows and orphans of the city."

As Colin and Victoria joined in the wrapping, Jesse touched a hand to Lana's swollen stomach. "Are you sure this isn't too much right now, love?"

"The doctor said I'm his healthiest patient. Besides, the baby isn't due until mid-February."

"Which will give you plenty of time to recover before we set sail for Europe in the summer."

The others exchanged smiles, because the entire household had been included in the plans. They were, after all, family now. And all of them, including Withers, were looking forward to the coming journey.

"Have I told you how absolutely beautiful you're looking?" Jesse loved the flush that stole over his wife's cheeks at his scrutiny. "You're positively glowing."

"And why not, with all of you spoiling me?" Spying Maria entering with a tray of hot chocolate, Lana added, "Wait until you see the food Clara is planning for the party."

"All guaranteed to have the children begging for more, I'll wager." Jesse winked. "And topped off by dozens of her famous sugar cookies."

Lana nodded. "And cut into the most amazing shapes. Little stars and bells and tiny wreaths. Oh, Jesse. I can hardly wait to see their happy little faces."

As she settled down on the floor between Colin and Victoria, Jesse sat beside her. He picked up a sheet of colorful paper and began to wrap a toy.

At her arched brow he chuckled. "You didn't think I was going to let you have all the fun, did you?"

Fun.

Lana looked around the room and felt her eyes fill. Ever since she could remember, her life had been a constant struggle just to survive. Now here she was, living a life even finer than the one she'd dreamed of all those years ago. Not only a fine big house with lovely gardens, but a home filled with people who had become her dearest friends. She had broken her own hard-and-fast rule and had lost her heart to a rogue, only to discover that he was fine and noble and eager to share this wonderful life with her. A life now filled with love and laughter and the greatest gift of all—family.

It had been a long journey from Ireland to America, from desperately lonely orphan to wife and mother. As she studied the happy faces of all those she loved, Lana knew that the best part of her life's journey lay ahead.

"'Tis fun, isn't it?" She wrapped her arms around Jesse's neck and kissed him full on the mouth, much to the delight of the others. "I wouldn't have missed a minute of it for all the world."

"Nor I." He gathered her close, feeling complete. For a man who had been prepared to live his entire life without real love, every day with his adored Lana was another gift to be opened, another delight to be cherished.

He'd gambled his heart and won the biggest prize of all: the love of a lifetime.

Turn the page for a special preview of
Ruth Ryan Langan's next novel

HEART'S DELIGHT

Coming soon from Berkley Sensation!

Chicago, Illinois—1890

H ODGE E GAN PICKED up the cards dealt to him and eyed the pair of aces without expression. About time, he thought as he lifted the tumbler of whiskey to his mouth and drank. He'd been donating to Jasper Sullivan's wallet for two hours. It was his turn to win a jackpot.

The overhead chandelier, aglow with dozens of candles, was reflected in the U.S. Marshall badge pinned to the lapel of his black coat. When he picked up the expensive cigar and bit the end, a pretty woman with yellow dyed hair and a gown that revealed a great deal of pale, firm flesh reached over his shoulder to hold a flame to the tip. He puffed, adding to the pall of smoke that hung over the table. As soon as his glass was empty, the woman poured another drink from a crystal decanter. When she glided away, her perfume lingered.

"I'm in." Jasper, the chief of police and cousin to the mayor, tossed a gold piece in the center of the table.

"I'll see you." Maxwell Body, who owned a nearby stock yard, flipped his coin and watched it bobble before settling.

"Me, too." Emmet Harding, who owned one of Chicago's finest restaurants, took a coin from his neat pile and leaned forward to add it to the pot, all the while holding his cards close to his chest.

"Marshall?" Cyrus, the bartender at the Beal Street Hotel and Gentleman's Club, who was filling in for the regular dealer, looked over.

"May as well." Hodge kept his tone casual as he added his gold piece to the pile. "Been losing the whole night. Why stop now?"

The men around the table shared wolfish grins, each one waiting as Cyrus dealt the next of their cards.

Hodge watched their eyes as each man studied his hand. Jasper blinked hard, and Hodge knew the man wasn't happy with the outcome. Maxwell kept his gaze fixed on his cards, refusing to glance around, which only confirmed that he had what he hoped was a winning hand. Emmet glanced left, then right, as though trying to assess his chances against the others.

Only after he'd studied the others at the table did Hodge look at his own cards. He fought to keep his composure as he saw the third ace. He was going to thoroughly enjoy raking in all that money. Not that he needed it. His pay as a U.S. District Marshall was generous, and his lifestyle simple. But the win would guarantee him bragging rights among his cronies for weeks.

"Jasper?" Cyrus nodded toward the man on his left.

"I'll call."

"Maxwell?"

The man's bushy beard twitched with humor. "You'll have to pay to see mine, Jasper." He glanced around the table before tossing another gold piece and accepting his last card. "You'll all have to pay to see these little darlings."

Emmet tossed down his cards. "Too rich for my blood."

Cyrus turned to Hodge. "Marshall?"

"I'll pay to see them. In fact, Maxwell, I believe I'll just fatten the pot." He tossed two gold pieces and had the satisfaction of seeing Maxwell's eyes go wide.

"Thanks. I'll be happy to relieve you of all that. . . ."

"Marshall!" A breathless voice was shouting hoarsely from the doorway.

Hodge glanced over with a twinge of annoyance when he recognized Will Stout, the kid who worked at the train station and ran the telegraph.

"Marshall!" With the air of one who had the attention of everyone in the room, the boy hurried over and announced loudly, "There's been a bank robbery in Madison."

"That's in Wisconsin, boy."

"Yes, sir." Will took a moment to catch his breath. "The robber shot a clerk working at the bank, then shot the bank president, before taking off with all the money. Before he left town he shot the police chief."

"How badly are they wounded?"

"They're all dead."

"Anybody on the case?"

The boy shrugged. "Don't know. With the police chief dead, they said they want you there as fast as you can ride."

Hodge swore, low under his breath. Damn the timing. He tossed down his cards.

Seeing them, Maxwell whistled. "Too bad you couldn't have toyed with us a while longer, Hodge. I figured my hand for a winner. Doubt I'd've quit until you ran me up a couple hundred more."

Hodge snarled. "Cash me out fast, Cyrus. I'll use it to buy my train ticket."

As he pocketed the gold and strode out the door, he swore again. The train would take him only as far as Milwaukee. If the thief decided to make his escape into the back country, he could be weeks on horseback in some godforsaken wilderness before he'd know the luxury of a gentleman's club again.

He hoped this wasn't a sign that his luck was about to desert him.

MOLLY O'BRIEN SET out across the field. She studied the rich, black earth, alive with green growing crops. While her neighbors raised wheat, acres of it, she grew corn, beans, and best of all, hay. Hay to feed her herd. Enough hay to cut and store to get them through the long Wisconsin winter.

It never ceased to amaze her that her big brother had settled in this spot, so far from the place where he'd been born.

Molly had left Ireland at fourteen, and now, at twenty-six, she still felt a tug on her heart whenever she thought of that lovely green land across the sea. Her family farm in Cork would fit in one corner of this vast farm. There'd been no more than a dozen or so cows. A snug little cottage. A bit of land for growing things. And yet, with the help of her grandmother, her mother's mother who'd come from Scotland, they had turned their little dairy farm into a profitable business. And all because of her grandmother's recipe for making cheese.

It had been her brother's dream to bring the recipe to America, and have a dairy farm that would be the envy of all.

With the death of her brother and his wife, along with her parents, Molly had been forced to scale back that dream. Now, it was enough if she could feed her family of four growing girls, all of whom had been left homeless until Molly took them in. What was left over she used to barter for their necessities. It was satisfying to know that her neighbors were eager for her milk and cheese. Each time the people of Delight tasted it, they went into raptures over the smooth texture, the sharp tang of it.

Her grandmother would be proud.

Up ahead she saw two saddled horses grazing, their reins trailing. Dismounting, she picked up a man's blood-stained jacket lying in the grass. Checking a bulge in one of the pockets she discovered an enormous wad of bills. Though she didn't take the time to count it, Molly knew that it was more money than she'd ever seen in her lifetime.

Was he a banker then? A wealthy rancher?

Had the other man been trying to steal this man's money?

It made sense. A wealthy man, and a thief determined to steal his money, by whatever means possible. The thought sent a ripple of unease along her spine.

A little farther she found a second coat, though she nearly stepped over it since it was half-buried in sand. She stooped to pick it up. As she did, she felt the stab of something sharp prick her finger. Turning over the jacket, she saw the grimy badge of a U.S. Marshall pinned to the lapel.

Going through the pockets, she found several documents addressed to Marshall Hodge Egan. There was a remnant of a train ticket from Chicago, ragged and torn no doubt by the conductor's hand. One of the papers, carefully folded, was a poster, listing the name of Eli Otto, wanted for murder and bank robbery. Though there was no picture of the thief, he was described as tall, with dark hair and eyes. The poster carried a warning that he was armed and extremely dangerous, having already killed three people, one of them a lawman.

A thief. A murderer, who was extremely dangerous.

Molly thought back to the two men who were now lying in beds in her farmhouse, more dead than alive. Both could fit that description. She'd had to struggle to lift all that bone and muscle into and out of her wagon. Both men were tall, strong, with dark hair, though she couldn't describe their eyes.

Walking in methodical circles around the area she retrieved a rifle, two hand guns, and a very sharp, very deadly knife that had a flat piece of metal which folded over the blade, no doubt to conceal it in a pocket or boot.

It was clear to her that each man had used everything available to fight off an opponent.

As she tied the coats behind her saddle, her mind was racing.

No wonder they had fought with such desperation. It truly had been a life-or-death situation.

Under her roof at this very moment she was harboring both a man of the law and a dangerous criminal, with no way of telling which was which.

Even worse, she had left her four girls alone with them. And though one of those strangers might be willing to give his life to save them, the other would do whatever necessary to escape, even if it meant harming helpless children.

Catching up the dangling reins of their two horses, Molly pulled herself into the saddle of her mount and urged the old mare into a heart-stopping, pulse-pounding gallop.

With each mile, the accusation rang through her mind. What had she just done? Oh, sweet heaven, she was giving aid and succor to a dangerous gunman who had killed before, and would no doubt do so again, given the opportunity. But she could see no way out of this dilemma. Without knowing their identities, in order to save an honest man, she would have to fight to save the life of a man with no conscience, as well. And she would have to do all this while finding a way to keep her little family safe from harm.